PRAISE FOR WAITING FOR BEIRUT

Driving Rebecca Dimyan's charming first novel, Waiting for Beirut, is the compelling voice of young George Lahoud, son of Lebanese immigrants who live in a Lebanese community in a small 1950's Connecticut town where everyone knows one another's business. The details of Lebanese-American life are as rich and savory as the *kibbeh nayyeh* and *baba ghanouj* that Ummi, the mother of the clan, makes for her family.

Written in understated prose that nonetheless oftentimes rises to the elegant, this is a rare first novel that is at once insightful, compelling, and thoroughly relevant to today's world.

Michael C. White, author of *Soul Catcher* and *Beautiful Assassin*

"Many lives ago, I encountered Rebecca Dimyan's Waiting for Beirut in first draft form. It's been such a joy, a decade later, to see this manifestation of Geoge Lahoud's poignant tale. There is so much to admire: Dimyan balances the conversational and the lyrical so elegantly in a story that is not easy to tell. She can step out of herself with the ease that only someone who really listens and observes and lives can. As a result, the reader can't help but look at this portrait of longing from so many lovingly rendered angles. It's a deeply moving Lebanese-American mid-century epic, and it's also a very necessary novel that challenges so many multicultural assumptions and heteronormative tropes of generations past."

Porochista Khakpour, author most recently of *Brown Album: 's on Exile & Identity*

WAITING FOR BEIRUT

A NOVEL

REBECCA DIMYAN

RIZE

Waiting for Beirut, A Novel
text copyright © Reserved by Rebecca Dimyan
Edited by Cody Cisco

Published in North America, Australia, and Europe by RIZE. Visit Running
Wild Press at www.runningwildpress.com/rize Educators, librarians, book clubs
(as well as the eternally curious), go to www.runningwildpress.com/rize.

Paperback ISBN: 978-1-955062-75-6
eBook ISBN: 978-1-955062-77-0

For Giddo, Titu, and anyone who ever dared to dream.

PART I
THE STRANGER

Danbury, CT
September 1951

PROLOGUE

WASHINGTON, D.C.

The letter weighed heavily in my pocket. It tugged at my tweed jacket like it had its own fingers. I ignored it in favor of another glass of gin. I focused on the way the alcohol burned my throat as I swallowed it in a single gulp. My knuckles were beginning to swell, but the ache was dulled by another glass. A pair of businessmen smoking cigarettes in the corner of the bar laughed at some exchanged confidence. I overheard a bit about the removal of lavender lads from the State Department.

"You think it's true? That many homosexuals working in the government?" the shorter gentleman with a round, hairless face asked his heavyset companion.

"Sure, sure. I mean, it is DC. There are all kinds of vermin here. Bound to be communists and cocksuckers, too." Their laughter amped up. "Just listen to McCarthy..." The rest of the dialogue was lost to the music.

A piano at the far end of the bar had been taken over by a blonde, freckle-faced young man whose rosy cheeks suggested he'd imbibed at least a few cocktails. He started playing boogie-

3

woogie blues and then a group of what appeared to be his friends—twenty-something young men in argyle socks and oxford shirts and their young ladies in pleated skirts—pushed tables and chairs against the oak-paneled wall to make room for dancing. Swinging hips, stomping feet, twisting bodies, and wild arm movements followed. Within a few minutes, several more patrons joined the bonhomie.

The electric tempo and booze-fueled euphoria starkly contrasted with my mood. By the third or fourth drink, I couldn't ignore the letter any longer. I took it out, unfolded it, and let it shake in my hands. It had been crumpled from my haste to forget it, torn in the struggle that followed several hours later, and a smear of blood—Jacob's or mine, I couldn't be sure—blurred some of the words, but my brother's message remained clear: *Bayee is dying. You need to come home.*

This was not the way it was all supposed to end—drinking alone in a crowded bar on M Street. Silhouetted strangers planted on nearby bar stools like stage dressing. Georgetown was to be my raison d'etre. I had planned on bodies and blood and injury and death, but not all at once, and not quite so intimately. I was going to be a doctor. And before I began university, I had been a butcher's apprentice. I've always been familiar with the sound bones make when they crack and the way raw meat feels in bare hands—these things do not disturb me. Animals die. People get hurt and sick. But these were my injured hands. This was personal. This was Jacob.

I blamed the assault on my brother's letter, on the news of my father's decline, on the drinks we shared earlier in the evening, on the way he leaned in for something more than a goodbye hug. Perhaps it was all these things. Perhaps it was something else entirely. The only facts I could be sure of sitting at the bar in the aftermath were these: Bayee was dying. I was dropping out of school to return home so that I could run the family grocery store. And I beat my best friend until he was a mess of damp flesh. The image of his cracked, black-framed glasses lying in the road beside my shoe as he stumbled off into the DC night, his sobs discernible even amid the traffic and echoes of music was a memory that a bottle of gin couldn't seem to mute. But saeadani ya rabi, so help me God, I would drink until it did.

I didn't know how late it was, and I didn't remember leaving the bar. I recalled vomiting in an alley behind a dumpster that smelled of spoiled milk and expired foods. I recalled sweat or tears stinging my eyes. I remembered the sunrise looked like a cigarette just before it burns out. I also remembered, for an instant, Jacob's last words to me: "I see the real you." And mostly, I remembered my father, the last time I saw him and the way my face burned after he slapped me.

Then everything went black.

CHAPTER ONE

George Lahoud, my father, my bayee, was a butcher and a drunk. He was the proprietor of a small grocery store on the corner of Beaver and Elm Street, which I inherited along with a language that belonged to the old country, our Lebanon. Most times, my brother Michael and I referred to our parents by the Arabic terms bayee and ummi although we used mom and dad, too. I think these words were artifacts that my parents clung to in both love and nostalgia like the cedar tree in our backyard or the recipes Ummi lovingly followed.

Bayee spent his days stocking shelves, sweeping floors, preparing cuts of meat and acquiring produce to fill rows of large wooden bins. Although he took great pride in his butchery, fruits and vegetables were his passion. He scoured the region for the best purveyors of produce to supply his seasonal collection. These fruits and vegetables were treated with the paternal affection he lacked in tending to his own children. I once saw him trace the web of white veins on a cantaloupe with such tenderness, I found myself jealous. He held the fruit up to the fluorescent light, admired its alabaster threading like it was a Rembrandt painting, and watching him I longed to be loved like that. But I was just a boy then, and I would have settled for a hug.

Although not an effusive man, my father spoke eloquently of the best strategies for selecting the perfect watermelon. He waxed on about multipurpose radishes (he swore they could cure indigestion), impossibly delicious wild berries that could reconcile enemies, and he proclaimed that good, seasonal foods could fix any trouble—from heartache to the common cold. He curated the sweetest melons in the entire tri-state area. Cigarette draped over his thin lips, he recited techniques and facts about produce like they were lines of poetry and he was Kahlil Gibran. It would be many years before I realized that my father saw himself as an artist—not a butcher or grocer.

Bayee's store was his sacred place. The prayers he didn't say and the bedtime kisses he did not give his sons—everything —was reserved for Lahoud's Market. But this market was more than my father's religion, it was the very heartbeat of the Lebanese community in Danbury, Connecticut. It was the place where Mrs. Auon came for Ummi's meat pies after her husband died. "They were Eddie's favorite," she said through a mouthful and tears. It was the place where Sammy Issa came for bread and cheese when he lost his job at the fur factory. My father gave him basic supplies on credit for weeks until he secured a new job as a janitor at New Street School. It was the place where Michael and I played hide-and-go-seek until Mrs. Sadi caught us and yelled at Bayee for letting "his boys run loose like chickens with no heads." When she left scowling, thick bifocals sliding off her large nose, white hair in a school marm bun, he laughed and joined our game, covering his eyes and counting to ten in accented English.

And it was the place neighborhood children ran to hide from Tita Um'Asad, the old lady who perhaps was more folklore than real nightmare. When the kids of Elm, Beaver, and George Streets misbehaved, our parents threatened to send us to Tita Um'Asad's rundown house. Tita Um'Asad was a thousand years old, made of brown wrinkles, menthol cigarettes, and fingers deformed from years working as a seamstress. Rumor had it that she used her sewing needles to prick the behinds of tots who wet their pants or argued with their siblings or generally caused trouble. However, while the fear was universal, no one had actually ever experienced her terrifying tools of discipline or, for that matter, anything beyond her Arabic cursing, which was primarily reserved for the several feral cats that lived in her overgrown yard. Eventually, it was concluded that she wasn't more than a threat used by our parents to keep us in line.

In the backyard of the store, a cedar tree grew. Years earlier, Bayee left a village somewhere near Mount Lebanon. He arrived in America with a small leather steamer trunk containing one suit, five Syrian pounds, a steel knife, and the seeds of a cedar tree. He got a job in a local fur factory until he'd saved enough money to buy a rundown two-story house in the midst of Danbury's little Lebanon. The first thing he did, even before hanging a shingle, was plant the seeds in the small parcel of land. Like his produce, he tended to this seedling until it grew dark, scaly bark and branches that sprouted clusters of light green needles. I asked him once about this tree. He replied, "We are nothing but cedar trees planted in American soil. Don't forget that, boy."

When he lost the deed to the store in a game of cards, it wasn't simply devastating—it was life-altering. The night we learned of Bayee's loss, Michael and I had just returned home from seeing *The Adventures of Robin Hood* staring Errol Flynn. We were sword fighting with wooden spoons borrowed from Ummi's infinite supply of kitchen utensils, I playing Sir Robin and Michael stuck with the role of Prince John.

"But you always get to be the hero. I hate being the bad guy," Michael was whining when we were interrupted by an unfamiliar sound: Ummi was yelling.

Before that night, I had never heard her raise her voice above a soft tone. Her voice, then and now, was a cool breeze through an open window. Apparently, Bayee had been gambling at the Lebanon-American club and had lost the store in a game of poker to Albert Hokayem. My father didn't even try to defend himself. He sat quietly and let Ummi scream and cry and curse him. It was the only time I had ever heard my mother swear. It was two years before my parents would be able to buy the store back. Bayee stopped playing cards, but he began drinking more. Perhaps that is the moment something cracked in his head, when he went from social drinker to secret drunk.

But this was history, lost to aging memories and black-and-white photographs stored in dusty boxes beneath beds. Now, I was back in Danbury, standing in front of the small store that raised me, watching my father sweep as if I had never left, as if it hadn't been two years since I'd last seen him, and as if he wasn't dying.

In stained apron, cigarette still dangling from his lips, Bayee cleaned the shop floor with slow, stiff movements. Arthritis had made his body sore; my mother's cooking made him over-weight; drinking had made him jaundiced and ill. He placed the broom against the wall, next to the checkout counter, and resumed his place at the register after a few minutes. I watched as he helped himself to a handful of olives from the large barrels behind the counter.

My father had aged a decade in two years. This man before me had red eyes and yellow skin. He repeatedly wiped his nose with a handkerchief, but a steady stream of snot persisted. His hands shook as he removed the cigarette from his chapped lips, flicked the ash onto the ground, and placed it in a glass ashtray already filled with half a dozen shells. Although he did not look well, he did not look as though he was on his deathbed. If he was so sick, how was he still working? Of course, I knew my father and he'd likely insist that everyone else was incompetent, that he was the only one capable of running the market. I was sure that he'd take his final breath in the store.

I felt a lump rising in my throat, and my body went cold. I could not help but remember our last interaction, the vein that danced in his left temple, the sneer revealing cigarette-yellow teeth, and the alcohol breath that slapped me before he did. I remember knocking over the tray of knafeh as I ran out of the store, the shredded dough and cheesy pastries smashing into a pile on the floor, leaving my father trembling with adrenaline and rage. Now, I couldn't help but think this was his punishment, karma. His hands cursed with tremors, condemned to shake every morning until he'd drunk enough to settle them. These were the hands that broke me once. These were the hands that taught me the art of butchery, the hands that led me to church on Sundays and folded in prayer before evening meals. These were the same hands that administered punishment when my brother and I misbehaved, as little boys often do. These were the hands that made me.

I lingered outside, watching him in the bay window for a few minutes. A group of schoolboys ran past me on the sidewalk, kicking a tin can and laughing as they went. The air stunk of sulfur from the waters of the Still River, purple in hue from the dyes of the local hat factories. Shanty houses thrived like weeds in the dirt plot across from the store. Towering, leafy elm trees lined the street, their cool screen providing shadowy protection from the bright sun and equally bright gaze of strangers and acquaintances. Yes, this was home; my constant, my constant impasse.

CHAPTER TWO

B efore Jacob walked away from me bloodied and broken, we shared drinks at a bar on the edge of campus. The dimly lit, smoky room was filled with lively banter, unspoken secrets, and too much pretense. Thick red lips smiled from a corner. A raven-haired woman sang songs about misbehaving. Couples danced, friends laughed, and Jacob and I pretended that I wasn't leaving DC the next morning.

Jacob drank most of his gin in a single gulp. It was almost as if my friend was the one dropping out of Georgetown. As I watched him, I imagined he was the kind of man who sang in the shower. *But men don't imagine other men in the shower.*

"This was a great idea," Jacob shouted over the cacophony of music and conversation.

I caught the eye of a woman drinking a glass of white wine in the corner. I smiled at her, knowing she found me handsome. I noticed Jacob also taking in our surroundings. From the moment I met him, I sensed that, to Jacob, people were words to be memorized. He often watched passersby longer than was conventionally appropriate. He seemed to be studying everything from the creases of their clothing to the crow's feet beneath their eyes. In conversation, he stared as if he was trying to learn every laugh-line, dimple, or blemish. While some may have felt unnerved by this sort of interest, I appreciated it. It showed he was invested in people, invested in life.

Jacob's hair was all wild curls and defiance, fitting for the budding journalist. After a few moments of quiet between us, in a thin voice lacking its typical cadence, he said, "My parents cut me off, you know." Before I could respond, he continued, "Said I needed to learn how to be a man even if I wasn't going to act like one. Or something like that. Who really knows what parents say in anger? Anyway, it's why I work at the café. My scholarship isn't enough."

I was unsure how to react. Jacob was from money. He didn't act like a man is supposed to act, according to his parents. He was resentful, or, at least, his tone was bitter. I settled on: "I had a rather contentious parting with my folks, too."

"Did they question your moral fiber?"

I shook my head and took out a cigarette.

Jacob smirked and swilled his drink.

"What're you smiling at?" Puzzled by his sudden and apparent amusement.

"Nothing. Forget it." Jacob's cheeks flushed. "Has anyone ever questioned your manhood?"

I felt my face grow hot. The room was hot. "I'm getting another gin." I got up from the table and made my way to the bar, offering no other response. Navigating the sweaty, smoky bodies crowding the bar, I stumbled closer to drunkenness and to memory. The first time I met Jacob.

* * *

Shortly upon arriving in DC, I discovered a café on N Street. Café Sorriso served strong coffee and pastries baked in-house. Vinyl cushioned seats and plenty of tables provided an ideal reading environment. Often, I read *The Washington Post* as men in suits took their lunch breaks, read their newspapers, met their mistresses. These men, always so polished, so effortlessly masculine, smoked cigarettes and smiled and tipped hats like they came from Hollywood films. I liked to find a table by a window so that I could watch the unfolding metropolis. It was all so quintessentially American: reading a newspaper in a coffee shop surrounded by businessmen talking politics and women smoking cigarettes as their babies slept in strollers.

It was September '49. The streets of Washington DC were teeming with former GIs, returned from Europe or the Pacific a few years earlier, taking advantage of the GI Bill and studying at one of several universities in the area. Other men home from the front resumed careers as businessmen, lawyers, doctors, journalists, politicians, shop keepers. Pretty women in foulard silk scarves, full skirts, and heels clicked down the sidewalks, many with swollen bellies, gloved hands full of bags from the shopping district in the Northwest quadrant. The presidential election of the previous year had stirred up support for New York Governor Thomas E. Dewey, and, although he'd lost the election, vestiges of his campaign were still visible in some parts of the city. Someone had even scrawled his slogan, "You know that your future is still ahead of you," in loopy black paint on a bench at the bus stop across the street. As popular as Dewey was, I was happy when Truman, the underdog, won.

The man who worked the counter at Café Sorriso had slight features, almost effeminate, and had slicked-back curly hair. He wore thick, black-rimmed glasses and his nose had a Semitic curve.

"Coffee, black. And the pastry du jour?" he asked.

"You're a quick study." I had been having the same drink and dessert every afternoon for the last two weeks.

"Don't let this apron fool you. I'm studying at Georgetown." He handed me my steaming brew.

Recent ink stains bloomed like bruises on his small hands. "You're studying journalism? English Lit?"

"Journalism. How'd you figure?"

"It was either one of those or ballpoint pen-making."

The man laughed as he arranged a cheese danish on a small white plate. He handed me the pastry, made a halfhearted attempt at wiping away the ink on his apron, and extended his hand, "Jacob. Jacob Eisenburg."

"George Lahoud." I shook his hand, which was surprisingly soft.

"You're a student?" Jacob asked, then looked, almost nervously, over at the door, probably to make sure he wasn't ignoring any customers. The café was almost empty. An older gentleman sat at a table in the window, sipping a hot beverage and reading a newspaper. Wood-paneled walls matched wooden tables. Black tiled floors reflected the ceiling fans and shaded lamp sconces filled the walls.

"Georgetown." I smiled at him. "Bio major."

"Hadn't pegged you as a science type." Jacob smiled and began wiping down the brass counter.

I took a sip of the coffee. "What do I strike you as?"

He looked up, stopped wiping, and folded his arms across his chest. "I thought you might be a kindred spirit."

I laughed. "A journalist?"

Jacob grinned. I noticed his front tooth was slightly crooked. His face was smooth, hairless. He paused a moment before saying, "A writer or poet, perhaps."

"I'm not nearly unstable enough to be a poet. Or drunk enough."

We both laughed. He went back to cleaning, and I started to make my way to an empty table at the back when Jacob added, "You should come to O'Malley's tonight. A bunch of us get together, talk politics and poetry, have a few drinks. You know, work on getting drunk enough to be decent writers." He took out a cigarette from a tiny gold case and offered me one. "We won't bite, I promise."

"Alright." I took the cigarette, let him light it, and inhaled deeply. Jacob smiled, lit his own, and blew blue-gray puffs of smoke out of puckered, off-centered lips.

"We usually get there around 9:30. Know where it is?"

"Sure."

I took my coffee, which had cooled considerably, and danish, and sat down as a blonde woman in a pencil skirt and brimmed hat walked into the coffeehouse. A black fly had landed on my cup. It didn't move, just stayed there, humming. It crawled insidiously onto my thumb, and then finally buzzed off as I reached for the danish. I nibbled at my pastry, but I wasn't hungry any longer. My heart raced with the thrill of new friendship. I sensed Jacob was the kind of man who took what he wanted, who believed life owed him things, and he would not be satisfied until he had taken everything from it. I wanted nothing more that afternoon, in that coffee shop on N Street, to be counted among this man's friends, to become an important— if not vital—part of his existence.

* * *

"Two glasses of gin," the bartender announced as he handed me the drinks, disturbing my memory. I returned to the table to find Jacob playing with a gold-plated lighter. He was smoking a freshly lit cigarette and offered me one as I sat. A mound of burned-out shells already filled the glass ashtray on the table, but not all of them were ours, and I suddenly felt the urge for a calming hit of nicotine—a perfect complement to my increasing gin buzz.

Too much alcohol prevented the rest of the night from remaining complete inside my head. I do remember this: heart-beats and breaths and minutes evaporated. Dust-glazed bar tops and sweat-dusted foreheads shining in the soft light. A loose curl stuck to Jacob's damp brow. We talked about school and dreams and all the things we looked forward to after gradu-ation—the graduation we both knew would never come for me. His semester was going to start on Monday; I'd be back at work in the family store hundreds of miles away.

And then Jacob nearly fell out of the chair in an attempt to leave. I couldn't stop laughing but helped him up, throwing his left arm around me to keep him upright. Once out of the bar, I paused, leaned us against the cool stone of the building. We were in a narrow and empty alley. The lamplight illuminated our fedoras, and both of our jackets were draped over one arm as the other arm tried to steady my drunk friend. Jacob's hair took on a wild quality in the unseasonably humid weather: curls spilled from under his fedora and stuck to his pale fore-head. His black-framed glasses reflected moonlight and some-thing else.

Jacob turned his face abruptly and kissed me hard on the mouth. My reflexes were delayed; I might have kissed him back, but probably not. I remembered the taste of gin and sweat. I shoved Jacob to the ground. I punched him, once, maybe twice. His arms flew up defensively and he looked up at me like he was an animal caught in a trap and I was the hunter about to kill him. The sound of his cries blended with the distant traffic. Maybe I was crying, too.

And then all at once it was daylight, and I was at the train station. Final footfalls echoed in the DC afternoon. A train screamed into the platform, exhaling men with darkly colored fedoras and briefcases. I shoved the steamer trunk towards a Negro porter, tipped him more than I could afford, and sat on a wooden bench overlooking the platform. A clock chimed, catching in the congested air like a gasp. I picked up a copy of *The Washington Post* lying next to me. I tried to read an article on recent proceedings by the House Un-American Activity Committee, but the words remained empty blocks of letters. My headed pounded and my mouth was incurably dry. And then there was Jacob. I would never have the chance to apologize, not that he would have forgiven me. I wouldn't have forgiven me. And there was Raina, too. My sweet cousin. When would I see her again? She had been so sad, almost distraught at the news I'd be leaving. *Take care, darling.* Raina's simple parting words, punctuated with a dab to her smudging eyes. She was too consumed by her own emotions to notice my cut and swelling knuckles.

By a quarter after two, I had discarded the paper and made my way onto the train. I wiped beads of sweat from my forehead with the back of my shirtsleeve. The September heat, a relic of the scorching summer, overwhelmed passersby who seemed to move more slowly, the rose-faced conductors checking tickets at the door left damp fingerprint souvenirs, even the flies stagnated over steaming garbage pails. The coal steam settled in the folds of heat layering the air.

I reached into my pocket and produced a ticket. I handed it to the middle-aged conductor who took it perfunctorily, stamped it, and handed it back. Before making my way into the car, I turned around and cast a scattered glance across the bustling platform. I tipped my hat, but I had nobody there to bid goodbye.

CHAPTER THREE

B ayee eventually looked up from his papers and noticed me standing outside. I entered the store and was hit with the smell of sawdust and cheese. He must have just finished oiling the floor. Once a week we laid the sawdust down to absorb the oil. Assorted cheeses—parmigiano, feta, halloumi— the brined mixture of goat and sheep's milk—emitted the tangy, rich perfume of home. The tin ceiling offered an elevated air to the otherwise small, simple market.

"Your apron is in the back," my father said as the door closed behind me.

"Missed you, too," I muttered under my breath. More audibly I added, "I'm going upstairs first."

He grunted and retreated to the storage room where I imagined he had hidden bottles of gin or arak. It was obvious by his breath he had not stopped drinking, and if, as Doc McDermott claimed, these were expiring breaths, why should I stop him? Anyhow, I knew my father. He wouldn't have listened.

The store had not changed. Produce nestled in wooden bins that lined the compact aisles. Mutton, lamb, and beef hung in raw slabs over the back counter. Shelves were crowded with small bottles of saffron, coriander, cinnamon, countless other spices and mesh bags of pine nuts and chickpeas. I scanned the front of the store and remembered days running around with Michael, shoving each other until one of us inevitably knocked something over and paid for it with a good swat or kick from Bayee. A tabletop radio still occupied the shelf behind the register. The rounded, dark wood device buzzed news of the first transcontinental TV broadcast by President Truman. Large posters of Asmahan, the raven-haired, fair-eyed, Syrian-Egyptian singer, and the equally lovely Egyptian singer-actress, Umm Kulthum, hung on the wall behind the counter. Faded black-and-white stills of some village in Lebanon and vaguely familiar strangers also filled the walls.

Before I could make it to the back staircase, which would lead upstairs to our apartment, Michael came barreling out of the back room, apron splotched with blood, black hair tousled in his usual unkempt way. "Georgie!" The swinging door whooshed back and forth behind him.

He moved to embrace me. "Don't even think about it!"

Michael looked down at his streaked apron, animal-scented and sticky. "What? Not a fan of eau de mutton? We can't all be as dapper as you." My younger brother looked me eye to eye and laughed. Uninterrupted fraternity—one of the things I missed.

"Nice to see you, too."

"What happened to your hand?" A knot began tightening in my stomach, and, for a moment, I felt like I might vomit.

I gave a short laugh. "Just a disagreement solved with fists. You know, liquid politics."

"Politics or broads?" Michael chuckled. "How upset was Ummi?"

"About to find out." I grabbed the trunk with both hands,

took one look at the steep staircase, paused, and added, "Give me a hand with this, will you?"

"Big brother needs to borrow my muscles, huh," he laughed.

"Never mind. Keep an eye on the register. Dads in the storage room." I snapped, perhaps a bit too defensively.

Michael rolled his eyes, let out a long sigh, and said, "Of course he is."

Maybe it was the note of concern or frustration in his tone, but my brother seemed suddenly older. Maybe he'd given up dreams for Bayee, too.

Before heading upstairs where my mother was likely cooking as she waited for her eldest son's return, I surveyed the store once more, and the day I left crashed into my brain like a head-on collision.

* * *

Bayee fiddled with the rounded dials of the tabletop radio. A man babbled about the recent FBI report naming Hollywood figures as members of the Communist Party. He continued for several minutes about J. Edgar Hoover's work with the House Un-American Activities Committee to expose subversives in the film industry. I had never been sure if he actually listened to the news or if he just enjoyed the consistent buzz and crackle of the stereo. My father turned to a stack of papers on the counter—lists of produce, meats, spices, nuts, dried fruits and bakery items. The store was quiet. It seemed like the perfect moment to tell him the news I'd put off for three weeks.

I stopped restocking shelves with mesh bags of pistachio nuts and walked over to him. "I have something to tell you." He barely looked up at me from the sheets of inventory. My palms began to sweat.

"I'm going to Georgetown. I got a scholarship." I could feel the rush of blood to my cheeks.

"What about the store? Who do you think's gonna run it, huh? Your brother?" He looked me in the eye. "Mujdoob.You know better than your father? Huh?" My father's eyes had that pinched, glassy look that always came when he had crossed the threshold from boozy and functioning to intoxicated and angry. "You think you're smarter than me, boy?"

I felt a lump rising in my throat. "Yes." I folded my arms across my chest. The rush of the challenge coursed through my body, and I felt bigger, stronger than I actually was.

Bayee's fists were balled and the vein in his left temple was dancing. The paperwork on the counter was all at once pushed askew. A sneer revealed cigarette-yellow teeth.

Instinctively, I took a few steps backward and bumped into a tray of Ummi's freshly made knafeh. It fell to the floor. Bayee lunged.

His breath slapped me before he did.

I was eighteen. The same five feet six inches as my father, but stronger. The muscles in my arms tightened. Before I had realized what was happening, I wriggled free of his grasp, easily defeated his dipsomaniac senses. But I didn't stop at the escape; I shoved my father hard. So hard he almost fell backwards into a bin filled with apples. Despite his initial shock, Bayee recovered with a hard slap to the left side of my face. He stood, shaking, breathing hard gusts for a moment. His eyes were large, black disks floating in bloodshot white. His nostrils flared and he clenched his jaw, gritting his teeth. The brief, adrenaline-fueled confidence dissipated quickly. Before I ran out of the store, I noticed the cigarette still dangled from his red-purple lips.

* * *

I shoved open the second story door into the kitchen where disfigured vegetables lay strewn about blue and white ceramic countertops, their curling skins peeled but not yet discarded. Steaming pots bubbled on the gas stove. Outside, it began to rain. I dropped the trunk on the linoleum and crowned it with my fedora. I breathed in the aroma of lamb, crushed wheat, and lentils. This was the cooking of my ummi, who sat at the table, dainty hands molding ground meat into oval shapes. My mother was a quiet, serious woman uncomfortable with affection, but her cooking provided any nurturing or comfort I could need. While she had a severe disposition, it did not take away from her beauty. I long admired my ummi's light features—her blonde hair and blue-gray eyes. Her eyes belonged to a far-off place. When I was a young boy, I thought she lived there, this elsewhere, and I longed to know this place as she did if only to know her better.

"Ya habibi, my son. Praise God." Ummi's soft Arabic was the greeting I ached for and savored. Wiping her hands on her faded blue apron, she rose from the table and stood on tiptoes to kiss my cheek. I shoved my hand, knuckles still tender, with broken skin, into the safety of my overcoat pocket. How long, I wondered, before Ummi noticed?

My mother let go of me and glided to the stove. Light caught in her sun-colored hair. She smiled and set a plate of baked kibbeh down on the table. "You are hungry," she said. "Sit. Eat." Her smile evaporated and she was familiar again: tragic, beautiful, distant. "You haven't been eating enough. Look at you, nothing but skin and bones. Don't they have food at your Georgetown?"

I pulled out a chair. "Not like home."

The word *home* burned my throat. Two years at Georgetown, medical career aspirations, a longed-for winter break in Lebanon with Raina and Joe—memories and dreams that would now drip like blood and gristle down the sink drain in the back of the grocery store. I had relinquished the surgeon's throne to reclaim the butcher's chair.

I shoveled the kibbeh into my mouth with my left hand and relished the sweet, soothing taste of ground lamb, onion, cinnamon, and allspice.

Across the table, Ummi sat watching, shaking her head, the lines of her face relaxed into comfortable melancholy.

"Very good," I managed to convey in Arabic between mouthfuls. She knew enough English only to apologize for understanding so little English. "Raina sends her love."

"And how is my dear cousin?"

"Vivacious." I smirked at Ummi, whose face tightened reflexively in the semblance of a smile.

She smoothed her apron, got up, and moved toward a stack of dishes in the sink. "Have you seen Bayee?" The mention of my father made me choke on the kibbeh.

"Yes." I didn't elaborate, and she knew better than to press.

We need you home, my brother's letter implored. *Bayee is dying.* I swore he was dying on purpose, to spite me, to ruin my plans. I had no choice. I would have to return home. Michael could run the store during the last days of summer but not in September, when he would begin his senior year of high school. It was September now and the time had come to put aside my dreams, let them collect like old tires dumped into the Still to float downstream and settle behind the bridge and abandoned milldam. It was September and gray and the rain had begun to beat loudly against the roof.

Slouching in the wicker chair, I took in the yellow rubber gloves that covered Ummi's small forearms, the squeak of her sponge against ceramic plates, the rush of water from the spigot. A tabletop radio played Beethoven's "Moonlight Sonata," Ummi's favorite, from a small wooden table with spindly legs under the picture window that overlooked Elm Street. I ate in the comfortable silence.

After some time, Ummi shut off the faucet and removed her rubber gloves. Laying them carefully beside the sink, she reached for a pack of Old Golds. She took out a cigarette and struck a match. My mother turned toward me and exhaled with smoke and a demand. "Go downstairs and talk to your father."

CHAPTER FOUR

After the fight with Bayee, I left Danbury a few months early and sought sanctuary at my cousins in DC. I arrived at the Jowdy's doorstep, trunk in hand. The house was red brick; bracketed cornices lined the uppermost part. The white door, complimentary trim and black shutters created a warm but regal air, fitting for the lady of the house, my mother's first cousin, Lorriane Jowdy. Raina, which was the name she preferred, citing its glamourous, Hollywood elegance, was a petite woman, foreign in her beauty and extravagant in her tastes.

"George, darling! Come inside!" Raina exclaimed as she rushed past an attractive copper-skinned maid in a meticulous gray dress to greet me at the door.

Ebony hair fastened in a chignon and dressed in a pale blue blouse and black skirt, she hugged me as if I was her own son newly returned from the war. Not unlike fattoush with its subtle crunch of toasted bread and zesty dressing, Raina was a woman of wonderful contradictions. Both reticent and exuberant, at times she would retreat from conversation for a quiet cigarette and glass of wine, preferring solitude to anything else. Others, she longed for convivial dinner parties where she could flaunt expensive dresses and make merry well into the early morning hour. Her husband's position at a top law firm in DC afforded her the luxury and lifestyle she dreamt of once as a little girl in a poor mountain village in Lebanon.

I returned the embrace. "I can't thank you enough for putting me up until school starts."

"Don't be silly. You're family." As the maid struggled with my trunk, Raina led me inside. Persian carpets in shades of royal blue, crimson, peach, and salmon mostly covered the hardwood floors of the large rooms. The scent of warm honey, rosewater, and walnuts caressed the air, indicating freshly made baklawa. Artie Shaw's "Frenesi" spilled in airy notes from a phonograph in the living room. Raina Jowdy had a penchant for clocks, evidenced by the erratic ticking coming from every room: scattered cuckoo clocks, an imposing grandfather clock in the hallway, a 19th century German porcelain clock on the coffee table, a gingerbread clock resting on the ledge of the kitchen window, and, my personal favorite, a French gilt-bronze three-piece clock garniture prominently occupying the center of the mantle. The competing tick-tocks, the disharmony, was soothing.

"Sit darling. You must be hungry. Anita, please bring us a tray of pastries and coffee, will you, love?" she asked as the woman entered the room looking slightly less meticulous than minutes earlier. Raina took a seat on a crimson divan and gestured to the velvet sofa across from her. "You'll be staying in the guest room. I hope you find the accommodations to your liking." Her brown eyes darkened to a shade of midnight.

"Any room in your household could be nothing less than perfect." I removed my jacket, handed it to Anita, who left the room quickly and silently, and sat across from my cousin. I exhaled deeply and relaxed into the soft cushions.

She beamed. "Celia must be so proud! Her son—Georgetown-bound, future doctor."

I smiled. "I can't tell you how much I appreciate this." The image of my father's balled-up fists and red face popped into my head along with a soft echo of Ummi's parting words: remember who you are, remember where you're from. Surveying the opulence and comfort around me, I was keenly aware of where I was from and equally aware of where I intended to go.

Raina shook her head but smiled. "Really, darling, Joseph and I are more than happy to have you. It's been a few years since we've had any children in the house. Joe Jr. lives close by, just outside of DC in Virginia and Evelyn and her husband are in Arlington, but they're all so busy with their lives. No time for their ummi." She grabbed a pack of Old Golds from an end table. Balancing the cigarette between red-lacquered nails, Raina lit it and exhaled through matching red-painted lips. "It'll be nice having a young man in the house again."

Anita returned just then with a sterling silver tray carrying a porcelain dish of baklawa, two glass bowls of rice pudding garnished with saffron and honey, and a small pot of steaming Turkish coffee with two small cups. My belly grumbled as she carefully placed the tray on the table between us.

"Enjoy!" Anita smiled widely showing off a set of large, perfectly white teeth.

"Thank you, love. Take the rest of the day. I can manage. I want to catch up with my dear George."

"Yes, ma'am. Thank you, ma'am." Anita looked at me, smiled again, and left just as silently as she entered the room.

"Now, darling, tell me everything. Don't leave a thing out. I want all the gossip!" Raina laughed and poured two cups of coffee, cigarette dangling over pouty lips.

"Well, you know the Lebanese, we are never short on gossip!"

She laughed and abruptly stood, walked over to the sofa where I sat, and wrapped her arms snugly around me for a moment. When she let go, Raina cupped my cheek with one hand, and held the lipstick-stained cigarette in the other. In that moment, Ummi and Raina made sense in the way Lebanon itself made sense: Ummi was Qurnat as Sawda', the highest peak of Mt. Lebanon; Raina was the accessible nadir, the Mediterranean Sea.

CHAPTER FIVE

The first days back home slipped like raindrops through the gutters. A rainy September dripped and blurred into a gray October. My hands healed well enough, and, for some unknown reason, Ummi did not pursue an explanation. The lack of verbal lashing was far worse than the ramifications I had expected. This non-response terrified me in a way I had never been terrified; it almost suggested she knew what had happened that night at the bar, that night with Jacob. But I did my best to banish thoughts of Jacob, thoughts of the biology and anatomy tests I should have been taking, the studying I should have been doing on rainy October days in Riggs Library. Instead, I settled into a familiar routine: early mornings breaking bones and slicing thick cuts of meat, days unfolding in the grocery store, evenings with the family, reading George-town's newspaper *The Hoya*, which I had continued to subscribe to, sometimes cards and drinks with childhood buddies in Art Negri's coffeehouse on Liberty Street. This was the life of an immigrant son, not an American man.

One morning, in the middle of October, I walked into the

backroom, and took in the smell of suspended carcasses and fresh Turkish coffee. Large and small boning knives, a meat saw, hooks, cleaver, and swivel glinting silver against the chipped wooden table bid me good morning. I took down the hanging lamb and placed it on the table. The art of the butcher was a vulgar, beautiful thing. The skill I had begun to harness in biology labs at Georgetown, which I had intended to practice one day as a surgeon, served me well and set me apart as a master craftsman of all cuts of meat. With precision, I guided the knife from the top of the pelvis, smoothly down the side, through the spine. Next, I sawed cleanly through the space where the spine and pelvis met, pausing for a sip of the thick brew beside me and leaving a smudge of blood on the white mug. I placed one hand inside the ribcage, the other outside, feeling for the bones. Separating the loin, I cut from the spine to the belly through the last rib. The tearing flesh sent tiny pieces of gristle and flecks of blood into the air, decorating my apron in splotches. I sawed the bones of the rib cage, a perfect desecration. I scraped away the membrane cushioning the inside of the ribs, eradicating it with simple flicks of my knife. I would french the ribs, trimming the flap between them and tidying up the ends of the bone. I wrapped the resulting rack in heavy wax paper, bound it with twine, and placed it in the freezer for customers.

The tabletop radio buzzed on the window ledge; the baritone sound of Nat King Cole took me back to DC, to musty bars and gin-soaked banter, filled the small room as I sat preoccupied with the fore end of the slab. I whistled to the tune of "Mona Lisa," analyzed the reddish-brown color of the mutton, almost the same hue as the rich post-dawn sun. Michael would be joining me in the store in a few hours. He would stock the shelves with pistachios, dates, and figs and then deliver weekly groceries to several households comprised of elderly women who were either too sick to leave their houses or who had difficulty finding reliable transportation to the store. Louie Deluca would show up shortly thereafter with a delivery of fresh bread: pita, Italian white, baguettes, and rolls baked that morning by Louie and his wife, Carol, the owners of their eponymous bakery at the end of Maple Street. In the meantime, I enjoyed the early morning solitude, the music from the radio and the pounding of the cleaver against raw meat. I lit a cigarette and inhaled deeply. Former muscles, having grown soft with academic pursuits, were already returning: biceps, forearms, triceps tightening. Fine ripples under fine black hair, one benefit of working at the store.

The October day passed without incident. The usual montage—customers, sales, customers, stocking, inventory, customers, close—played and then dissolved into a rainy evening. The tall, twisted gray beech tree on the corner dropped leaves of rust-orange, red, and yellow, which clumped in the puddles, clung to my thin shirt and fedora, and tangled in brown suspenders. I hadn't thought to bring a raincoat so I hurried to lock the door and dash upstairs before the icy fingertips of rain managed to turn my dark skin white with their cold graze. The street was lined with Plymouths, Cadillacs, Ford Coupes, all blanketed in leaves and sheets of silver rain. I tried to avoid the swelling puddles without success and though it only took me a minute to make it upstairs and inside, I looked as if I had jumped into the Still River.

"Ya habibi! Let me grab you a towel!" Ummi took one look at me and rushed off to the linen closet.

I took it gratefully. After removing soggy shoes, I went into my room. My carefully pomaded pompadour more closely resembled Michael's tousled black mess of hair. Instead of sculpting it back into place, I dried it with the towel and let the hair remain wherever it fell. I studied my face in the mirror.

Dark brown eyes that were almost black, a shade Ummi referred to simply as "midnight." The tiny black mole on my left cheek which sat prominently apart from the faint shadow of beard that had begun to appear. I changed into dry clothes and went back to Ummi in the kitchen.

"Your brother's out with Marlene." She didn't turn from the eggplant she was peeling.

I walked over to the sink and washed my hands.

"It would be nice if you had a young lady, too." The deep purple skin fell easily from the vegetable.

I took a place next to her at the counter, grabbed a large spoon and knife from the drawer, and sliced and scooped out the eggplant she had already peeled. "How's Bayee?"

She continued peeling. "Same."

The rain was loud as it slapped against the window over the sink. I looked out into the gray that had deepened to black. The streetlamps had turned on, illuminating the swaying beech trees and the tapestry of falling leaves carried by the wind. Raindrops danced like fireflies in the gilded light. The dimly lit kitchen, heat from the stove adding just enough warmth. Skeins of eggplant skin filled the porcelain sink. Salt, pepper, coriander, lemon juice littered the laminate counter. We worked in wordless tandem, peeling, slicing, scooping, and sprinkling the various ingredients.

The eggplant was frying in a pan on the stove and nearly perfect.

"What about Doris Naim? She's around your age, lovely girl."

"I'm perfectly capable of deciding whom to date. Umm."

"Yes, you and your great brain. So smart. You know everything. No use for your ummi." Unshaken, she continued, "Eleanor Rizkallah? Her father owns that fur factory, he—"

"Enough!" I slammed the utensils drawer closed. "Enough."

She fell silent, moved towards the fried eggplant, and arranged them delicately on a plate. She stuffed the eggplant into fresh pita bread making a sandwich. Walking over to me at the sink, she said, "Eat this, habibi."

* * *

Later that evening, I met a few buddies at Art Negri's coffeehouse on Liberty. The coffeehouse did not actually serve coffee. The basement of a two-story brown house owned by the Italian proprietor of a deli on the corner of Liberty and Main served as a meeting place for local guys looking for a few drinks and a game of cards. The poker games were run illegally out of the dark, smoke-filled room and, for the most part, remained problem free, although the street itself was frequently pocked in multicultural brawls. Pockets of Portuguese, Italians, and Greeks, among other ethnicities, collected like dust in the cracks of Danbury's Barbary Coast, the city's underbelly.

I reached sloping, narrow Liberty as the rain let up. Dimly lit two- and three- family houses lined the street. Residual suppertime smells leaked from cracked windows. The competing scent of kabassa, sausage and peppers, and kibbeh lent to the ethnic ambiguity of Danbury's Westside. A cluster of schoolboys convened under a streetlamp on the corner. They seemed not to notice me, or, at least, not to care. "Andiamo! Andiamo!" one of the boys yelled to the others as I passed. I walked onto the wrap-around front porch of Art Negri's house as they rushed off, kicking a can into the street. The door was tucked behind a white trellis knotted with rose vines. Mrs. Negri, a short, stocky woman with black hair tied back, a few strands plastered to her shiny forehead, answered the door. The middle-aged Italian woman with her hands on her hips, sleeves of her dress rolled up to the elbow exposing beefy arms, and a cigarette drooping from her mouth was a boiling tea kettle of a person.

"Downstairs." She indicated the staircase on her left in a husky, Italian-laced voice.

The dark wooden stairs led into the basement. A single bulb affixed to a ceiling fan lit the stairwell just enough to distinguish each step. The bottom of the stairs opened into a musty, capacious room. Wood-paneled walls, no windows, cement floor. The air was thick with cigarette smoke, sweating men, and the strong scent of garlic. A few men in the back corner were smoking narghile from a long, serpentine mouthpiece attached to a glass-based waterpipe.

"Pull up a chair, Georgie," Louie "Grizzly" Auon greeted from a table where he sat playing a game of cards.

I shook Art Negri's hand which was slight compared to his wife's. Then, I helped myself to some gin and took a seat next to him. "You fellas giving Grizzly all your dough again? Figured you'd learn by now." I smiled and slapped Joey Buzaid on the back as the other men laughed.

"Nah, they're saving it up for you," Grizzly replied as he laid his hand down. "I'm out, boys." The tall, broad-shouldered Grizzly, with his dark mane of hair, loosened his necktie and tipped back his chair.

"I'm in next game. Got to warm up first." I lifted my half-filled glass and grinned.

"Don't think I can afford to play with Georgie tonight." Joey ran his fingers through heavily pomaded hair and adjusted his glasses.

Ed Shaker and Jimmy Deegan peeked at their hands and decided against calling it a night. Jimmy took out a pack of Pall Malls and pulled out a cigarette. His fair skin was pock-marked and his eyes a deep blue, like a pair of cerulean stars surrounded by craters. "Artie boy, wanna fetch us another round? Think the night just got a little longer." He took a match from a book on the table and lit the cigarette, exhaling blue-gray twists. "So what's this I hear about you being back for good, Georgie? Georgetown too tough for you?" He laughed energetically while the other men fell still. A radio played upbeat music from a corner somewhere. My hand tightened around the glass. *Little boys laughing, throwing rocks. The ringleader's blue eyes dance. He was my friend—before and after.*

I felt my face grow hot. "What's it to you, Deegs? You still sore about Ruthie McGinty? That was high school. I can't help it if the ladies find me irresistible." *She liked me. He liked her. I liked him.*

"Knock it off both of you." Joey removed his glasses, wiped them with his shirt, and put them back on.

"Come on. Let's just play cards." Ed tried his hand at diplomacy, but I could feel my blood buzzing and my fists clench.

Deegs must have tasted the tension and liked it. "Sure, Eddie. Come on Doc Butcher-man!" he snickered. "Let's play."

Before anyone could react, I was on top of Deegan, punching him in the face, pummeling his flesh like he was just a slab of mutton. My knuckles elicited blood from some orifice, I felt it running hot on my skin. Grizzly pulled me off him before I hurt him too badly. Trembling and heart beating fast, I looked down at my hands livid with another man's blood. Again.

Art Negri began yelling at me in Italian, gesticulating wildly, showering anyone close to him with spit. Grizzly guided me out of the basement, up the stairs, outside. Autumn's cool breath felt good.

"Go take a load off, George." The large man, my friend

since we were schoolboys, stood on the front porch, thumbs hooked in his suspenders. Before turning to go back inside, he added, "I didn't know you and Ruthie McGinty went together."

"We didn't. We were friends." My recently healed knuckles were beginning to hurt and the rain started up again.

"Right." Grizzly returned inside where I imagined he rejoined the drink-fueled bonhomie. And for the second time that day, I was walking in a cold, unforgiving rain.

The rain was sobering, but sober thoughts turned quickly to gin memories. The night with Jacob at the bar on M Street. Dim lights revealed fashionable men and women, laughing, seducing, engaging. Twists of cigarette smoke in the air. A pair of gin and tonics. A loose curl stuck to Jacob's wet brow. A misunderstanding and then rage. I assaulted him, felt his soft, white skin give under the strength of the punches. Eyes distorted, his broken image running and dripping like blood and tears forever in my memory.

CHAPTER SIX

Classes began. A first night at O'Malley's became many. I often sequestered myself in the Riggs Library, the smell of old books helped me concentrate. There was something comforting, like being home or drinking a hot cup of coffee on a cold day, that I felt when I was tucked among the cast-iron library stacks and seemingly infinite collections.

I relished the comfort of family, the comfort of Raina's companionship. It was almost time to return to Danbury for the holiday. I had yet to visit Ummi or Bayee since I'd left; Michael came down for a weekend. My brother told me that Bayee was becoming ill, more than just the usual hangover. He suggested I come back home for a few days, but I brushed him off saying that the term would end soon enough.

The last Sunday afternoon in Georgetown before Christmas break, I made red pepper and walnut mhammara dip with my dear cousin. In the same Lebanese tradition, we followed back home, we were cooking dinner early in the afternoon on a Sunday. My other cousins, Raina's children, would show up within a few hours and we would sit together and eat. Geography was irrelevant; food and family had no boundaries.

Bent over a garbage can scooping seeds from the red pepper, Raina still looked Hollywood glamourous. In a peacock blue dress, dark hair swept up in curls, dripping in sapphire and diamond jewelry, one hardly noticed that she was wearing an apron. Perfect red nails matched perfect red pepper. I ground walnuts, crushing them effortlessly.

"Georgie, darling? Has anyone ever told you how much you look like your father?" She looked up from the peppers and smiled.

My response was to take a cigarette from Raina's pack of Old Golds lying on the counter beside several bunches of drying herbs. I lit one and offered it to her. She took it, and I repeated the process for myself.

"It's not just your looks. You've got his charm." She exhaled gray curls of smoke.

I snickered. "Charm?"

"Yes, charm." Raina put the red pepper on the cutting board. Instead of reaching for the knife, she reached up into the cabinet and pulled down a bottle of brandy and two crystal snifters. "Afternoon cocktail?"

"Please." I pushed the crushed walnuts aside and leaned against the counter, taking a half-filled glass from Raina.

"The idea of your father as debonair surprises you?" She took a sip of the drink. Then, before I could respond, "I suppose it would also surprise you that Joe's an asshole." She laughed a reckless melody.

"Joe? An asshole?" I tried to sound incredulous, but the fact was, while he was as generous and affable as they come, he was a terrible husband. His love of horses and women did not leave much room for his lovely wife.

"Darling, thank Heavens you're going into medicine. What

a terrible lawyer or politician you'd make!" Raina finished her brandy and refilled the glass, exhaling smoke and confidences as she did so.

"Maybe he's not the best husband, but I'm sure he loves you." I swigged the rest of my drink and held it out to her. She refilled generously.

"You don't have to be polite, George." Her dark eyes seemed overcast as she leaned against the counter, extinguished her cigarette in a crystal ashtray, and folded her arms across her bosom. The late-afternoon sun caught the blue of her dress and the sterling silver of the candle sticks lining the windowsill. Shadows moved like secrets about the room. "Enough of this silliness! The family will be here soon, and we have much to do. Hand me those walnuts will you, darling? This dip isn't going to make itself." Before returning to the food, Raina cranked up the radio and began to sing along to Dinah Shore's "Buttons and Bows." She would have sounded almost identical to the real Ms. Shore but for her slight Arabic accent.

"I wish we were all going to be together for Christmas," she declared when the song had come to an end. Before I could agree, she continued, "Next year, you should come to Lebanon with us. Come home with us, darling."

Overwhelmed with sudden happiness and excitement, with affection for my favorite cousin, Ummi's favorite cousin, all I could do was smile my assent. Christmas in the old country; another attainable dream.

CHAPTER SEVEN

Our family, like our Lebanese community, communicated in food. We spoke companionship in sweet, savory bites of kibbeh; honey-glazed baklawa was reassuring maternal kisses; tightly wrapped grape leaves meant "everything will be ok." We were a community fluent in the language of food. Sometimes a gap existed between Arabic and English, meanings lost in translation; but food, food was universally spoken. Affection was limited with Ummi, but her cooking filled the space between words and gestures, the disconnect between us.

The autumn continued in a gray drizzle. I spent Saturday cooking with Ummi in preparation for Sunday dinner. Most of the weekend was dedicated to baked kibbeh shells, stuffed grape leaves, hummus and tabbouleh, roast chicken stuffed with rice and pine nuts, dried bean stew, falafel, kafta meatballs in tomato sauce, and an assortment of dried figs and pistachios. For dessert, knafeh—sweet string pastries with creamy vanilla filling. Ummi, in her usual fashion, worried there would not be enough food for the four of us and whoever stopped by.

Glancing up from the sieve, I stopped pressing the cooked chickpeas momentarily to reassure her. "It's plenty, Ummi, relax."

She shook her head but resumed kneading a mixture of ground lamb, parsley, onions, and spices for the meatballs. Her small hands worked vigorously, pounding the meat compact and smooth—her authority certain. A chorus of sizzling onions, boiling chickpeas, the percussion of knives against cutting boards, fists against raw meat and the sifting of the sieve against soft vegetables rang through the kitchen like a song.

Michael barreled into the kitchen and reached for some pistachios. "I'm starving!"

"Habibi, here, take some bread." Ummi abandoned the kafta mixture to wash her hands and find some pita bread for Michael who leaned against the counter crunching.

"Zis good, Umm."

I mocked his response, and Michael threw a pistachio at me, which missed and landed on the linoleum.

"Shut up, I like pistachios." Michael smiled through a mouthful of nuts.

"Ya habibis, enough. Michael, see if Bayee needs anything."

"Sure, Ummi." Michael grabbed a final fistful of pistachios and left the kitchen.

* * *

Marlene, the Lebanese girl Michael was seeing, and Uncle Taffy were the only people who joined us that Sunday. Loud, animated Arabic drifted from the makeshift dining room. Marlene was speaking quietly into Michael's ear, but my brother was intently focused on the food that was being set on the table in front of him.

"Everyone, quiet. Let's say grace and eat. Celia, say the

prayer," Bayee bellowed from his seat at the head of the table. His color was slightly better, but his plate was almost decorative with its obvious white space.

Ummi gave a short blessing and encouraged us to eat until we were too full. Dinner commenced, conversation resumed, and thoughts wandered like Bedouin ancestors, traversing the lonely desert of my mind. I would have been studying for finals in Riggs right now. Or in the coffee shop with Jacob. Was he working today? Maybe studying? Or nursing a hangover, drooping over some left-wing piece due later for *The Hoya*. I smiled at the thought of his black-framed glasses sliding down his nose, his hand smudging Blackwell ink. And then I remembered the last time I saw him, his black-framed glasses cracked, broken like his bloody mess of a nose. We had been very drunk when he had crossed the line, when I had crossed the line.

"Marlene, dear, we're so happy to have you join us." Ummi served Uncle Taffy kafta meatballs.

"Thank you, Mrs. Lahoud." She shot Michael an expectant glance, which he completely missed in his fervor for more hummus. Marlene was a very pretty Lebanese girl, petite, curly dark brown hair, tan skin, dark eyes. Her nose curved prominently but was not too large for her oval face. She smiled often, perhaps to show off her unnaturally white teeth.

"Eat more, habibi; your plate is too empty!" Ummi began shoveling falafel across the table and onto Marlene's plate.

"That's plenty. I want to save room for dessert."

"You're so skinny, you can eat more."

Uncle Taffy abruptly brought the conversation to me. "George, I was thinking about your marriage yesterday."

"What marriage, Khali?"

"Your future marriage, my son. Your younger brother is about to beat you to the altar." Marlene flushed a lovely shade of crimson; Michael choked and began coughing. Uncle Taffy leaned back in his chair, clasped his hands behind his head, and smiled. His protruding stomach rested comfortably on his lap.

"What're you talking about?" My tone was not as controlled as it should have been.

"You're a virile twenty-one-year-old man with a reliable business. Perfect husband material. Hell, I'd marry you." He gave a hearty laugh and nearly toppled the chair over with the force of it. The near-accident cut his joviality off.

"It's time. You should have a son sooner rather than later." Bayee grumbled before taking a deep drink of *arak*. "The family line needs to continue. You're the eldest."

Before anyone could respond, Uncle Taffy continued as if Bayee had never spoken. "Lots of Lebanese girls with good families ask about you. One, in particular." He paused for a bite of food. "Very sweet girl. Lovely family." A pregnant pause to let the significance of the impending name build. I almost expected a drum roll. "Eleanor Rizkallah."

"What about her, Khali?" My exasperation oozed with each word.

"She asked about you, that's what!" His words were barely audible through the mouthful of kibbeh.

Bayee exploded with, "He's saying you should court her, adjab!" He slurred the punctuating insult.

"Thank you, Bayee. I understand that. I'm asking *why* should I date her?"

"Yeah, there're plenty of prettier girls," Michael added. "And Georgie has no problem in that department anyway." Marlene slanted her eyes and scowled in his direction although he remained oblivious.

"Michael, don't be rude! Eleanor Rizkallah's a lovely girl with a lovely family," Ummi chimed in.

"That's not the point. I don't need anyone's help."

Before anyone else could weigh in, Uncle Taffy, in

complete momentary abandon of his crusade, began yelling at Michael who had just picked up another kafta meatball with his hand and put it on his plate. "Germs! Germs! Why are you using your hands like that, boy? Use this serving spoon!" He was brandishing the silver spoon like a weapon. "You people are all barbarians! Don't you understand the nature of germs?"

Affecting a serious expression, Michael smirked an apology. Everyone else, even Bayee, tried not to laugh, though Marlene looked mildly frightened.

Uncle Taffy, sitting with his arms folded and face flushed, gruffly stated, "I just wanted you to know she asked about you. That's all."

"Well, thank you. Thank you, everyone. Now if you don't mind, I'm going to eat my supper in peace!"

* * *

As the holidays approached, Bayee became sicker. Perhaps the time of year induced a bout of nostalgia, or, maybe, I had finally begun to accept the fact that my father was dying. Either way, I began remembering. Memories regarding Bayee were mostly black, burned, charred by flames of resentment, but one existed untouched among the kindling.

It was 1940 and I was ten and Michael was eight and we were helping Bayee organize shelves in the store. The summer heat was unbearable. I would have sworn it to be a thousand degrees in the shade. Small puddles of sweat pooled under my arms, soaking the white, short-sleeved shirt, rendering it soiled and undesirable.

Bayee stopped his paperwork, looked at us from behind the counter. "How are those shelves coming?" Drops of perspiration decorated his tanned forehead. Even then, his hair was receding and thin, although completely black.

46

"Almost done. Sort of." I responded timidly, afraid he might take his frustration with the heat out on us.

"Let's take a break then, shall we?" He walked over to the door and turned the open sign to closed. "Come on, follow me." Obediently, we made our way behind him, to the back of the store, through the back storage room littered with wooden crates of spices shipped from Lebanon and bins teeming with recently delivered watermelons and cantaloupes. Wooden coffers heaped with shisha lay waiting to be sorted. A heterogeneous blend of the Mediterranean tobacco, pungent citrus, olives, coriander, saffron, and freshly baked pita bread blended, and intensified by the heat, created a distinctly Arabic scent. Bayee led us out the door to the backyard. To the right were stairs leading up to our apartment.

The tiny yard, enclosed by a tall, unpainted picket fence, was a shade of blonde, parched by the oppressive heat and lack of precipitation. A garden hose, coiled and sleeping serpent-like, was all at once disturbed by Bayee. Turning the water on and unraveling it, he pressed his thumb partially over the mouth of the hose so that water shot off in all directions.

"Doesn't that feel better now, waladi?" he asked in a light tone. Michael and I danced like little dervishes in the water falling on us like rain. Whirling in circles and watching the water catch in the sunlight, breaking like hydrogen cobwebs upon us, we laughed until our sides cramped. Bayee held the hose and continued spraying us as Ummi stood on the upstairs porch watching and smiling, her gold hair glowing in my memory's sun. After an eternity of bliss, Bayee stopped and returned the hose to its proper place. Before heading back to the store for the day, he dug deep into his trouser pocket for a few cents. Handing the money to me he said, "Ibn, why don't you and Michael take the day off. Go buy yourselves an ice cream at Woolworths."

Michael and I said, "*Shukran, Bayee!*" in unison and ran in the direction of The Five and Ten.

But that was nearly a lifetime ago. December revealed itself in the snow dust that had begun to frame the ground. The wind had teeth; it nipped and nibbled at skin without discrimination; children in scarves and heavy jackets and older folks equally swaddled in winter attire wore the pink and red evidence of its bite. Bayee's yellow complexion had become normal to us then, but the swollen legs and feet to match the swaying belly were new. His breath seemed to tangle in his lungs. Distorted, rounded nail beds made his fingers like miniature clubs, like the sausages we sold at the store. Sometimes, I noticed residual blood on the toilette seat, a souvenir of his frequent vomiting. And while his body continued its wretched crawl towards death, alcohol continued to expedite the process. I tried to focus on the memories in which Bayee was alive and paternal.

But December was not just a time for remembering; it was a time for regretting. I should have been on winter break. I should have been with Raina and Joe in Lebanon. My favorite cousins, my constants and confidants in DC, had included me in their holiday plans, their plans to return home, home to a land that, while I had never been, was a vivid memory forged by Ummi's stories and old photographs on walls in the shop. Lebanon: land of ancestors and dreams. I was the cedar tree in our backyard, a product of Lebanon, which had rooted and thrived in American soil, the soil in the back of our store on Elm Street. But I was out of place among the native trees, the beeches and birches and elms. I longed to be the beech tree on the corner, tall and twisted and regal. Maybe a trip to Lebanon would help me understand why, embrace the cedar tree that seemed so out of place in our backyard. But instead of exploring our homeland with Raina and Joe, I was home, watching my father kill himself.

Michael, in complete disregard for winter, came barreling into the kitchen one evening wearing a simple sports jacket and lugging several brown bags from Ali Bez's Fruit and Veggie Stand. His mop of hair crowned the tall paper bags, and his chapped hands were conspicuously lacking gloves.

I looked up at him from my spot at the kitchen table. The bags tipped in his arms and a few rogue oranges dropped to the linoleum floor. Michael shot me a look that was equal parts irritation and accusation. "Don't worry, I don't need any help. I'm obviously using my superhuman strength to manhandle these bags into submission."

"Great. Didn't plan on getting up." I glanced at him from T.S Eliot's *The Waste Land* and smirked.

A few seconds later, after nearly dropping one entire bag as he tried putting it on the counter, he added, "I may have overestimated my skills."

I laughed, walked over to the counter, and relieved him of his load. "What happened to your superhuman strength, little brother?"

"I exhausted it fighting the cold." He rubbed his hands together in an attempt to warm them.

I smiled and rolled my eyes. "So, what're you doing tonight? Taking on Father Winter for round two?"

"Funny. What's it to you?" he responded sheepishly.

"You have another date with Marlene Buzaid, don't you?"

"So, what if I do?"

"That's great, she's a pretty girl, from a good family, too."

"Don't say anything to Ummi. She'll start pressuring me to propose. It's only been a few dates and half the town has us married after graduation."

"You? I can't go to church without mothers offering up their daughters for dates! St. Anthony's dating service. Father Hayek himself came up after mass last Sunday. 'Jeorje, have you met

Ms. Eleanor Rizkallah? She's a nice girl, Jeorje. Very nice girl.'"
I aped the old priest's harsh "g" sound, residual Arabic present
in the syllable.

Michael and I laughed until Ummi breezed into the
kitchen. "What're you boys laughing about in here? Bayee is
resting and if you two wake him..." She waved a slender finger
at us.

"Sorry, Ummi. We'll be quiet," Michael apologized before
she could go off on one of her lectures.

Ummi shook her head and muttered under her breath
before returning to the living room to a pile of clothing that
needed mending, and to the radio that buzzed an Arabic
diatribe.

"I'm not really going out with Marlene tonight," Michael
whispered, drawing my focus back to the kitchen.

"Really?" I had resumed my seat at the table and was about
to return to reading when my brother continued.

"I've been going with this other girl, Kate Hanrahan. Real
Irish spitfire—blonde hair, dark eyes, legs that go from here to
the old country. I think she might put out soon. I usually take
her to a movie or for a shake at The Five and Ten. Bayee lets
me take the Lincoln so afterwards I park behind the old farm-
house, and we fool around in the back seat."

A rush of warmth hit my cheeks. "My little brother is
becoming a man!" The pride was sincere; so was the
jealousy.

Punching me in the arm, he gloated, "I *am* a man, brother!"
He had a cocky tone but retained a goofy grin. "There must
have been some fine ladies in DC, a nice Southern belle,
perhaps?" I imagined how easy life must be for my younger
brother. So uncomplicated.

I grinned, hoping the erubescence of my cheeks would be
perceived as confidence. "You know how suave I am."

"Come on, give me some details. What did she look like?" I blessed him and his obliviousness.

"Which one?" I winked and he just looked at me, radiating fraternal admiration. It had been so long since I'd felt such gratitude course through me.

"Don't know why I'm surprised. So typical." Michael reached for an orange, choosing to peel it instead of putting it away and ignoring the rest of the fruit collected on the bottom of the grocery bag.

"Yeah, that's me. Such a ladies' man." I tended to the ignored oranges as Michael chomped on a piece.

"Staying in tonight?"

"It's too damn cold outside to leave the house, unless you're a superhero, of course."

"Or have a date with a beautiful woman!" He smiled as a trickle of juice escaped the corner of his mouth. He expunged it with the sleeve of his shirt. "Better go change. Gotta looks dapper for the lovely Miss Hanrahan."

I shook my head and smiled at my brother, who grinned and left the room. I wanted to drown in the words of T.S. Eliot, but my thoughts were surfacing in DC. Making red pepper and walnut mhammara dip with Raina, preparing for a Bio test in Riggs, debating Middle Eastern politics with Jacob at the café on N Street—a kaleidoscopic view of a life I once called mine.

* * *

I was asleep when Michael came home later that night.

"George, wake up!" Michael sat at the edge of my bed, shaking me awake.

I swatted at him with the arm not tucked under the pillow, half certain he was nothing more than a waking dream, a nighttime mirage.

He had resorted to nudging me repeatedly until I opened my eyes and sat up.

"What the hell?" I rubbed my eyes until Michael was clear, smiling goofily, his perpetually tousled hair more tousled than usual.

"I need to tell you something."

"Seriously? This can't wait until I'm awake?" I propped myself up on an elbow. "Did you make it with Kate?"

"No, Georgie. I had an epiphany!" His dark eyes were wild. "I took Kate to see *A Streetcar Named Desire*, you know, the one with Vivien Leigh? God, Vivien Leigh is something. Really beautiful—"

"Your epiphany is that Vivien Leigh is beautiful? Seriously, Michael, it's like one in the morn—"

"No! I'm getting to it. Like I was saying, Kate and I saw *A Streetcar Named Desire*. Afterward, we drove to our usual spot. We start kissing, her dress comes off, she's just in her corset, breasts look like they are fighting to get out and then... I have an epiphany!"

"About Kate's breasts?"

"That I'm in love with Marlene!" He jumped off the bed at this point as if to emphasize the significance, highlight his foolery.

"What the hell does that have anything to do with everything you just told me?" I was sitting erect, fully awake now.

"Don't you see, George? I could have had Kate right then and there, but all I could think of was Marlene and how upset she would be if she knew I was about to make it with Kate Hanrahan. Christ, George, I'm in love!"

"Well, that's a hell of a way to figure it out. Congratulations. Now can I please go back to sleep?" I fell back onto my pillow before he responded.

"Of course. Sweet dreams, brother!" And with that,

Michael collapsed onto his twin bed next to mine and was snoring almost instantaneously.

Now wide awake, I looked around our small room dressed in nighttime black: the navy blue and white vertical striped wallpaper, a singular window overlooking the corner of Elm Street and Beaver, and the prominent crucifix hanging on the wall between two twin beds. These things were hardly distinguishable from the quiet darkness. I closed my eyes and prayed for sleep.

CHAPTER EIGHT

It was December and I was no longer a student at
Georgetown and Bayee was dying without any kind of
grace. Or so I thought. One day, weeks before his death, Bayee
seemed almost to recover, if only for an afternoon, if only for a
swan song.

Michael and I were stocking the shelves when Uncle Taffy
burst through the door and knocked into a bin of high-piled
melons, which subsequently crashed to the floor.

"I'm going to make one million dollars!" he exclaimed
breathlessly.

"Only *one million*, Uncle?" Michael feigned incredulity.

Taffy ignored his youngest nephew and spoke directly to
me, "I have an invention. It's genius!"

"What is it, khali?" I tried to look interested. Michael rolled
his eyes as he scooped up the melons and returned them to
their rightful place.

"Hair tonic." He grinned.

"Hair tonic?" I asked as I placed bottles of saffron on the
nearly empty shelf.

"Yes. I have created a solution using very, very secret ingredients. You apply to the head, and boom, the hairs start growing in few weeks! Cure for baldness!" He threw his thick arms into the air for emphasis.

Michael was nearly doubled over with laughter, and I was struggling to maintain composure. Uncle Taffy was completely bald and had been for as long as either of us could remember.

I stopped stocking bottles and turned towards my uncle. "Did you use this tonic?"

"What kind of question is that?" Shaking his head, he turned and walked out of the store as abruptly as he had come in.

"He's priceless," Michael remarked as he replaced the last of the disturbed melons.

I went behind the counter to attend to sheets of weekly inventory. I glanced up at the clock above the cash register. Half past ten. "Would you go out back? Ali Bez should be pulling up any minute with the produce."

"Sure." Michael picked up a few empty crates and walked into the storage room leaving me alone with a half-empty store. Mrs. Saadi and Mrs. Issa were making their way through the store more engrossed in a conversation about the next Ladies' Guild meeting than their respective grocery lists.

I heard the back door swing but assumed it was Michael. I didn't realize it was Bayee until the garrulous women stopped talking to each other and Mrs. Saadi exclaimed, "George, dear, how wonderful to see you!" The short, middle-aged woman in dark framed glasses rushed over to Bayee and kissed him twice, once on each cheek.

Mrs. Issa followed, mimicked the greeting, and added, "You look great." Their partially filled grocery baskets hung from their arms like second pocketbooks.

"Lydia. Georgette. Good to see you, ladies. Both ravishing

as always. I'm surprised your husbands let you out of their sight!" His smile elicited schoolgirl blushes. "How're Jimmy and Ed doing?" His face bore traces of warmth.

"Keeping busy," Lydia Saadi responded for both of them. Her short, dark coiffure complemented her sharp features.

"How's Celia?" Mrs. Issa asked, tucking a loose curl into a tightly fastened chignon.

"Saint-like." Bayee laughed as the women smiled affectionately. He wore a freshly pressed pale blue dress shirt and black slacks. His swollen belly hung over his belt, drawing attention to how skeletal his limbs had become. "I'll leave you ladies to your shopping. Let me know if you need anything."

They both watched him walk away. "Great seeing you, George."

Bayee walked around the counter and stood next to me, glancing down at the sheets of half-completed inventory. I noted only a whisper of gin. "I see you're holding down the fort."

"I see you're not upstairs resting."

"Can't get anything past you, huh?" He lacked the usual antagonism. "Everything is good? People happy? No problems?" He folded his once-thick arms over his chest, leaned against the register, and surveyed the store like a Bedouin sheik taking stock of his possessions.

"I know what I'm doing." I didn't look away from the inventory.

"I know, son." He placed a hand on my shoulder and squeezed it. "I know."

I looked into his tired brown eyes; blood vessels decorated the whites like explosions of fireworks. The muscles in his jaw tightened visibly. Bayee nodded and headed towards the backroom. He returned minutes later with a pocket of pita bread stuffed with minced raw lamb balanced between his withering fingers. The smell of the fresh meat mixed with the scent of onions, olive oil, and mint.

"Try the new shipment of lamb. So fresh." An ephemeral memory seized me. I was a boy, Bayee was not sick, and we ate kibbeh nayyeh in the backroom while poking fun at the old Lebanese ladies trying to read small print on small spice bottles. The afternoon sun dimpled store shelves and the old women's bifocals.

"I'm good," I said. "Thanks though."

Bayee chewed slowly, savoring the kibbeh nayyeh as if it would be his last.

"Hey, Georgie! Shipment's here and everything's accounted for!" Michael announced as he came in from the back storage room, licking fingertips, savoring the remainder of the snack he had just shared with Bayee.

Mrs. Saadi grabbed him to help her before I could respond.

* * *

Christmas was a week away, and Bayee had resumed dying. The afternoon in the store had been strange, but it had rekindled a hope in Ummi that had burned out long before his liquor-breath. Despite the progression of his disease, Ummi remained more certain than ever that Bayee could get better, that he would get better. Perhaps it was this wifely devotion that was the most heartbreaking thing of all.

Bayee and Ummi were their own unique love story. While my mother was neither demonstrative nor verbose, her affection for my father was undoubtable. And my father, too, lavished upon Ummi his own kind of adulation. Long before alcohol laid siege to his organs and his mind, Bayee was generous—to a fault. Any extra money he made went to buying gifts or to card games and drinks at the Lebanon Club. He couldn't save a penny if he'd tried. One day, Bayee came home from a long day at the store with a pair of pearl earrings for Ummi. He smiled adoringly at his wife the entire hour she reprimanded him for spending money we didn't have on such frivolous items; however, she put the earrings on that day and almost never took them off.

The next day, she made his favorite dessert—knafeh, a Lebanese cheesecake of sorts, delicious shredded dough, a salty ackawi cheese, and Ummi's orange blossom syrup drizzled on top, garnished with chopped pistachios. Bayee savored each bite as Ummi sat across from him at the table drinking a cup of steaming Turkish coffee and occasionally touching the round, smooth pearl decorating her right lobe. The silence between them was comfortable, affectionate. This childhood memory represented the essence of Bayee and Ummi: clipped words, sweet, seductive bites of a favorite dessert, lost money, spent money, fastidiously micromanaged money. Ummi was a solemn prayer sliding off the lips of children: deliberate, dutiful, pious. Bayee was a drunken song, passionate, overwhelming, full of life. For years, they compensated for each other's peccadillos.

Now he waddled on swollen legs and ankles, distended stomach swaying with the effort. His jaundiced skin shimmered with perspiration. Tufts of still-black hair peeked through a thin, sweat-drenched white undershirt. His teeth had become blood-stained and yellow from vomiting. He hissed at Ummi as she tried to help him into bed.

"I'm not an imbecile, al'ama! I can walk from the bathroom to my goddamned bed. If you want to be useful, bring me another arak." He fell into the bed, emitting a loud groan. "Jesus Christ."

"I'm sorry. I know you're uncomfortable. I'll grab—"

"Just stop talking! You're giving me a headache."

Ummi threw her hands up and walked over to the kitchen.

She smoothed her French blue cotton housedress, ran her slender hands over the crisp white apron. She didn't say another word but maintained a martyr's silence.

I didn't bother to say anything in her defense. Instead, my eyes burned him an angry glance. I handed him the newspaper and followed Ummi downstairs.

Our apartment was small. It occupied the floor above the grocery store. It was comprised of a good-sized kitchen, a living room that doubled as a dining room for Sunday dinners and special occasions, a bathroom, and three bedrooms. Michael and I shared one room, Bayee and Ummi had one, and the third was a spare room that held Ummi's sewing machine and various boxes of anonymous items. Now, Ummi slept in there so Bayee could rest more comfortably. However, her restless shuffling and quiet prayers had become synonymous with other nighttime sounds. It certainly explained the deep gray shadows framing her lovely blue eyes.

"He shouldn't talk to you like that." I came up behind her at the sink and put my arm around her; she remained tense.

She held the frosted bottle of arak for a moment and then poured the potent liquid into a tall glass; a tear fell softly into the drink. Ummi patted my arm in response. We walked back to Bayee's room where he had tossed the paper on the floor in a fit of protest.

"I can't focus on that right now." He wiped his forehead with the back of his hand. His bald head reflected the light fixture on the ceiling.

"Here's your drink. Careful not to spill it on the sheets, I just changed them." Ummi handed it to him. A strand of hair freed itself from the tight chignon at the nape of her neck. She tucked it behind her ear.

Without any acknowledgment, Bayee turned the conversation to me. "Why haven't you found a wife yet? There's plenty of Lebanese girls with good families around here. What's wrong with them, huh? You think you're some kind of city boy now? Better than us because you had some college? You think you're better than us?" *Better than a man who gambled and drank everything he ever had away? Better than a grocer, a butcher?*

Ummi cringed.

I was fuming. "I am better than you, that's what I think!" I was shaking so hard, I put my hand on the post of his bed to steady myself.

He leaned forward, suddenly strong with his rage, and threw the arak in my face.

White flames blazed through retinas and corneas and sockets: *Make it stop! Make it stop, God! Make it stop!*

Ummi must have grabbed water and helped me flush out the *arak*. She must have been quick to act, but it was a thousand years and I had died and God had turned his back on me.

My mother helped me sit at the kitchen table and brought me a glass of water to drink, my eyes still burning. As she placed the glass in front of me, she said, "Don't you ever think you are better than your father. Remember that he came to this country with nothing. He made a life, habibi, a beautiful life for us. For you. You are who you are because of your father. Don't you ever forget that." She walked away without another word, and I remained seated, eyes stinging.

I wasn't crying. I didn't cry. And I really did believe I was better than my father.

* * *

Ummi and I began cooking for Christmas three days beforehand, the same day we brought home the tree. She had put Michael and me in charge of getting the Christmas tree, a task whose success became a highly contested issue. After an hour of arguing over which tree would better represent our family's needs, we eventually resorted to a coin toss, which I won with a declaration of "heads."

The one I had selected was a five-foot Douglas fir, a tree only a few inches shorter than Ummi. There were several large gaps between the sparse branches and the trunk slanted prominently to the right. It had more character than any other tree on the lot. When the silver tinsel was piled on, a bit too generously, the large multicolor lights draped abstractly, and the ornaments hung in awkward bunches (due to the uneven clustering of the branches), the Christmas tree was the most beautiful I had ever seen. Bayee even commented, "It has personality."

We prepared sugar-coated almonds and baked cabbage stuffed with ground lamb shoulder, cinnamon, and white rice. Eggplant fried in lemon and olive oil along with baba ghannouj and hummus were served with warm pita bread. For the main course, we roasted a chicken and stuffed it with rice, ground lamb, and pine nuts. I helped Ummi grind leg of mutton to make baked stuffed kibbeh, which we also served as a main dish. I made rice pudding using orange blossom water, powdered caraway, and cinnamon, and when it was finished, I decorated the pudding with blanched and slivered almonds. Ummi and I also spent time on an assortment of pastries which we began making a week in advance of all the other cooking.

Aside from my parents and brother, we were joined by Uncle Taffy, Marlene, and Father Hayek on Christmas Day. The old, rotund priest sat at the table laughing a jovial sound with Bayee, who occupied the head. Yellow-coated eyes tried futilely to smile, to accompany the sanguine complexion of the priest beside him. Uncle Taffy joined them in the crystal snifters full of licorice-flavored arak and the tobacco-filled narghile water pipes. Skeins of gray smoke danced to the sound of Christmas tunes coming from the tabletop radio. Michael had taken Bayee's Lincoln to pick up Marlene, and I was helping Ummi arrange the appetizers.

"Let your Ummi do that, boy. Come join us for some arak." Uncle Taffy exhaled a plume of smoke and passed the narghile to Bayee.

"I will in a minute, Khali. We're almost done." I finished the placement of pita bread around the bowl of hummus, arranging the triangular pieces like petals around a chickpea blossom.

"Should we've gotten you an apron for Christmas, boy?" Bayee spit from his seat at the head of the table.

I chose to ignore him. Uncle Taffy began explaining his revolutionary hair tonic to Bayee and Father Hayek. At that moment, Michael and Marlene walked in with rosy, snow-stung faces. Marlene's mink coat was covered in a fine layer of white, as was Michael's camel jacket. Her dark, curly hair was perfectly coiffed beneath a stylish black hat also dusted in white.

"Just in time for appetizers, sit down, sit down!" Ummi exclaimed as she adjusted a cloth napkin, refolding it to meet her expectations.

"Smells wonderful, Mrs. Lahoud!" Marlene gave her mink to Michael and made her way to the table in a black taffeta dress. "Can I help with anything?" Michael's young girlfriend was genuine, always smiling, and often laughing or joking right along with my brother. It occurred to me then that she was the female version of Michael.

"No, no. Just eat!" Ummi walked around to Bayee and placed a small hand on his shoulder. He reached up and covered it with his for a moment before she rushed off to grab more pita bread from the kitchen.

Returning to the table, she took a seat at the opposite end of the table from Bayee. I sat to her right. Marlene sat beside Michael, whispered something in his ear while puffing out her cheeks and widening her eyes. He started laughing hysterically.

Father began what would be a seven-minute Christmas blessing, one which I spent eyeing the food spread out on the table before us. "Bless you, George and Celia, for your hospitality. God will look favorably upon you and your household."

Ummi thanked Father Hayek for honoring us with his presence, which signaled to those of us who may or may not have paid attention to the prayer that eating could commence. *I could have been eating this dinner in Lebanon right now. With Raina and Joe.*

Ummi began serving Father Hayek some stuffed cabbage.

"Celia, I need more arak." Bayee requested from the head of the table.

"Of course." She rose from her barely occupied seat, abandoned her own still empty plate, and took his glass. Ummi wore a crimson silk dress with a single strand of pearls hugging her delicate neck, her fair hair pulled back into a French twist. She could have been a European among Arabs.

"Celia, ukhti, grab me some, too, if it isn't any trouble." Uncle Taffy asked his sister as she made her way into the kitchen.

"It's no trouble at all, akhii." Her black pumps were muted by the deep indigo Persian carpet.

"On second thought, I'll help you. I just want to make sure our glasses don't get mixed up. Germs, you know." Uncle Taffy stood up, a napkin falling off his lap. His bald head shone like the globe of a streetlamp in the soft gilded light of the dining room. His facial hair couldn't be considered a beard but rather a few days' worth of scruff.

"What *does* he mean by that?" Marlene quietly asked Michael.

He just shook his head and stifled a laugh.

Ummi and Uncle Taffy returned to the table with two nearly full glasses of arak. She set one in front of Bayee and the other in front of her brother, who had resumed his seat.

"Celia, your stuffed cabbage is the best I've ever had!" The old priest said in Arabic as he shoveled a generous helping into his mouth.

Ummi nodded at Father Hayek. "Thank you, Father." She had finally begun to fill her own plate with the food we spent so much time preparing.

"Tell me, Jeorje, have you taken my guidance seriously?" Father asked between mouthfuls of cabbage.

"Excuse me?" I focused on the plate in front of me, choosing to ignore the eyes stuck to me like bits of dried eggplant on the bottom of the frying pan.

Turning to Ummi, the old priest explained, "I've decided Eleanor Rizkallah would be a wonderful match for your son. Wonderful!" A shadow of a smile appeared on Ummi's lips. *To be on the other side of the world, far away from this conversation.*

"Georgie works all the time, Father. He doesn't really have time right now for anything else." Michael's defense was unexpected. I smiled at my younger brother.

"Yes, yes, of course. But I'm ready to perform your marriage. You're young still, son. Don't spend all your time in that store of yours. Your brother here is capable, too." Michael frowned at him, but the old priest was too preoccupied with the delectable spread before him to pursue the conversation much further. Everyone fell into comfortable consumption as Frank Sinatra sang of his dream of a white Christmas, the very kind we were enjoying.

* * *

Snow danced in gray light, piled in frenzied drifts. Christmas was over like a breath, but winter remained. I remained, remained obediently, in my cage with its bars made of shadows. I continued to subscribe to Georgetown's newspaper. One afternoon, not long after the holiday, I picked up the previous semester's final issue of *The Hoya*. I had neglected it when it arrived, too busy peeling the flesh off animals with the ease of tearing wrapping paper from Christmas gifts. Too busy cooking with Ummi; too busy insulting my dying father.

The headline read "Hoya Editor Dead of Apparent Suicide." I stumbled over the words and continued reading, and finished, and returned to the beginning, masochistically reading a second, third, fourth time. Jacob Eisenburg was dead. He had killed himself. The article left out the details. A cruel montage, stuck on repeat, played over and over and over in my mind: sleeping pills, dead; gunshot, dead; jumping into the Chesapeake, dead. Repeat. I sat at the edge of my bed holding tightly to reality, focused on the snow. But I was slipping towards memory, the fist of regret clenching my throat, choking me.

Jacob is dead. The trees were already dead; ice had taken up in the bark, in the limbs. *Why?*

The final night in Georgetown, I stumbled upon him, waiting for me perhaps, on a bench in center of the Quad. Jacob Eisenburg. Returning from a bar where I had just said goodbye to some of my other friends, I saw Jacob scribbling in a notebook under the lamplight. A rain began to fall softly, collecting in Jacob's fedora like tears on a pillow. He looked up from his notebook as I approached and smiled in his lopsided way—one corner of his mouth higher than the other, giving him a distinctly mischievous look.

"Nice night for working outside."

"Who doesn't love writing on soggy paper?" He tucked the notebook inside his jacket. "I was going to call it a night anyway." He got up from the bench, walked towards me and said, "So you're going back to Connecticut."

Something twisted in my abdomen. "It seems that I am."

"You weren't going to leave without saying goodbye?"

"Of course not." We stood under the lamplight as the rain continued to paint our hats and jackets. Jacob's hair took on a lion quality in the weather: curls framed his head and stuck to his pale forehead like a mane. Two friends, two young men, just beginning to experience life, not yet shaped by its inevitable cruelty.

Rain drops smudged his black-framed glasses. "Let's grab one more drink." We both knew it would probably be the last one we'd ever share.

And now I was sitting in my bedroom trying to digest the fact that Jacob was dead, and I had never said "I'm sorry." I couldn't sit still any longer; the snow was making me dizzy. I got up and went into the kitchen and pulled a bottle of Bayee's gin from the cabinet. I poured half a glass and drank it in almost a single gulp. Ummi sat with her sewing, Michael was out. Bayee was dying, probably still drinking in the bedroom. I retreated to the safety of my own room, bottle tucked under my arm. *Why, Jacob? Was life so terrible?* I threw the copy of *The Hoya* across the room, but I was not satisfied with that impotent gesture. I picked it back up and tore at it, clawing it with animal rage. I ripped it even when it was already shredded. *You've deprived me of the chance to ever say I'm sorry.* Eventually, I collapsed on my bed again, abandoned the glass and drank directly from the bottle.

Gin thoughts became gin memories. I begged the remembering to stop, begged for sleep instead. But gin made me seven years old again. The snow outside the window became a tapestry of leaves. It was autumn. I remembered the trees along Elm Street were colorful, like the red and orange kites Michael and I flew at Candlewood Lake every summer.

This particular day—branded into my memory as if with a cattle iron—I belonged to a group of average schoolboys playing in an average schoolyard. We had been running around, maybe playing tag or hide-and-go-seek or cowboys and Indians. Whatever it was, the game had ended. I was flushed, energized from the adrenaline and the recklessness of little boys. I hugged my friend and pecked him on the lips. I was happy, and I smiled at him. But he didn't look happy, and he didn't smile back. Boys don't kiss boys. I needed to learn this lesson, they explained as they pushed me to the ground and kicked me hard in gut. *"But if I like him, why can't I?"* Such a stupid question mandated a few additional kicks.

Later, when I ran home, my sides and stomach aching, I took a circuitous route, cutting through a deserted field by the train tracks. Bums, casualties of the Depression, sometimes spent their days there. On this day, the area was vacant except for some discarded items—empty bottles, cigarette butts, and an old tire almost hidden by the overgrown weeds. I sat on the tire, and, through tears, I looked up at the cloudless sky and asked God, *"Why?"* He responded by spilling sunlight all over me, drizzling it over clear shards of glass, frosted amber fragments, dark green broken bottles. The jagged edges caught the light and cast it in all directions. When I had stopped crying, I stood up and began slowly, carefully toward home, my arms clutching a still throbbing gut. Walking through the crystalline detritus, I thought of a mosaic, broken but still beautiful.

I didn't know it then, but I would only ever be broken.

CHAPTER NINE

As the days became shorter and colder and death crept closer to our doorstep, I spent a lot of time remembering. I remembered the Danbury Fair and a younger, happier Bayee.

Fair day was a holiday in our household. My father closed the shop and dressed in church attire. Donning his one gray suit, bowler hat, and freshly shined shoes, Bayee verged on dapper. He even wore cologne—a musky sent like leather and cardamom that complimented the heavy notes of tobacco that stuck to his skin and clothes. His hands were scrubbed nearly clean, but the stained cuticles and callouses that decorated his fingers betrayed his blue-collar trade.

My mother was especially elegant on Bayee's arm. Pale pink dress, button down jacket and matching hat, her fashion was simple yet beautiful. Outside of Sunday mass, my parents rarely dressed up and went out together—fair day, weddings, and funerals were the only exceptions.

For ten days every October, 52 acres of wetlands was transformed into the sprawling fairgrounds. Nearly forty-foot-tall fiberglass sculptures of Uncle Sam and Paul Bunyan were set up among the animal and farm-grown food exhibits. Bayee was in his element, sampling and purchasing homemade wines and produce from the fruit and vegetable stands. Manufacturers' tents displayed locally made hats, boots, and other items. Each year, Bayee would buy a new hat for Ummi who, eyes fire-lit in a way that rivaled young girls in the throes of first love, would swoon over the gift, but, mostly, over the attention her husband lavished on her when he was flush with adrenaline from the great Danbury State Fair.

The twenty-five cent admission gave entrance to the rides, food stands, and races. We always went during the first five days which were when the horse races took place on the track. My father smiled and laughed as if he, too were a young boy, and I couldn't help but fall in love with the excitement of the horse races if not to have something in common with him.

Crowds of people were as thick as the patches of pachysandra growing in our backyard; beyond the gate, it was impossible to move without bumping into folks of all ages, from all parts of the state who came to enjoy the fairgrounds. The scent of popcorn and peanuts, sausages sizzling on grills, and sawdust pricked the cool autumn air. Hot dogs, oysters, clam chowder, chicken pot pies with gravy—food of all kinds filled the concession stands that made up restaurant row.

In 1946, John Leahy, a local oil tycoon, purchased and reopened the fair after it had been closed during the War. Retaining some country fair elements but adding a new showman flare, he incorporated circus animals and transformed the track into the Danbury Race Arena where midget and stock cars raced all year, even through the summer months. Although Bayee continued to love the fair, he could never hide his disappointment that his favorite equine element had been replaced with vehicles.

But before the race track was paved and still hosted horses,

I remembered attending the heats with my father. I remembered high school students skipping classes for the day to attend the fair and congregating at the rides. I remembered once seeing a little blonde girl, maybe seven or eight, polishing apples with rags to display in large carts. Other blonde children, probably her siblings, were arranging the apple stand which included candied fruit dipped in caramel and chocolate. I remembered my father making his way through a crowd of teenagers to purchase four caramel apples—one for each of us. I remembered the way he handed them to Michael and me, his smile so broad I wanted to reach out and grab onto it. We took those caramel apples—Ummi, Michael, Bayee, and I—and we found a spot in the crowd lined up behind the fence and waiting for the next horse race to begin. I remembered my brother and I would take turns sitting on Bayee's shoulders so we could see the horses and the way his muscles tensed and his voice bellowed when the horse he liked pulled ahead of the others. I remembered eating the caramel apple and not realizing the caramel had dripped, warm and gooey into his already thinning hair. I remembered the moment he realized it, the fear that seized my insides, and then the relief when he began laughing. My father laughed and laughed even after the horse he liked lost and the race was over.

But mostly, when I remembered the fair of my childhood, I remembered how much I loved my father.

* * *

We all knew it would be Bayee's last holiday. We did not know that he would die only a few weeks later. Our tiny, insular world still resembled the one of Frank Sinatra songs: snow frosted homes, children's imperfect snowmen, and ice skating on the frozen Still River. Michael stayed with Ummi during the day so he could help her with Bayee, who was now completely bed ridden. She protested at first, insistent that he not miss any school. He'd be graduating in just a few short months, and she feared he'd get behind. But Michael was stubborn, and she didn't have the strength to argue. I worked the store by myself, trying to forget. Jacob was dust in my mind that had collected in the space reserved for dreams.

People came and went from the house, visiting Bayee and bringing food. Mrs. Saadi came every Tuesday with stew and would stay for a few hours to help with household chores. Jeannette Moses showed up on Wednesdays with varying dishes. Mr. and Mrs. Issa came and sat with Bayee for a spell on Fridays, often bringing cigars, a fact Ummi and Mrs. Issa weren't happy about, but allowed, as it seemed to perk Bayee up a little. Even Father Hayek, per Ummi's request, visited daily. Almost the entire Lebanese community stopped by at some point during the three weeks between Christmas and the day Bayee took his final breath.

The day he died, I was working. The store lacked customers, and I busied myself stocking shelves with a new shipment of pine nuts and pistachios. I was listening to the radio babble about the raging war in Korea when Ummi came rushing into the store from the back room. "You must come! It's your father!" Her hair was loose, rebellious in pale waves.

"What's wrong, Umm?" My stomach seemed to freefall at her entrance.

Tears painted her flushed cheeks. "Come, George!"

"I'll be right there!" Nearly dropping the mesh bag of nuts, I tossed it on the shelf and rushed to lock the door and turn the sign to "Closed."

I took the steps two at a time, but still a full eternity passed before I got upstairs and into Bayee's room. Ummi held his hand with both of hers, as if she believed holding on would keep him from slipping into death. Michael sat on the other side of the bed, rubbing Bayee's emaciated shoulder, tears welling like rain puddles in his eyes. A clock ticked, a pendulum swung. Bayee was gaunt, his face hollowed out and empty. The pigmentation of his skin was yellow, the color of the sun if it could stale. His eyes were closed and the swollen belly beneath the covers rose and fell intermittently and with effort. It was a challenge to take in air, probably even painful. Beneath the covers, his legs and feet were swollen and bulbous. I walked to the end of the bed.

Bayee's eyes flickered open. Sunken and yellow, life was already missing from them. But he was cognizant still and began to move the hand not clasped by Ummi. He seemed to be motioning the hand towards me so I moved closer, next to Michael.

"George..." The name caught on his tongue, stuck in the threads of spit that stretched across his barely open mouth.

I switched spots with Michael and leaned in close to him.

"Closer." The words were barely audible.

"I'm here, Bayee." I leaned towards him until my face was inches from his. So close I could smell something like blood.

"A...al...alone..."

"You two should leave," I said to Ummi.

Reluctant to let go of his hand, Ummi just stared back at me through swimming eyes. "I...I..." She couldn't leave him or speak or move.

Michael kissed the top of Bayee's head and walked over to Ummi. Taking her gently by the arm, he walked her out of the room. She never took her eyes off her husband.

Bayee swallowed hard, opened and closed his mouth a few times, created new threads of spit to block his words like a web. "You...you're...smart boy...but..." The word became lodged in his throat, he choked on it, coughing violently.

"No, I'm sorry I said—" I began to say but Bayee raised his hand, authoritative, even in death.

"Um...Ummi needs you...the family needs you." He managed to squeeze out of his dying voice box. His mouth remained grotesquely open, a gaping hole struggling to take in air but instead emitting a high-pitched, deflating sound that slicked skin with goose pimples. The web of spittle bubbled in the corners of his mouth.

I stroked his shoulder, not knowing what else to do. "I know. I'll be here for her, for you."

Death sounds pricked the room like the ticking of the clock. Minutes or maybe hours passed before Bayee spoke again. "The tree...I want to see...the tree..." Bayee articulated in half-breaths. "Tree...please..." His finger lifted, pointed towards the window. "Home...tree..."

I realized he was talking about the cedar tree in our back-yard, grown from seeds he had transported from his village in Lebanon. The cedar tree was a remnant of home, of his coun-try. Of course, he wanted to look upon the familiar tree; he wanted to look upon home. It took several minutes to help him from the bed to a chair by the window. He could not walk or move. Instead, I carried him, my father, light with age and death. I sat my bayee in the old suede chair facing the window so that he could look upon his cedar tree, crippled with winter as he was with death. And he gazed into the cold gray, his yellowed eyes resting upon his cedar tree, his Lebanon. Bayee smiled and took one last strangled breath.

I stood beside him, over him, with him, taking in the cedar tree. I didn't think of the drinking, the temper, the selfishness. In those moments, I remembered the way my father laughed when he caught me sneaking a pastry before dinner once. *Your mother will be furious! He'd laughed as he joined me, grabbing a freshly baked piece of knafeh.*

A thousand oceans away, Ummi wept.

* * *

Bayee died while Raina was on the train from DC. She was coming back to Danbury to help her dear cousin Celia with her dying husband. She was coming back to say goodbye to George Senior, the man she once described as charming. Raina did not make it to Danbury in time.

I hadn't seen her or spoken to her since I left Georgetown four months earlier. She showed up on our doorstep the day before the funeral in a belted coat and with a leather valise, stylish even in grief. Raina cast aside the door as if it were a barrier. Her red-painted lips formed a smile despite the tears glinting like broken glass on her cheeks. We hugged tightly and, despite her grief, she was as lovely as melting snow in springtime. I took her coat and valise and led her to the kitchen table where Ummi sat in silence. Raina removed her gloves, handed them to me as well, and began flitting about the kitchen like it was her own. She found the coffee pot and immediately made some fresh Turkish brew which she brought over to her cousin.

"I couldn't get here sooner, Celia. I'm sorry." Raina hugged Ummi close to her but she remained stiff and resistant to the gesture.

"You came, dear cousin." She put a hand on Raina's arm and kissed it.

"It wasn't soon enough. I didn't get to say goodbye to him, Celia. I didn't say goodbye." She let tears flow freely, not embarrassed to show her emotion. Ummi remained steadfast in her lack of tears and instead comforted her cousin. My mother had wept alone in her room all through the night, a sound I wouldn't soon forget. But in the presence of anyone, even her dear cousin, Ummi would be composed.

"It's alright, Raina."

I sat at the table with them, drinking coffee, taking a moment to return to the dishes I had been doing before Raina arrived. The store would be closed for the next few days.

After several minutes of tears or lack thereof, I decided I should bring Raina's things to my bedroom where she would be sleeping. I was giving her my bed and sleeping on the couch in the living room while she stayed with us.

"I'll bring your things to my room."

She looked at me through smeared eyes. "I'll come with you." Turning to Ummi, she added, "Need anything, Celia, dear?"

"No. Go with George. Get settled." She remained seated, the steam from her untouched coffee sputtering in the air as it cooled.

I led her through the hallway and into the room, carrying her valise and guiding her with my hand on the small of her back. She was familiar with the layout, but it had been many years since she'd been here last.

Once in the room, Raina sat on my bed and asked, "George, honey?"

"Yes, Raina?" I stood in the doorway arms crossed over my chest.

"Did he suffer much? At...at...the end?"

"It doesn't matter. He's at peace now."

"Yes. Yes, I suppose that's right." She dabbed her eyes with a lacy handkerchief and slipped off her pumps.

"Raina?"

"Yes?"

"It's good you're here."

She attempted to smile, but her mouth couldn't quite force the movement.

* * *

Later, when I would remember the day of the funeral, it was difficult to distinguish between hail beating the roof of the church and the sounds of pipe organ pummeling the air. Aramaic chanting rose like spirits from the crowds, crowds of family, friends, and many others from the Danbury community and surrounding towns. Prayers were spoken, words expressed the significance of Bayee's life, and finally, his casket was lowered into the waiting earth. Ummi was the color of snow in her black garb. I noticed she was missing an earring; it must have fallen out this morning when she was readying for the service. I felt my cheeks warm painfully. Michael held on to a crying Marlene like he was afraid to look at the coffin, like if he didn't see it, his father could still be alive.

Although the coffin was closed, I could imagine Bayee, his dark blue suit just a little too big and the dark, stained nails not quite clean. Ed Shaker would have spent a great deal of time on the body, adding makeup where color was necessary. The decades of animal blood and other foreign particles had weathered his hands, broken down his nails, and probably frustrated the fastidious mortician. But they were rough, calloused, stained, and even death could not change the hands of a butcher.

I dug my hands deep into my pockets. These hands were not stained or broken—yet. I took time after each day in the shop to soak them in a bowl of warm water and baking soda. My hands, still clean, belonged to me.

The hail and rain had changed to sleet and then snow. The weather itself was plaintive. People in black cried softly under black umbrellas. They came up to me at the cemetery, offering the words expected of them.

"I'm sorry, George, for your loss."

"Senior was a great man."

"We are here for you, son."

"So sorry, George."

"I'm sorry for your loss."

They couldn't begin to understand the loss that had settled into my soul. The loss of education, the loss of experiences not available in Danbury. My flawed butcher of a father. The man who fashioned me in his own image. The man who gave Michael and me money to buy ice cream on hot summer days, even when we hadn't much. The same man who drank too much and yelled too much and pushed too much and loved too much.

In spite of the cold, dimples of sweat stuck to my forehead, began to tangle in the hair on the back of my neck. Another hug, another kiss, another genuine condolence and I would have to punch someone or break something.

"Ummi, I need a minute."

She probably hadn't heard me. She was staring into the hole that now claimed her husband.

I did not return to the church for the mercy meal, another opportunity for expressions of sympathy. I found the Lincoln beside the twisted branch of a birch tree, another victim of winter's pillage. I drove home through gray, dirty snow and vacant storefronts. It must have been Sunday. Downtown Danbury—Ed's Cigar shop, the Capitol Theatre, Feinson's, the Savings Bank of Danbury, the Post Office—was all darkened and barren, devoid of passersby or activity. I continued through the urban Lower Elm Street neighborhood, Lester Wong's Ho Yen, Bizzarian Fish Market. Up the hill, through Upper Elm with its large, affluent houses and wrap-around front porches coated in snow.

And then I was running up the steps to our apartment above the store. Raina was sitting at the kitchen table. I wondered for a moment why she slipped away from the funeral and how, but then, who was I to ask. She didn't notice me, distracted by a cigarette and her tears. Red-lacquered nails seemed to be the only color for miles. Without waiting for her to see me, I closed the door and ran down the steps and into the empty store. I did not stop until I reached the back room.

I took a fresh lamb carcass out of the freezer and hung it from a meat hook in the butcher room. The transition from cold to heat elicited steam from the raw animal, and, before it had begun to thaw, I punched the frozen flesh. I pounded it and pounded it, my knuckles turning from pink to red to bloody. *Surgeon's instruments traded in for the butcher's tools.* The lamb swung and I hit it more. Grunting, visceral sounds came from somewhere within me. Muscles tensed as if they would snap. I pounded the carcass until I could scarcely breathe. *A lifetime of pounding carcasses. Bayee, the carcass.* I looked at the swinging meat, the burgeoning red and flushed purple, the exploding threads of white fat. I ran my fingers across the slick flesh. *The moist thickness of his lips. Jacob.* Everything burned —eyes, knuckles, insides. Lips met exposed carcass, face pushed into the meat, inhaling cold, salty hardness. *Kissing him, salty tongue tango.* The need to beat dead animal to a pulp over-whelmed me again; I overwhelmed the carcass with my fists. *I pushed him so hard to the ground. The overwhelming need to assault him with my fists.* Time stopped. An animal sound, a sound like the final scream of a slaughtered lamb came from somewhere. I couldn't feel my hands anymore, but I kept hitting. *Jacob was dead. Bayee was dead. I was dead.*

CHAPTER TEN

After Bayee passed, Ummi had difficulty sleeping. She would pace back and forth, back and forth, for hours at a time; the faint sound of her voice in prayer could be heard above her restless steps. In a strange way, her pacing was comforting. I fell asleep each night to the sound of crickets, the distant rushing of engines, and Ummi's footfalls. She greeted me at dawn with a fresh pot of Turkish coffee, the thick brew already bubbling in a ceramic mug as I set out to begin the day. Ummi was still meticulously put together, even at that hour, but her eyes revealed the toll of her nocturnal routine. It was not the lack of sleep—but death—that had collected under her eyes in deep gray shadows.

Heartbeats and foot beats continued falling like the wet snow of February and March. And then, one day spring revealed itself in blooming yellow daffodils and crocus buds. One Saturday afternoon in May, Michael whistled an off-pitch tune and smiled to no one, to the air, to the new shipment of Honey Dew melons he was stocking.

"What's with the good mood?"

He pulled a black box out of his pants pocket. Inside, was a small, round diamond on a gold band. "Think Marlene'll like it? You don't think it's too small, do you? I couldn't afford anything bigger."

"Congratulations, brother!" I slapped my brother hard on the back and hugged him tight. My little brother was getting married. First.

Michael turned to me and grinned. "I asked Mr. Buzaid if I could propose to Marlene. But I still have to ask her. Nothing's official yet." I noticed that my brother's hair wasn't unruly. When had he started using pomade?

"It's beautiful. She'll love it." *Marriage; younger brother; aisles and brides and flowers; happy Ummi.* "I'm so happy for you!" Walking over to the counter, I reached underneath the register and pulled out a hidden bottle of Plymouth gin. Bayee had concealed it in the drawer among scrap papers and ballpoint inkwells, and we all pretended we had no idea it was there. "Let's have a celebratory drink. For the old man."

"Yeah. Okay." He took a hard swig of the alcohol and handed it back to me. I took a few more swigs than I probably should have, but Michael didn't seem to notice. I fiddled with the dial of Bayee's radio, changing it from the usual news broadcast to a station playing "Blueberry Hill."

Michael tapped his foot along with the song. I took another swig of gin, put it back in its spot, and turned the volume up a little louder. Jacob loved Fats Domino; he was a terrible dancer, had the rhythm of a rock, I told him. I started moving to the music, and Michael laughed from the fruit bins. All at once, the door opened, and Eleanor Rizkallah walked in. I lowered the volume on the radio and refocused on the list of inventories in front of me. *A bit too serendipitous.*

"Why'd you lower the music? I love Fats Domino." She smiled under a black pillbox hat.

I half-smiled and turned up the music. "Wouldn't have pegged you for a Domino broad."

"And what would you have pegged me for?" Eleanor strolled over to a rack of spices.

"Don't know, maybe Rosemary Clooney or Frank Sinatra."

"They're good, but I like a little Domino." She picked up a bottle of saffron.

"You have good taste then."

"I do, but you're not exactly the standard for good music." She smiled sweetly enough.

"My opinion counts for something, doesn't it?" I remained behind the counter, arms folded, leaning against the wall.

"I suppose. Your opinion on mutton is something I would take very seriously." Eleanor grinned. I took her in. She had generous pink lips, a fair complexion, and short dark hair. Average height, curvaceous, plain, almost lacking features, an honest smile. Eleanor wore a long, red tweed jacket with matching gloves. She had the kind of face that blend into a crowd, but a personality that overcompensated. The simple features and assertive disposition made me think of a dash of salt in a spicy dish—undetectable but important. In the unremarkable brown of her eyes, I recognized a glint of something familiar. Impetuousness? Desire? I couldn't quite be sure.

I laughed and walked over to her. "With all due respect, Miss Rizkallah, I think you need to reevaluate your priorities."

"Thank you, Mr. Lahoud, for your insight, but I think my priorities are just fine. Now about that mutton." She moved towards the meat counter near the back of the store, passed shelves stocked with freshly baked breads and pastries. Mrs. Harmon, an attractive Black woman in a beret and a belted coat who lived around the corner, reached for a loaf of French bread and reprimanded her five- or maybe six-year-old son who was begging her for a pastry.

My head buzzed bumble bee thoughts. It could have been the gin, but expectations mixed with urgency and Michael was getting married and I would not go back to Georgetown and Jacob would become a shadow and this is where I was and would always be, standing in our grocery store helping customers pick out mutton.

"Why don't you challenge my opinion further at the church festival Friday night? We could argue some more, maybe dance a little, too?" I reached into the cooler behind the meat counter and pulled out a freshly cut flank.

"Sure, okay." She remained composed, her voice resistant to any note of emotion; I imagined it was what she wanted, hoped for even, but Eleanor Rizkallah was not the kind of woman who was accustomed to attracting the attention of male suitors.

"Pick you up at six?" I handed Eleanor the mutton wrapped in wax paper and bound with twine.

Michael cast a curious glance over the empty fruit crates he was carrying to the back. Passing Eleanor, he said, "Afternoon, Miss Rizkallah."

She turned, acknowledged Michael, and said, "Hello," and then, to me, added, "Sure. Better ring me up. I've got to get home." She was suddenly anxious to make her purchase and leave the store, but her smile remained stuck on her round face.

"Down the street, big white house, right?" Everyone knew the Rizkallahs lived in the big white colonial on Elm.

"Big white house. That's me." Eleanor grabbed the mutton and carried a few bottles of spices over to the register.

I rang her up and bid her adieu with, "See you Friday." My smile elicited a rose color that overwhelmed her already rouged cheeks.

"See you Friday." Eleanor took her bags and left the store.

"Well, that was unexpected." Michael emerged from the back and joined me at the counter.

"Eleanor's a nice girl. She's got bite."

Michael laughed. "Bite and bucks."

Slightly too defensive, I responded, "So?"

"Just saying, she's not really a looker. Plain Jane, brother."

"She's not bad looking. And she's sweet."

"And her family is loaded." Michael took a broom resting in the corner and put it to work as I turned up the volume of the radio and hummed along to Rosemary Clooney's "Come On-a My House." Mrs. Harmon and her son approached the register with a basket filled with sundry items, the little boy happily nibbling at his pastry while his mother pursed her lips and shook her head. A tinkling of bells signaled the entrance of more customers.

The sun slanted through the window of the store and broke into pieces over the counter, the paperwork, my hands. Gilded bars of light warmed the surfaces. And I smiled at the vigorous applause in my head, the overwhelming approval, Ummi's approval, Bayee's approval, the entire community's heartfelt approval.

* * *

Friday arrived and I told Ummi I had a date with Eleanor Rizkallah. My mother's lips tightened and the corners of her mouth raised as she nodded her head, an action suggestive of approval. "She goes to church with her family every Sunday."

"I know, I know."

The dark clouds under her eyes seemed to lighten. "Are you picking her up now?" She crushed a half-finished cigarette in an ashtray on the kitchen table. A week-old copy of *The Saturday Evening Post* lay disturbed beside it.

"Yeah. I'm taking the Lincoln."

"Yes, yes. You must do that. Where're you taking her?"

Ummi got up from the table and, arms folded, appraised my appearance.

"I figured we could attend the festival at St. Anthony's together"

"Yes, good." She clicked her tongue, nodded again, and smoothed my carefully pomaded hair. Something about her in that moment reminded me of Raina. I kissed her on the cheek and made my way to the car.

Eleanor wore a black skirt, a matching fitted jacket with narrow sleeves, white lace gloves, and a strand of pearls. Dark hair was fastened in a chignon at the nape of her neck, and she wore a black pillbox hat decorated on one side with flowers made of black beads and tiny pearls. Black kohl outlined her dark eyes and red lipstick brightened her mouth. I couldn't help but be impressed by her meticulous style.

"Feel like dancing?" I looked over at her in the passenger's seat, twisting a lace handkerchief in her gloved hands.

"Perhaps." Eleanor tried to conceal a smile.

"Well, I have my dancing shoes on, so here's hoping."

* * *

The mahrajan was hosted by St. Anthony's Church, however, five other Maronite churches in Connecticut collaborated to make it a spectacular annual event. Large white tents were set up in the church parking lot and garden behind the church. Long banquet tables were filled with families both local and from out-of-town parishes. Teenagers from town even attended with their friends as it was an event that served alcohol to whomever ordered it. Every kind of traditional Lebanese food was prepared by the Ladies Guild and the delectable scents of kibbeh and shwarma, among other dishes, were ubiquitous. Cigarette smoke amalgamated with hookah. A band played Lebanese music and people danced feverishly.

The weather was unusually warm for May. We found a corner of a table with two empty folding chairs. I pulled out Eleanor's seat and then excused myself to grab us some beverages. When I had returned with a gin and tonic for myself and a white wine for Eleanor, she'd removed her jacket to reveal a silk blouse, the top pearl button of which had come undone, exposing an alabaster neck.

"Thanks, George." Her voice was uneven, like she was trying to control her nerves, but they were stronger than her resolve. The way she emphasized my name was like a reminder to herself that she was actually on a date with a good looking fellow named George. This name, my name, sounded clumsy tripping off her lips. Eleanor took a long sip of her drink.

I drank deeply from the sweating paper cup. The gin tasted good, like dancing in the rain after a heat wave. "So, Eleanor, tell me something interesting." I leaned back in the chair and brought the drink to my lips. The cup cast a long, sideways shadow across the table. *Sideways glances and longing and Georgetown. Focus.*

"Is this like an interview or something?" Red-lacquered nails stood out against the white paper tablecloth. She leaned intimately forward and smiled. Her plain features lit up. "I like cooking and shopping in Westport. I work as a secretary for my father, and I have a goat named Fatimah who I may or may not have encouraged to pick up a cigarette habit. Speaking of cigarettes, mind if I have a light?" She reached into her purse and pulled out a Camel. *Her conversation is sharp.* I remembered, then, the story of her childhood, the death of her mother when she was only a young girl. I imagined that Eleanor's fierce character was the result of growing up the only female in a household of men.

"You have a smoking goat?" I laughed and produced a lighter and a cigarette for myself.

"Fatimah has a proclivity for nicotine." She exhaled a tuft of smoke and tucked a rebellious curl behind her ear. "My poor father almost had a heart attack when he spotted her from the kitchen window one day, not chewing an alfalfa stalk but actually smoking a cigarette. Thought he was having a hallucination." She laughed and sipped her drink. "Can you imagine? Looking out the window and seeing a goat staring at you from her pen, just puffing away? My brother got the biggest kick out of it. Dad, not so much." Eleanor laughed.

I was laughing too. "Was it hard to teach her?"

"Not at all. Goats are very intelligent creatures, you know. I was feeding her some alfalfa stalks one day, enjoying a cig myself, and she kept cocking her head at me. I don't know why, but I just got the idea in my head." The smoky air was alive with the tablah, daf, and lute as a rich voice sang of a home ocean away.

"Wish I had thought of that. We used to have goats some years back, but sold them off when things got slow at the store." *And Bayee gambled away a month's salary.* I drained the remaining gin from my cup, letting the ice cubes clink against it. "I'm going to grab another. Want one?"

"I'm fine." She smiled as I got up from the table. Her earlier nerves seemed to be unraveling, replaced by the charming wit and confidence I'd experienced during our initial encounter at the store.

I sifted through the thick crowd, brushing against men in spicy-sweet cologne and damp oxford shirts. "Gin and tonic, please." I shouted to the bartender manning a makeshift bar set up behind a folding table, a fifty-something man with salt-and-pepper hair and glasses, a moist curl stuck to his forehead. He had an irritated look, as if his wife had begged him to contribute to the festival and this was the compromise they'd reached.

"Thanks." I took the paper cup filled with mostly gin and walked back over to Eleanor. She sat stirring her drink half-heartedly with a red-painted pointer finger. *Red stirs in twin drinks in Georgetown, slipping towards memory—again.*

"Did you get lost?" She grinned. Grounded in playful banter.

"Yeah, you wouldn't believe how tricky it is to find the bar. I almost gave up and called it a night." I smiled at her, or rather, into her. It elicited the blush I hoped for. Lively Arabic music punctured the air. Jacketless men stood up from tables, leading their female companions to the dance floor set up in the center of the tent. In perfect imitation, I stood up and extended my hand. "Dance with me."

She gave me her hand. Pleasantly buzzed couples filled the space, dancing clichés all around us. A flushed-face gentleman pulled his blonde date closer as their bodies twisted and bumped to the rhythm of the music. Their faces were so close it seemed as though they would kiss, the woman gazing expectantly into her beau's eyes with a look that was something between hope and hunger. Bachelors eyed full-bodied beauties dancing with each other in pairs, or they conversed with each other, passing narghile amongst themselves. Clusters of parents with young children filled tables surrounding the dance floor as some of their older children joined the energetic dancing. Elderly couples moved to the music as if they did not have arthritic joints or bad hips. I pulled Eleanor to me, moved perfectly with the song while she tried to follow my lead. She stepped once or twice on my foot and, embarrassed, tried to pull out of my arms. "This is a great song. You can't sit it out." It almost didn't matter that she had two left feet.

When the song ended, we returned to the table. "I'm sorry, I'm not light on my feet like you." She avoided my gaze.

"Don't be silly. Fred Astaire would have two left feet comparatively." I was reassuring; she was relieved. Something about her insecurity was attractive. *You're not the only one out of your depth.*

I had finished a fourth or possibly fifth drink. Eleanor was talking; I watched the shapes that shadows made on tent walls, on faces, in a room of aspiring lovers, contented families, children filled with hope and dreams and too many sweets. I knew I shouldn't have any more gin. Detachment. Eleanor's words slipped through cracks in my mind. Chanel No. 5 in the corner or in front of me or over and under me. Eleanor flicked the ash of a dying cigarette. I still needed to drive her home. "What'd you say we head out? I have to be at the store early in the morning." At last, a truth.

"I shouldn't be home much later, anyhow." She cast dark eyes towards a half-finished drink.

I took a longer route home, passing the tall brick columns that marked the Malloy Hat Factory, scattered parked cars filled with necking couples in Richter Park, and railroad tracks that bisected a field of overgrown stalks where shards of broken glass had once glinted in the sun like crystalline flowers.

I walked Eleanor to the front door, witnessed a light go off somewhere on the second floor, and kissed her gently on the cheek. "Let's do this again next weekend."

Eleanor's face flushed pink and she grinned. "Who said I want to see you again?"

Not anticipating the sarcasm and feeling heavy with drink, I faltered, but only for a moment. "So I'm still only useful for picking out mutton?"

The sound of our laughter stuck in the night air like damp curls on foreheads.

* * *

The day of Michael's wedding had arrived, and I was assaulted by lavender taffeta, calla lily bouquets, and boldfaced expectations. After a five-month engagement, Michael and Marlene were entering into holy matrimony. All the Lebanese families, the wives, mothers, fathers, husbands, sons, daughters, and grandparents of every living person of Lebanese descent for miles around were in attendance. St. Anthony's couldn't hold another person, couldn't squeeze in another white rose or daisy. It was perfectly traditional. Marlene was dripping in satin and lace, her dark curls crowned in white, and a gold crucifix hung around her delicate neck.

A few weeks before the ceremony, we had been working in the store, Michael was stocking shelves, and I was taking inventory, when he made an incendiary comment.

"I hope you aren't too sore I'm tying the knot first. Figured if I wait for you to get hitched, Marlene and I'll never get married!" He laughed so carelessly, so insignificantly.

"What're you trying to say?" I looked up from the papers in front of me and nearly knocked them off the counter.

"Jesus, Georgie, I was joking! Why so sensitive?" He continued placing bottles of saffron, coriander, cumin, and cinnamon in their proper places, but the clanking of the glass against wood shelf was a chorus of insects buzzing when all you want is sleep.

"Don't manhandle the spices. We can't afford another shipment." I walked over to the counter, turned up the volume on the radio so that the news broadcast would drown out Michael's response. "And, I'm clearly dating Eleanor Rizkallah."

He mumbled something but refused to speak aloud or even look at me for the rest of the afternoon. The day seemed to drag and clunk and irk me with every ignorant question from customers. *Mrs. Issa, you've been coming to the store for nearly twenty years and you still don't know where we keep the rose water?* Even the group of young boys who came into the store for a soda in the late afternoon irritated me with their boisterous antics and horseplay. However, a small boy with disheveled hair who appeared to be someone's younger brother, a tagalong, did make me smile when he began to badger a taller, lanky boy for ice cream. The mis en scene, a distant but familiar memory. My anger was misplaced; Michael was still my boyish younger brother, and he was happy.

The next morning as I poured a fresh cup of Turkish coffee before going into the store, I apologized to a sleep-drunk Michael.

"All's forgiven. I need a best man after all, and you're the only brother I have." He stretched and yawned loudly.

* * *

We easily fell back into comfortable brotherhood. I brought Eleanor to the wedding as my date. A reception followed the ceremony in the church basement. Traditional Arabic food was served: tabbouleh, kibbeh balls, chicken and lamb kebabs, roasted lamb with rice, assorted fresh fruits, and, of course, pastries served with the Bavarian cream wedding cake. Most of the men, and a few women, smoked narghile from long stemmed, glass-based waterpipes in between eating and dancing. I sat back and inhaled strong tobacco from the mouthpiece, exhaled curling wisps of gray.

"You and Eleanor Rizkallah next?" Johnny Nassif, a close friend of Bayee's and a retired attorney, asked as he reached over and changed the mouthpiece on the narghile, brought it to his fat lips and took in the smoke.

"We'll see." I smiled pleasantly enough and Johnny accepted it.

He clasped his thick, ruddy hands over his protruding stomach, "Nice girl. Good family."

"Georgie Porgie! What's this talk of you marrying Eleanor Rizkallah?" Joey Buzaid, Marlene's brother and a childhood friend, walked into the conversation and reached to take the piece from Johnny. The tall, almost scrawny Joey, with heavily pomaded hair and glasses inhaled the narghile. I responded by shaking my head and laughing.

Grizzly Aoun and Ed Shaker strolled over to the group with twin glasses of arak. "Joey running his mouth again, Georgie?" Grizzly teased and knocked back a swig of the clear, potent liquor.

"Nah. Just talking about the lovely Miss Elea—" Joey choked on the narghile and Grizzly intervened.

"Shut up, man!"

"She's a proper broad, isn't she?" Johnny added and then, expressing his need for more food, left the group.

I took the piece back from Joey. "There's certainly enough. Satinah! Eat!"

Ed Shaker mumbled under his breath, "Just what Johnny Nassif needs—more food." We laughed agreement, and I sat down on a folding chair next to the hookah. Then I let the narghile tangle with the alcohol in my system as I watched Eleanor dancing with the other women and a few men. She wasn't as confident as the others or quite as good, but she laughed and smiled more than any of them. She clapped her hands, swung her hips, indifferent to the pearls of sweat taking up on her forehead. Eleanor Rizkallah was electric despite her obvious failings, and it was that, as much as what she lacked, that drew me in. She looked over at me and waved.

"George, come dance! They're starting the dabke!" Eleanor

interrupted the relaxing sensation coursing through my body, the pensive state. Who could turn down the dabke?

A troupe of Arabic singers had been brought in from New York City. They were playing the traditional Arabic folkdance. Not a single person remained seated, everyone rushed to join hands and form a line. If Bayee were alive, even he would have abandoned his seat and joined his wife in celebration. Bayee: cold, dead, absent. Ummi led the dance, lovely in pale blue chiffon, twirling a silk handkerchief and stomping her dainty foot to the beat. She laughed a sound that was as rare and musical as the celebration; the lute, reed clarinet, drums, and tambourine beckoned. Eleanor beckoned.

"Dance, my son! Dance!" Ummi called out as she passed me, leading the dance procession to the back of the church basement, around the tables and chairs. She summoned a pair of older women who had remained seated. I took Eleanor's hand in mine. Her hands were strong, not dainty. Her palm was moist, firm. She squeezed mine tightly. Her foot bumped mine repeatedly as she stomped and kicked, always a beat late. The smell of Chanel No. 5 overpowered narghile smoke. We stomped and moved together, as one, winding our way around the room, laughing and smiling, until our faces hurt as much as our feet. Our hearts knocked in unison against chest cages, matching the beat of the drummer's hands against his instrument, and, for a perfect eternity, we danced the dabke in celebration of love, of family, of each other. The music stopped, but Eleanor continued holding my hand. And I wasn't sure that I wanted her to let go.

The wedding ended sometime after midnight. I was drunk from the festivities. Eleanor had gone home; she was tired and had to wake up early to prepare food for the Rizkallah Sunday dinner. The remaining guests sent Michael and Marlene off in a borrowed white Cadillac, bidding them fruitful lives with showers of rice. Not too long after departing for The Groveland Hotel, where they would spend their wedding night before leaving in the morning to honeymoon in the Catskills, the rest of the guests dissipated along with Ummi and a few high school kids we hired to help with the food and cleanup. I did not want to head home quite yet, my thoughts thick with alcohol and memory. I walked instead outside the church, enjoying the effect of gin and narghile and the way the stars swam in liquid black.

Something drew me back inside St. Anthony's. Maybe it was the stained-glass windows, alive against the night. Light flickered behind the images, gave them a dream-like quality. I stepped inside, overwhelmed by the smell of incense and lilies. I made my way down the incarnadine nave, pausing to genuflect in front of the altar, in front of God. Deep gold from twin candelabras danced with shadows across the alabaster marble. I sat back in the hard wooden pew, lacking prayers or penance. Ummi had been so happy today. She nodded approvingly at the way Eleanor drew close when I was next to her. Ummi had noticed, of course. She had been worried, the younger son marrying first. But she was reassured, and she glowed. The marble saints, Anthony and Charbel, watched from their lofty position.

The sound of the oak doors opening startled me. Father Hayek waddled down the aisle, heavy under the weight of too much food, drink, and narghile.

"Son, you have not left? What kind of spiritual guidance do you seek at such a late hour?" Father's eyes were puffy and wandering, his complexion warm. I felt satiated just looking at him. He sat in the pew in front of me, turning around to face me. "Tell me, Jeorje, what's on your mind?" The last word was marred by a loud belch. Father laughed and excused himself. "Might have had a little too much nourishment tonight!" His booming, rich laugh was magnified by the empty church.

"I'm happy you enjoyed yourself, Father." Parsing through confusion, doubt, and too much alcohol, I decided the old priest may be just the person to talk to. After all, it was his job to give counsel, to impart God's Will. "Father? Have you read Kahlil Gibran?"

"Yes, yes indeed. Quite enjoy him. Brilliant man."

"How about the parable of the madman? Are you familiar?" I searched for recollection in his face.

"The parable of the madman, you ask?" He squinted his eyes in concentration. "The madman. Yes, the madman! The narrator is in a madhouse conversing with a young man. He asks him 'why are you here?' The boy says he has tired of people attempting to mold him into their own image. The young man feels he can only be himself within the walls of the asylum. How is that for an old, drunk man's memory?" He patted his belly. "But tell me, son, why do you wish to sit in a church discussing Gibran at such a late hour? And after your brother's wedding?"

"I read the parable a few days ago. Just can't seem to get it out of my head. A young man seeks sanity in a nuthouse. And those final words..."

"The final words?" Father Hayek folded his arms across a wide expanse of chest and furrowed his brow.

"The boy asks him if he, too, was driven to the madhouse by the well-meaning people in his life. He says he is simply a visitor. Then the boy says, '*You are one of those who live in the madhouse on the other side of the wall*'." I felt a dull headache encroaching as if I was sobering up. "That's the last line."

"Yes, I remember now. A profound man, Gibran. His prose so simple, yet so complex. I admit, sometimes even I find his meaning elusive. Especially when I'm drunk." Father began a series of uncontrollable hiccups. "It's so late. Aren't you tired?"

"Sometimes I feel like the visitor." I pressed my middle and pointer fingers against either temple, easing the pressure of a building headache.

Father Hayek laughed. "My boy, you are like Gibran to me right now. Why don't we call it a night? We can talk tomorrow, over your dear mother's kafta meatloaf?" He stood slowly, and slapped me on the back.

"Of course, Father," I smiled warmly. Father Hayek left me alone in the empty church, which, only hours before held so many people—my newly married brother, his lovely wife, old friends, well-wishing family, and my beaming mother. A feeling coursed through my being along with the intoxication, a feeling which had percolated throughout the day, maybe even started days before. It was a feeling amplified by the recent memory of Eleanor's hand in mine. I was the visitor.

CHAPTER ELEVEN

When Michael and I were young boys, school-aged, I would wake often, in the darkest part of night, terrified from some unremembered threat. Michael, always the faithful sleeper, remained undisturbed. I would run to Ummi and Bayee's room, creep softly to the right side of the large bed, Ummi's side. I would tug on her arm until she had woken without stirring Bayee. Wordlessly, she'd get out of bed, pull on a paisley robe, and guide me into the kitchen. Her hair in rollers and sleep-muted eyes not quite lit, she would sit me at the table. She'd heat a pot of milk and pour the steaming beverage into two ceramic mugs. Sitting beside me, her mug clutched in her hands, Ummi would pull a cigarette from a pack of Old Golds and light it. In a voice that reminded me of the leaves of an elm tree swaying in the wind, she told stories of a beautiful young girl. The girl was from a poor family who lived in a small village in the heart of Mt. Lebanon. In some stories, the girl would dance with the shadows of pine trees, read in the shade of a cedar grove. In others, she dressed up with her cousin in old clothes and sometimes she made the goats and the chickens take part in their sartorial games.

One night Ummi told me the story of how the young girl's family decided it was best to send her far away to a country many were talking about. America had opportunities, they said. Family friends had gone there, and they knew of a man looking for a Lebanese wife from the old country. They sent the girl by herself on a big ship that took her far away to this strange new land. There were no mountains or cedar trees, and even the brightest blue sky was not as bright as in Lebanon. She was afraid in this strange country, but her new husband was kind, and he comforted her. He was also young and handsome, something she had not expected. She also did not expect to fall in love with him, but she did, and they lived happily ever after. These stories soothed me like the tendrils of midnight smoke from my mother's cigarettes. After each tale, I finished my milk, and Ummi walked me back to my room and tucked me under the blankets.

I tried to imagine what it would have been like to be young Ummi, in a new place with a spouse she'd never even met before. I knew Eleanor and liked her well enough. And perhaps one day, I could really fall in love with her, too. These were the thoughts beating in my head as I tried to fall asleep after my brother's wedding.

The memory of my mother's nocturnal stories comforted me even though I was no longer a boy, and I carried this memory in my pocket always, a delicate whispering of butterfly wings.

* * *

Several nights a week I would end the day with a few drinks and a game of cards at the Lebanon American Club. Local

Lebanese men, many friends of Bayee's, would spend their evenings there after having supper with their wives and children. One night in October shortly after Michael's nuptials, I found an empty seat next to Eleanor's father.

Kamil Rizkallah was a dark, imposing man. His very appearance was something of a paradox—a perfectly bald head and a bushy salt-and-pepper beard that dominated his face. His belly was rounded by years of good Arabic cooking, but he carried his weight well. Eleanor had clearly gotten her fashion sense from her father, who was known around town for his expensive suits and collection of long, camel-hair coats.

The Lebanese community loved their success stories, and Kamil's was one that was very well known. He came to Connecticut from Lebanon as a young man, classically broke, with a wife and two children. With Eleanor, her older brother, Kamil Jr., and his very young wife in tow, Kamil took the only job he could get—as a worker in one of Danbury's many fur shops. The city's flourishing hat industry relied upon these fur shops for the animal pelts that were used to create the felt material needed to manufacture hats. Immigrants from Lebanon and Syria often found employment preparing rabbit and beaver pelts for these hat factories. The job of making these animal pelts suitable was a dirty, smelly job that many local American workers did not want. A notoriously arrogant man, Kamil decided that although he was an immigrant, he, too, was better than this degrading work. The city's rumor mills spun a story of a suspicious fire that destroyed a well-insured warehouse in Kamil's name. Other folks swear it was wealthy associates from the old country who provided the initial investment. Either way, eventually, Kamil established his own fur factory. He bought a large Victorian house on Elm Street for his young family, and the Rizkallahs were soon regarded as one of the community's wealthiest and most successful. But Kamil nearly became unhinged after the sudden death of his wife. While it is almost certain that she died from complications of influenza, many in the Lebanese community believed it was her fragile disposition wasted by the harsh American air (for it was commonly accepted that the air in the United States was nothing like the pure air of Lebanon) that killed her. Kamil never remarried although he was often seen around town with various beauties.

"Evening, Kamil." I punctuated the greeting with exhaled smoke.

He extinguished his cigarette in an ashtray on an end table next to the couch, picked up a crystal snifter, smelled the amber liquid, and took a deep swig. "Eleanor made a fantastic pumpkin soup last night. It was perfect."

"Sorry I missed it. Ummi needed help making knafeh. I wanted to sell some this week."

"Ahh. I must send Eleanor to the market then. Celia's string pastries are the best in town, and I don't say that lightly. Does she have a secret?" Kamil leaned forward.

I smiled encouragingly. "Orange blossom water. Adds some before baking them and then again when she takes them out."

"Really?" He stood up, rather abruptly, and made his way to a table of men playing blackjack and enjoying cigars. I remained where I was, choosing instead to study the arabesque pattern of the Persian carpet under my feet. A fire crackled in the nearby fireplace, bathing the overstuffed furniture in warm light. Raucous laughter and wisps of smoke smeared the atmosphere. I swallowed more gin.

"Georgie! Come play cards!" Uncle Taffy hollered from the card table. The old man's bald head reflected the light above him, and from where I sat across the room, it resembled an orb.

"Think I'll sit this game out, Khali. But thanks." I walked over to them anyhow and took a seat by my uncle.

"Perfect timing, George. I'm telling them about my latest business venture, *Taffy's Tonic* —hair tonic extraordinaire!" The old man quivered with excitement. His rheumatic knuckles assumed a purple-pink hue. Age spots bloomed like spilled ink on his hands. I hadn't noticed how old and frail he had become.

"I thought you called it quits on that one, Uncle?" I stifled a smile, noticing the others do the same.

"No, no, no! NEVER! This is my ticket, my golden ticket!" He looked horrified at the suggestion. "This tonic is created from top-secret herbs and spices and—No! I've said too much! You people might steal it!" He narrowed his eyes at the table of men he'd been friends with for twenty-plus years.

"We're all respectable men here, Taffy," Kamil reassured him.

"Well then, like I was saying, this tonic will allow the baldest of men to grow a full head of hair—like MAGIC!" He clapped his hands. "I have a special meeting with *Johnson & Johnson*." Uncle Taffy beamed.

"And when will you start using it, Taf?" Johnny Nassif asked from across the table, eliciting a round of chuckles.

"I'll not even dignify that with a response!" Uncle Taffy threw his cards, got up from the table and stormed out, a stream of laughter trailing behind him.

As the laughter died down, Johnny turned the conversation to more serious matters.

"Kamil, have you heard about the trouble Balmforth Avenue is giving the Shadeeds?"

Kamil sipped his drink, looked at his cards, and responded, "Are you referring to the petition they brought to the city council?"

"Yes, that would be it."

"What are you talking about?" I asked, genuinely curious about the local politics.

"You don't need to trouble yourself with things like this, son," Kamil said.

"The boy is not stupid, Kamil. He knows things like this happen," Johnny added.

Kamil put down his cards, folded his arms across his chest, and looked at me. "Some folks feel uncomfortable living next to 'dirty Syrians.' They are trying to stop good Mr. Shadeed from buying a house on Balmforth. They seem to think that the Shadeeds don't deserve to leave River Street." He smiled, picked his cards up again, and said to everyone, "But they will not prevail, of course."

The men in the room became quiet for a moment and nodded in agreement. I couldn't help but respect Eleanor's father. He didn't just provide a beautiful life for his family and the people he loved; he protected his entire community.

* * *

Michael and Marlene had settled into connubial bliss. I was running the store and spending most of my free time with Eleanor. She was not a dull companion, sharp-tongued and opinionated. And, by society's standards, an old maid. At twenty-five years old, several years my senior, she was considered past her prime. Most of her friends, cousins, female contemporaries, had married and were already mothers, Lebanese or not. Eleanor was not unaware of this fact.

One evening in late November we had left the Capitol Theatre after seeing John Wayne and Maureen O'Hara's new film, *The Quiet Man*. Sauntering down Main Street, her arm hooked through mine, Eleanor rested her head on my shoulder as we walked and exhaled the words, "Do you love me?" more whisper than question. I imagined her cheeks glowing in the lamplight, her heart accelerating more quickly.

My own cheeks grew warm and heart rate accelerated. "Yes." I surprised myself with the swift, confident response. I had grown quite fond of Eleanor and, perhaps, in a way, I did love her. She was strong-willed, at times impetuous, and she made me laugh.

Squealing with delight, Eleanor stopped walking, cupped my face in her gloved hands, and kissed me fervently on the mouth. I wanted to respond with equal fervor but pulled away after a moment. Unfazed, she returned her head to my shoulder and giggled at nothing. This newfound revelation, that I loved Eleanor, was the impetus I had lacked. There would be no better time than now to take the next step.

When I asked Kamil for his permission to marry his only daughter the next night at the Club, he surprised me with an emphatic, "Of course." He also insisted on giving me a few hundred dollars in cash. "Eleanor deserves only the best. I'm sure you'd choose something lovely but, well, let's face it, son, you're a butcher." I took the money and fought with every ounce of self-control I could muster not to throw it back in his face. The wallet weighed down my pocket like a leather onus. "I'll give my man Eli a call, best jeweler around. He'll take care of you."

* * *

Eli Razinkoff owned a small jewelry store in Manhattan. His custom-made pieces attracted a clientele that consisted mostly of Long Islanders and wealthy uptown socialites. I found the formidable gray corner store, large glass windows encased in iron bars, eaves dripping the tears of an earlier rain, and walked inside. Eli waited with sketches he had drawn up the moment Kamil phoned him with news of his daughter's impending engagement.

"George Lahoud? I've been expecting you." Eli was a short man with a narrow face consumed by a large, Levantine nose. He spoke with a heavy New York accent.

Rows of glass cases held a colorful assortment of jewelry: lapis lazuli in a platinum bracelet, blood red rubies made to look like miniature suns on gold bands, tiny clusters of mother-of-pearl on silver clasps, amethyst grapes with emerald leaves fastened together in a necklace. Cases of diamond rings—round, square, pear cut, heart shaped, emerald design—lay beyond the initial glass-entombed baubles. The store seemed to stretch far back until it finally opened to reveal a back room. Eli Razinkoff led me inside this room—a Spartan, closet-like space consisting of a desk, three wooden chairs, and a file cabinet—where he produced pages of intricate drawings, the only evidence I was in a jeweler's office.

"I've been making jewelry for Kamil for many years. Birthday presents, Christmas, Easter—you name the occasion, I've made something for his daughter. Lovely woman." Eli paused over a sketch of a 1.5 carat round diamond on a simple gold band. "What do you think of this one? It is large without being ostentatious, simple but not boring. Understated elegance." He moved the drawing closer, pointing at it with his bony finger.

"Perfect. She'd love it." I could see Eleanor wearing it. Her hands were not small or dainty, like Ummi's or even Marlene's; the ring would sit comfortably, elegantly on her finger, soften the bulkiness of her hand. "This is the one."

"You sure? You haven't looked at any others?"

"I'm sure. This is the one." He couldn't challenge the finality in my tone.

"Well, when you know, you know. I'll take the down payment at the register."

* * *

I left Mr. Razinkoff's store, crossing the busy New York intersection and made my way through Lower Manhattan, towards 7th Avenue and the Village to find someplace to eat. I had heard this area was home to a new movement claimed by some liberal artists and bohemians calling themselves Beatniks. I worried about being in this sort of area, wandering aimlessly in the streets called home by beaten-down, potentially nefarious souls. There were a few upscale restaurants, but I didn't want to stand out as a lone diner. An anonymous-looking place blended into the corner. "Chazz's Bar" looked like it could have been a residual speakeasy, the entrance inconspicuous at the bottom of a few rotting steps. I walked inside, found a seat at the nearly empty bar and sat down. It was dimly lit, walls a dark cherry wood with pictures of jazz musicians. A woman with skin the color of Turkish coffee sang in a husky voice to no one in particular as a pianist with thick, blonde hair accompanied her. I was reminded too much of a small bar in Georgetown, on M Street, too much of someone I had almost forgotten.

"Want somethin' to drink?" A gruff, grizzly bear of a man came over to take my order. His carefully pressed white shirt looked like it was struggling to contain bulging muscles. A faded bruise hugged the outline of his right eye. I imagined he was some kind of boxer.

"Gin and tonic, please. You have a menu?"

"Sure." He leaned under the bar and pulled one out.

"Thanks." The air in the place was muggy though it was cold outside. I took off my camel-hair jacket and draped it over the seat. My elbows stuck to the sticky bar, forcing me to roll up my sleeves.

"Gin and tonic." The bartender placed the full drink almost tenderly in front of me. Surprising for such a tough-looking guy. "Somethin' to eat? We gotta lotta good options. Not too many people come here to eat, but they'se really missin' out." He smiled broadly. He was probably Italian, definitely from the Bronx.

I ordered a burger, handed him back the menu, and took a sip of the drink.

"So, you ain't from around here, are ya?" The man seemed desperate for someone to talk to. Understandable. The only other people in the place besides the singer and pianist were a couple of well-dressed Wall Street types, fedoras shading their faces, having a conversation over a bottle of wine.

"Just in the city for the day." There was not a drop of tonic in the drink.

He had leaned back and folded his arms. I couldn't help but appreciate the twitching muscles in his forearms.

"I had to buy a ring. I'm going to propose to a broad I've been seeing."

"Congrats, boss! I ain't been so lucky in that department." He reached for a glass filled with a bronze liquid and brought it to his lips, downing it in one gulp. "How'd you know she's the one?"

I felt the need to finish my drink.

The bartender refilled both our glasses.

"She'll be a great wife." I took another deep swig.

"I believe in soulmates. I know I don't look like the hopeless romantic type, but, hell, I can't help myself." He laughed loudly. One of the Wall Street guys shot a hooded glance. The pianist missed a key.

"You're more teddy bear than grizzly?" I gave him an

uncomfortable smile. "Sounded funnier in my head." I glowed gin pink.

He laughed more and refilled my drink. "This one's on the house. Name's Tony, most of my friends call me Boomer."

"Name's George, most of my friends call me George." I extended my hand and his large ball of one swallowed it.

"Almost forgot about your burger." Boomer disappeared behind some swing doors and returned almost instantly with food.

"Thanks. I'm starving."

"No prob, boss."

I ate my burger quickly and washed it down with more gin. When I was finished, I asked Boomer for the bill.

"Sure thing, boss. Stop by again if you'se ever round these parts." Boomer put the check down, grazing my hand with his. I instinctively jerked away, and he diverted his hand to my empty plate. I ignored the shock his touch sent through me, the warmth it induced.

"Keep the change."

"Thanks. George?"

"Yeah?"

"Don't just marry the gal 'cause she'd be a good wife. Lots of gals would make good wives."

I pulled my jacket on and left Chazz's, the soles of my shoes sticking to the floor, smacking against the liquor coated linoleum like wet kisses.

* * *

I proposed to Eleanor Rizkallah on a gray December evening. We had dinner at Melillo's Restaurant followed by a walk downtown. I dropped to one knee under the soft honey-glow of the streetlight on the corner of Main Street, in front Feinson's

Men & Boys Store. Strands of multi-color Christmas lights were festooned from one side of the streetlights to the other side. White stars hung from the center of the strands above the road. Large green wreaths with red bows and gold ornaments filled shop doors and windows. The holidays had come again to Danbury, CT. She exclaimed, "Yes," and fell classically into my arms. Snow fell softly as if the entire scene was unfolding in a snow globe, and the world around us was quiet and beautiful. She looked at me through wet lashes and kissed me hard on the mouth. Images—an off-centered smile, a damp curl, kissing with fists—blanketed me like the cold flakes. Skin prickled and stomach tightened. Eleanor blinked away snowflakes and maybe tears.

"You're everything I've ever wanted." Such disclosure, such adoration.

"You're everything I've ever needed." Truth.

* * *

Months passed like heartbeats. The wedding was only a few weeks away. We sat in the Rizkallah's sitting room among bride magazines, cutouts, cigarettes, and a bottle of gin. The liquor throbbed in my throat. Eleanor sat prettily in oblivion. The ring glared at me from her pale hand; I glared impotently back.

"Calla lilies? What'd you think?"

"Sure."

Dust winked in the bars of sunlight circumventing the venetian blinds. Eleanor sat with one leg tucked beneath her on the crimson divan. Gold and black satin pillows were scattered along with magazines, books, picture cutouts. Eleanor's pink head scarf and loose-fitting pale blue blouse and slacks seemed incongruous with the rich surroundings of the Rizkallah's sitting room. She put out her cigarette in a yellow enameled ashtray. The enamel formed intricate patterns of wheat shocks and scrolls, which attracted narrow slivers of afternoon sun. Her cigarette stub joined several nicotine shells that I had contributed over the last two hours. A half-empty bottle of Plymouth gin occupied the end table. My half-empty glass sat next to it.

"Looks like you've got all the details under control." I moved to stand, feeling the gin overthrow my senses momentarily. I caught myself.

"Don't you want to talk more about centerpieces?" Eleanor looked up from a picture of an elaborate sculpture she had torn from the *Ladies' Home Journal*.

"Nope. Not at all." I turned to walk out of the room when Eleanor huffed loudly.

"You just don't seem interested in planning our wedding!" Equal parts accusatory, disappointed, and pouty. "I feel like it's just another day to you!" She put down the picture and folded her arms across her wide chest.

"I'm thrilled. Can't wait for the big day." The gin sharpened the irony in my tone.

Her lip quivered, childlike, and tears threatened to smudge brown eyes.

"Eleanor, seriously, you're doing such a great job with all the details. I just get in the way." My tone softened.

"That's not true." She sniffled but smiled up at me from the divan.

I sat back down and grabbed her hand, kissing it affectionately. Then the buzzing in my head started, but I couldn't determine whether it was my thoughts or the black fly hovering over a white ceramic bowl filled with green and purple grapes.

"Eleanor?"

"Yes?"

"Are you happy?"

"Very." She cupped my cheek in her hand. "But I'd be happier if you told me what you think of these centerpieces." Eleanor held out a picture of a peacock feather arrangement in sterling silver vases. *Raina in a peacock blue dress peeling pepper. Sterling silver candlesticks cast shadows that moved like secrets. Raina in a loveless marriage. This was always going to be my fate, wasn't it? But then, the touch of hands, skin brushing against skin, electricity and adrenaline. Could I have that along with the convenience and comfort marriage would bring? I heard, once, about places in New York City that men visit. These places always spoken of in hushed tones full of shame, like the simple utterance of their existence would damn the speaker to Hell. I could confide in my sweet cousin, demonstrative while Ummi remained cold, American while my mother clung to the old country, to Lebanon. Raina's dress in the light matched Ummi's eyes. Ummi can't know, she would never understand. Perhaps Raina wouldn't either. Or worse, what if telling her altered her affection for me? And Eleanor...*

"George! The centerpieces, do you think they're pretty?"

"Lovely."

Eleanor turned back to the cut outs, the magazines, the books. "Back to the flowers now, darling. I'm really not sure about the calla lilies. They're just so commonplace."

CHAPTER TWELVE

I suffered long and restless nights lying awake in bed with thoughts of weddings and flowers and Eleanor and DC and Raina and the future, and I clung to a memory of the horse track, of a first-time sexual encounter as I once did to Ummi's bedtime stories.

Washington, DC, 1950. Heart beats and hoof beats tangled in sticky May air. Clouds of dirt hung like diaphanous blankets, coating the lungs but dissolved by alcohol. I remembered the smell of horse shit and mud and the ubiquity of flies contrasted by sweet-smelling women with elaborate hats and men in polished suits. Finals ended the second semester. Raina's husband invited me to join him at the track forty minutes outside of Baltimore. I dressed in a camel-colored suit, black fedora, and matching tie, and we headed to the Pimlico Special in Joe's cream-colored Plymouth Special De Luxe Coupe. Tucked into box seats above the track, drinking gin and arak and smoking Camels, the atmosphere was electric.

"Thirteen-to-one odds is not what I would consider 'a sure

thing.' Don't know why you listened to the boy." Joe's brother, Jimmy, shot me a piercing glance and shook his head.

"George's good. Sometimes you just gotta have a little faith, Jim-o!" Joe leaned back into his chair, swigged some arak, and cast a naked glance at a fair-haired woman with a large, colorful hat in the box next to us.

"That horse, what's 'is name?" Uncle Taffy asked. He was visiting from Connecticut and had refrained from betting.

"Capot, Uncle Taf."

"Your nephew and my fat head brother made a damned straight bet! No bet to place or show, just straight." Jimmy wiped tiny glistening beads from his forehead. "You got some kinda tip or something, kid?" He stopped wiping his head and looked with interest at me. He was a clenched fist of a man: round, tightly wound, bald. His eyes perpetually ran and squinted.

"Only tip I have is this one right here," I slapped my lower stomach.

Joe laughed, but Jimmy shook his head again and sat back in his seat.

Joe smiled at me. "Don't take it personally, son. He acts like a bitch all the time."

Jimmy folded his arms and focused too intently on the track below us. Uncle Taffy was preoccupied with his handkerchief, repeatedly using it to wipe his glass of arak. Each sip mandated a summary wipe. Jimmy did have a point; the odds were crazy. Thirteen-to-one that he would lose. But I read the list of names and Capot attracted my gaze and my wallet like a magnet. He would win. The outcome of the race clicked into place in my mind's eye. That's how it was. I'd picked the last two winners without knowing how. I was just a natural. Perhaps visiting the horse races each year with Bayee had taught me something. Joe believed in me; I believed in me; Jimmy did not believe in me. Maybe Jimmy was right.

The blast of the horn started the race.

Capot broke from the gate, making up the unremarkable middle, the average. Jimmy was right; he wouldn't transcend the odds, the mediocre expectations. I panicked. But his flanks rippled with power, and he sprinted, sprinted towards the two horses leading the race. I had a death grip on the railing; I felt my knuckles grow white. Joe held onto my arm, his own grip tight. A series of impossible seconds. Capot's rivals closed in, almost caught up to him. Jimmy had stopped breathing next to me. He was right, he was right, he was right. The jockey took control of the horse, guided him towards the end of the track. My breathing probably stopped, too. But then Capot kicked up dirt in protest, asking how we could ever doubt him. He made an almost graceful demivolt and closed in the furlong pole: he knew in that moment the race was his. Capot won by a single length. My gut won by a single length.

Jimmy nearly toppled over, grabbing at his chest. Joe threw his arms around me, and I nearly cried. The adrenaline burned through my blood like gin. Uncle Taffy looked as if he wasn't quite sure what had just transpired. One box over, the fair-haired girl with whom Joe had been engaged in a serious eye tango stood up, as did her slightly less attractive friend, a redhead in a tan behemoth of a hat.

Absorbed in our celebratory drinks, I scarcely noticed the two women reappear just outside our box. Joe, however, had apparently been expecting them. He went over, encouraging me to follow.

"You boys just won pretty big, huh?" The fair-haired woman tried too hard to be suggestive.

Joe inhaled her words and grinned broadly. "Well, that depends on who's asking."

"Daphne. Daphne Brewer is asking." She extended a small, gloved hand and smiled with sex-red lips.

"Well, then, yes Daphne. We did win. Very big. Won't you and your friend celebrate with us?" He held her hand several moments past acceptable. A sad, blurred image of lovely Raina misted my mind.

"We can do that." Smiling and turning towards me, Daphne added, "This is Eileen." Winking at Eileen, she turned all of her attention to Joe, who was more than happy to have it.

"And you are?" Eileen had a round face, flushed pink, and copper hair piled high on her head.

"George." I smiled at the girl and lit a new cigarette. "Want one?"

"Please." She leaned in close, parting her plump lips slightly.

I obliged by putting the Camel in her mouth and lighting it, taking in the strong scent of nicotine, sweat, and vanilla. I was on top of the world and everyone from Joe to this random woman thought so.

"Come with me." Eileen grabbed my hand and pulled me towards the exit of the box.

"Where're we going?" I craned my neck around to find Joe. His eyes locked mine, assenting to the proposition before me, encouraging it. I realized he'd soon be disappearing, too, seeking some hidden, dark corner or perhaps leaving the track all together. Maybe they'd neck in his Plymouth for a while.

Eileen laughed an off-kilter sound. Leading me to a deserted corner, far beyond the track and the horses, separated from the throngs of people celebrating or drowning in their losses, and concealed by a poplar tree, this woman I had just met began kissing me with drunken fervency. The taste of salt and rum filled my mouth and her lips were hot on mine. I was caught off guard, unsure, shocked. Buzzing with confusion and alcohol and the thrill of recent victory, her tongue found its way to mine. I wanted so badly to feel something, anything. But all I felt was nothing and my lips grew cold against hers. She pulled away, but then she looked at me and began rubbing my crouch. I concentrated on the shadow of hair that lined her upper lip. *Dark hair above lips, throats rough, bearded. Deep, husky voices that fill bars and libraries and coffee shops.* At some point, this copper-haired woman, drunk and laughing at nothing, knelt to the ground, and took me in her mouth. I leaned my head back and breathed in air heavy with horse shit and cigarettes.

A few moments later, Eileen stood up and brushed her lips with her pointer finger. My cheeks burned with the sensation coursing through my body. I leaned down and brushed clods of dirt from her silk stockings.

This memory rippled like the flanks of horse's mid-race, and I kept it close as the days until the wedding fell away like the excess skin peeled from a carcass. I would be a husband soon, a lover. Eleanor was a virgin, but she surely had expectations. This memory was a reminder that when I trusted my gut, I could be a winner. I had to believe in myself, trust myself. I could be a traditional American man who drank and smoked and received sexual pleasure from pretty women. This memory gave me hope.

CHAPTER THIRTEEN

It was June, 1953, and my wedding was in ten days. Cars passed by the store and pedestrians in summer hats moved lethargically in the heat. Only little children remained indefatigable. Through the open windows, their shadows played on the surface of the counter like the schoolboys in the road at sunset with balls and brooms and makeshift toys forged from tree limbs or discarded boxes or borrowed pots and pans. They played their games until angry mothers in aprons called from kitchens that "dinner was ready" and "supper was getting cold." I had been a schoolboy once. Life had been simple once.

The store was busy. Customers clogged the narrow aisles seeking fresh fruits and vegetables, cuts of meat for upcoming barbeques, and cold beverages to calm stubborn streams of sweat. I focused intently on ordering the extra shipments of watermelons, strawberries, and cherries, the most popular summertime fruits. Instead of delegating, I stocked the shelves and organized shipments with Michael. I arrived at the store before sunrise to prepare extra cuts of meat. I did all this to keep up with the store but mostly to distract myself from the fact that I was ten days away from marrying Eleanor Rizkallah. And the heat was becoming intolerable.

Damp half-moons decorated the underarms of our white shirts. Michael brushed the superfluous moisture from where he could and continued in his routine. I felt compelled to dash upstairs on lunch breaks to change into a fresh, unspoiled shirt.

"Let's hope the church isn't this hot. You'll have to change your tux mid-ceremony." Michael had finished restocking the fruit bins for the third time that day.

"Hope not." I produced a beige handkerchief from my pocket and wiped a soaking upper lip.

"You know I'm teasing?"

"Sorry. It's just the heat getting to me."

"Heat or nerves?"

"It's a million degrees in here." Electric fans hummed like black flies in the doorway, in the window, overhead. Ten. Only ten.

"Sure is! Speaking of, you haven't changed your shirt in an hour. Shouldn't you head upstairs for a new one?"

"At least I don't look like a used mop." I laughed. Michael was drenched, but in ten days he would be handsome in a black-pressed suit and tails, my best man. The shadow of black hair that had taken up on his chin would be razed. In ten days.

"Sweat's a natural bodily function. Stop fighting it, brother." He chuckled his way to the storage room.

Stop fighting it. A crown of sweat glittering on a pale forehead, a dark curl stuck to it. Jacob. Men in spicy-sweet cologne, masculine, edgy, sharp. Ten days until matrimony, until Eleanor would commit herself too forever, to me. Forever. Forever. Forever. Ten days left until forever. *Stop fighting it.* Forever was coming. *Stop fighting it.*

"Excuse me, George, honey. Be a dear and grab me a pound of beef, will you?" Mrs. Moses, gold chains interrupting the lines of sweat hugging her thick neck, approached in a wide-brimmed straw hat.

"Of course, Mrs. Moses."

* * *

Raina arrived the day before the wedding. Beige trousers, a white blouse, a red neckerchief, dark hair newly shorn in waves. She stood at the doorstep with a suitcase and a cigarette. Looking at me with eyes that matched a summer night sky, she grinned and flicked ash onto the faded doormat. "Hello, handsome!" She planted a wet kiss on my cheek and tossed the half-finished cigarette to the ground. I picked up her heavy bag and followed her into the kitchen. "Where's my favorite cousin? Celia?" She began calling for Ummi before I could respond.

"She's out. Last-minute wedding stuff with Eleanor and Marlene." I put her bag on the cracked linoleum and pulled out a kitchen chair for her.

"Drink?"

"I'll take a cup of coffee, darling."

"Turkish, okay?"

"Is there any other kind?" She smiled easily, and I went about making a fresh pot. "So Eleanor Rizkallah, huh?" Her eyes glinted like the diamonds in her ears. The short hair made her fine features sharper, more focused. A not entirely new rarefied air. Raina of Lebanon, Raina of Hollywood.

"She's a great girl." The brew percolated like the half-confessions in my mind.

"Christ, Georgie. I hope you sound more convincing at the altar." She took out another cigarette from a diamond crusted case. "Really, darling, you aren't a very good liar." She exhaled through flared teardrop nostrils. She balanced it between two long, red-painted fingers.

Bile burned in a pit somewhere in my chest. A compulsion to turn around and run out the kitchen door, run away from knowing dark eyes, dark like the secrets I kept from everyone. Did she already know? Did she know about these dirty, inexplicable feelings? Did she know that I really wanted to be in love with Eleanor, but sometimes the thought of kissing her made me sick to my stomach? Did she know that sometimes the thought of kissing men made my heart race and my stomach hurt, too, but in a different way? A good way. Impossible. Unlikely. Just because she was adept at pretense, adept at playing the happy, subservient Lebanese wife, did not mean she understood what it meant to live a lie. But if anyone could, Raina would. Raina the cousin, Raina the actress. I watched patches of dust that had collected in the cracks of the pale blue windowsill. A spider danced in the corner, the skeins of its web glinting in the sunlight. As the coffee pot hummed, I stood at the counter and studied a glass bowl of pistachio nuts, silver tin canisters holding flour, sugar, salt, formica tops scrubbed clean, a folded blue-and-white checkered dish cloth resting by the porcelain sink.

"Honey, you could have any broad you want." She looked at me through heavily painted eyes. "Eleanor seems like a sweet girl. I'm sure your mother loves her. And, of course, I understand your marriage will come with some financial benefits." She inhaled and exhaled nicotine. "Just don't become Joe. Christ, George. Don't become me either. Please." Raina rested her chin on her hand and smiled up at me through uncharacteristically misted eyes. I had started to walk towards her but stopped. The secret had taken root in intestines, stomach, arteries, soul. But maybe I was ready to purge my body of it. Sunday dinners prepared together. The shared loneliness. But. But I loved the honey-sweet taste of approval.

"I'm going to marry Eleanor because it's the right thing to do." I stood transfixed by my boldness.

"But, honey, she's such a bland girl. Very vanilla." A moment passed between us like its own secret. Then all at once she stopped speaking. "Is she in trouble, George?" Raina assumed a serious pose, erect back, hands down, cigarette extinguished in the ashtray on the table.

"No. It's not that." I sat down in a chair across from her. Raina looked at me confused but determined. I was reminded of the way she dug up weeds in her garden in Georgetown, brown gloves on, determined to eradicate the very smallest root of unwanted plant. "I will never be in love, Raina. Not with someone I can marry." The aftertaste of the words burned my mouth like bile or cheap gin.

"What'd you mean?" Her brow furrowed.

"I mean that I'll never be in love with the person I marry so it might as well be Eleanor."

"Come on, Georgie. Don't say that. You're still young, honey. You'll meet the right girl sometime."

"I'm not capable of loving any woman. Not that way." It was the truth I had refused to tell myself.

"Huh." She reached for another cigarette. I shrank from her sudden comprehension. She exhaled a curl of smoke. "I think that coffee's done, honey." Raina looked at me like she had never seen me before. Every muscle in my body tensed.

I walked to the lazy susan for a ceramic mug, but it slipped from my shaking hands and shattered in pieces on the linoleum. Raina knelt beside me, pushed my hands away from the splinters. She took my hands in hers tightly and wouldn't let me pull them away, but I struggled free of her grasp. I reached for the shards of ceramic, not feeling them slice and prick my fingers and palms. Drops of blood fell, tiny bursts of crimson on white linoleum.

"Stop it, George! Stop!" Raina yelled.

I knelt on the kitchen floor, surrounded by broken petals and blood blossoms, languishing in the garden of my nightmares. The room smelled of allspice and ground lamb and coffee and spicy-sweet perfume mixed with cigarette smoke.

Raina's hands on my shoulders guided me from the floor to the table. She handed me a cigarette, lit it for me, all the while puffing on her own. Without a word, she moved to the liquor cabinet above the sink, pulled down a bottle of arak and filled two crystal snifters. At some point, she must have tended to the coffee pot, which was cooling off in the corner of the kitchen counter. The nicotine and alcohol steadied my nerves, my shaking hands.

"Do you think less of me now?" I asked, not really wanting to know the answer.

Raina just laughed and swigged her drink. "What do you think, darling, that you're the first man to ever have a secret? Don't be dense."

I drank the entire snifter of arak in a single gulp and leaned back in the wicker chair.

* * *

That night my memory was loosened. It was loosened by the satisfying release of truth to Raina. Her words looped in my mind, *what do you think, darling, that you're the first man to ever have a secret?* Bayee had had secrets, too.

I was six years old. School had let out early that day; Michael and I got home together, but I sent him upstairs to our apartment alone. It was a hot day, and I wanted to grab a cool soda from the refrigerator in the store. *Grab me one too!* Michael shouted as he scampered up the stairs and inside. The "closed" sign hung on the door, an indication that Bayee was taking his lunch break. I went into the store anyway, triggering a tinkling of bells as I walked in. Nobody was around. Bayee must have been eating in the storage room like he sometimes did, preferring the crowded area with his desk to standing behind the counter. I reached into the cooler, and grabbed two Cokes. Then I heard an unfamiliar sound coming from somewhere in the back. Soft but consistent. Was someone in trouble? It sounded like a woman. Was she hurt? I made my way slowly to the back of the store. It grew louder, it was coming from the storage room. Was Bayee in trouble? I put my sodas down on top of a shelf. The door was open slightly, wide enough so I could peer inside. And then I saw a raven-haired woman clawing at Bayee's back, her long legs wrapped around him as she called out for God. He seemed breathless from pushing towards her, moving her so the desk she was sitting on scuffed back and forth, back and forth. I stood frozen. Bayee was moaning, too. My legs forgot how to work so I just stood. All at once the woman opened her eyes and saw me staring back. *George! Oh God George stop!* I didn't know if she was imploring me or my father, senior or junior, but it was enough to restore me, and I ran until I collapsed onto my bed.

Where's my soda, Georgie? I'm so thirsty! Michael demanded.

Sorry, Michael. All out. I kept my face turned towards the bedroom wall.

Aw shucks! He walked off in a disappointed huff.

* * *

The night before our wedding, Michael, Louie "Grizzly" Aoun, Joey Buzaid, and Jimmy Deegan picked me up in Deegs' '51 Volkswagen Beetle. The car's top was down, and the guys' fedoras on for a night out on the town. Deegs and I had made up months before, chalking up the incident at Art Negri's coffeehouse to too much alcohol.

Michael was clean-shaven, hair pomaded, but sports jacket tossed recklessly over one shoulder. In his other hand, he stuffed the remainder of homemade kibbeh, our dinner an hour earlier. He was more excited for my bachelor party than I was.

"You're in for one hell of a night, brother!" Michael practically shouted as he climbed into the backseat with Grizzly and Joe.

I slid into the front bucket seat where Deegs was fiddling with the radio dial. He stopped when he found a song to his liking. "What the hell are you eating, Mike? Smells funny." He started whistling to the tune as freckles danced across the bridge of his nose.

"Kibbeh," he managed through a mouthful.

"Strange A-rab food." He smirked. Something lurched in my stomach although it was probably just the sudden acceleration of the Bug. I squeezed the end of the seat tightly.

Michael relaxed into the backseat crowded by Grizzly's large frame. "You don't know what you're missing, Deegs. Best food around."

The red Bug blazed through Danbury's streets. We passed Square Deal Homegoods Store, Mohegan Grocery with its dirty straw floors and produce-filled barrels, Lillian Garber, the high-end women's clothing venue, and Ali Bez's Fruit and Veggie Stand on the corner of Liberty and Main. A block over from the old man's produce cart, on the edge of the Barbary Coast neighborhood, we pulled up to a small establishment run by Grizzly Aoun's father, Louie Sr. The eponymous tavern and restaurant served Arabic delicacies, but on the weekends, it was known for beautiful belly dancers, usually recent immigrants from the old country.

"I'm iffy about your food, but your women, well, that's a

different story." Deegs grinned as he elbowed his way up to the crowded bar and ordered a round of drinks.

We found an empty corner and made ourselves comfortable on oxblood couches fixed with gold and black pillows. The ceiling dripped gold fixtures, which emitted dim lighting. Cigarette and narghile smoke tangoed in the atmosphere, a smoky sweet aroma. I swilled the gin drink in front me as I took in the opulent, Middle Eastern surroundings. I relished in the thought that Kamil's wedding gift to Eleanor and me was six months in Lebanon. In two days, I would be on my way to my parent's birthplace, the land of ancestors and dreams. Finally, a dream within reach. A dream I did not need to abandon.

Deegs walked up to us with the round of drinks. "Ready to get this party started, fellas?"

Almost on cue, the music began: quick, heated palpitations of the tabla drums, the high-pitched throbbing of the finger cymbals, a low moan of the oud. A woman emerged from the shadows of men, a Lebanese goddess, another opulent fixture. Hips and midsection moved independently of each other and with equal authority. Her lithe, tight body commanded attention, and I could not help but appreciate the way her body seemed to move of its own volition as if it was the very beating of the music.

The dancer twisted and gyrated her way over to me, the bachelor, the almost husband. She removed her crimson cape and revealed the fullness of her breasts, the twitching muscles of her perfectly tanned abdomen, the bell-laced wrap barely clinging to her lower body. Black satin hair fell to shoulders, crowned in a crimson and gold veil. Heavily painted eyes, red lips, gold bangles to match gold finger cymbals. The belly dancer draped me in her cape, made me the center of her universe as she teased me with the beauty of her half-naked movements. A primal hunger took up in the eyes of the men around me, in the eyes of Michael, Grizzly, Deegs, and Joe. This appetite, this desire was evident in the way they couldn't tear their gaze from her, the way their mouths parted slightly and bellies rose with a quicker breath. The woman moved like a song, accelerating heartbeats and adrenaline. She was beautiful; yet, I focused on the sadness in her lovely brown eyes.

* * *

Dawn broke against the sky in a thousand shades of gold. The mirror revealed a handsome man of twenty-two. The strong bone structure of his tanned face followed the tradition of his father's. He wore a classic black tuxedo, his dark hair pomaded and smooth. He smiled and a dimple appeared in the left corner of his mouth, just under the tiny mole on his cheek. I did not know this man who looked at me in the mirror.

Ummi walked into the bedroom in lavender chiffon. Her hair was swept up and pearls clung humbly to her neck. She was the human equivalent of sunlight.

"So handsome, habibi." She placed a tiny hand on the small of my back, her version of affection.

"You've made the family proud." Blue eyes betrayed a hint of tears. I savored the rare verbal praise, a sentiment Ummi typically communicated with knafeh.

"Ready?" I asked, more to myself than to Ummi.

"Yes, my son." The tone of her voice was tight, controlled, and did not allow for stray notes of happiness, sadness, or emotion of any kind. Her feelings could only be perceived in the lightness of her facial muscles and the traces of dampness by her eyes.

The elm tree on the corner quivered in the warm breeze. St. Anthony's beckoned, Eleanor beckoned, a future of domesticity, of obligations, of sex and children beckoned. Elm trees, maple trees, beeches, and birches shook. Ummi full of hope in the passenger's seat, Michael oblivious in the back next to Raina. Raina full of knowledge. Pale sunlight dimpled the tireless ivy; ivy clinging to the railing of the church, to the gray stone building of St. Anthony's, ivy clinging like pearls to Ummi's neck: classic, traditional.

"Ready to take the proverbial plunge?" Michael hopped out of the backseat of the Lincoln. Plunge. Cold water, cold feet, cold heart.

"Couldn't be more ready." A version of truth.

Raina appeared beside me, arm locking mine. "It's not too late to change your mind." The words were breath in my ear. "I don't think you should do this." She had stopped walking and held me back from following them inside the church.

"I said I'm ready." I didn't mean to be so curt.

"You're going to regret it, honey."

"Hurry, everyone. Yullah! We're late! Eleanor will be waiting!" Ummi herded us into St. Anthony's.

Splotches, dizzying blurs of people. I felt as a goldfish must, in a glass bowl being watched by people. I must swim for you or blow bubbles; you expect things.

I took the plunge, headfirst.

* * *

Eleanor stood at the altar beside me in an ivory lace gown. The dress hugged her curves in just the right way, and she looked beautiful. We exchanged our vows in front of what felt like the entire city of Danbury. Jeanette Moses looked on with an overabundance of smiles bordering on giddiness, her husband solemn beside her. Art Negri and his wife, Ed Shaker, Grizzly, Deegs, Joe Buzaid: splotches, dizzying blurs. Marlene, a bridesmaid. Michael, a best man. The mass of people crowded the small church, which already appeared crowded with large bouquets of calla lilies, amaranth, pink and white roses. Drafts of incense veiled the air and the organ pipes blared. Afternoon sunlight leaked through the open stained-glass windows and glazed the marble in crimson and gold. I stood at the altar, held Eleanor's gloved hand in mine, repeated the words. We promised to love, honor, and obey and with the final vows, "I do", the matrimony was complete. As soon as I had made the vow, accepted the promise, I looked up at the crucifix, at God, and for the first time in my life I did not feel fear. I felt anger.

The ceremony was followed by a reception in the garden of the parish. A large white tent had been arranged among the roses and other flora of Father Hayek's Garden. The same troupe of Arabic musicians that had played at Michael and Marlene's wedding were brought in from New York. The food was catered by a Lebanese family who owned a restaurant in the city and who happened to be good friends of Kamil. Kamil, dressed entirely in black, drifted about the party armed with a glass of arak and a perpetually burning cigar. He grinned widely through his generous facial hair at the guests who honored his daughter with their presence at her wedding. He offered me neither welcome nor congratulations until the end of the festivities, long after the dabke had finished winding around the bucolic surroundings, the narghile had extinguished, and the last crumbs of baklawa had disappeared.

"Long day, huh, George?" Kamil had unfastened the top few buttons of his shirt and had long since removed his jacket.

"Yes, sir. But perfect." I drained the final drops of a glass of gin.

He put his drink down at a vacant table and sat. I joined him. "Excited about the honeymoon?" Kamil leaned back in the chair and puffed on the Cuban in his left hand. Most of the guests had left, but a few had remained and were taking advantage of the open bar and the energetic music. Raina and Joe were one of several couples still dancing feverishly to the rapid percussion of instruments. Eleanor and her brother Kamil Jr. were keeping up tempo quite well, too.

"Very. I've always wanted to visit the old country." It was the truth. Leaving for Lebanon in two days was the only part of the honeymoon that did not make me anxious.

"As you should. Lebanon is quite beautiful. It's home." Stopping to puff on his cigar, Kamil then added, "And it would be a great time to work on giving me grandsons." He winked and slapped me on the back before standing up and heading over to the dance floor. "Come dance, son. The day's not over yet."

Ummi had joined the few remaining dancers. Her pale skin shimmered. She moved energetically with Raina whose hand she'd taken in hers. The dark one and the light one, the two moved in tandem. The day and the night were sisters, dancing in the bodies of two cousins. I took the hand of my mother and kept up with her, stomping my foot, twisting my hips, clapping my hands. Michael and Marlene looked on with smiles from a table by the dance floor. Michael kept his arm draped over his young wife, inhaling a cigarette and passing it to Marlene, who smiled at her husband as she took in a hit of nicotine. The air was thick with heat and the floral aroma wafting from the garden, which insulated us from the rest of the world. A crescent-shaped moon floated in a pool of black.

* * *

The honeymoon suite of The Berkshire Hotel was beleaguered by bright pinks, white lace, and a bevy of mint-green cushions. The cherry wood, four-post bed was steeped in colorful pillows that didn't quite complement the pink and white floral bedspread. An oval, gold-framed mirror hung above the bed. I watched Eleanor's reflection tighten as her eyes fell upon the bed. Her nervousness was paltry compared to my own.

"Today was lovely, wasn't it?" She removed a silk shawl and set it upon the bed. Her gloved hands trembled.

"It was." I picked up a bottle of Cuvee Femme from an ice bucket on the nightstand table. I filled two crystal glasses and handed one to Eleanor. The champagne unfastened the knot in my gut. It appeared to have a similar effect on Eleanor, whose cheeks assumed a pinkish hue. I removed my jacket and threw it over a desk chair. My trunk, brimming with as many clothes as it would hold, sat in the corner awaiting its return trip to the old country.

"It's warm in here, isn't it?" Eleanor took off her gloves and veil. Her thick fingers fumbled with the buttons in the back of her gown. I steadied her hands and unbuttoned the dress for her, helping her slide it off her shoulders and climb out of it entirely. She stood shyly before me in a white corset, white curves, white stockings. Her dark hair fell curled to her shoulders. Eleanor rubbed the sides of her wide hips. Her anxiety filled me up. My hands were strong taking hers, locking fingers; they reassured. I guided her to the bed with a hard kiss on the mouth. Her whole being rose up to meet me, but I pushed her gently back until she sat on the bed.

I took off my tie, my shirt, my pants, my socks and stood naked before my new bride. By the appetite in her eyes, I knew that she found me desirable. I walked to her and removed her undergarments. Eleanor lay on the bed. Yards of white satin sheets, yards of white satin skin, white satin breasts, pink roses on bedspreads, pink roses on breasts. A dark, wet place below. A dark, wet place in my head. *Spicy-sweet cologne. The shape of a damp curl stuck to his forehead. Rough, bearded throats.* I buried my face in the pillow, the pillow wet with saliva and sweat. Eleanor beneath me was wet, too. Wet with saliva and sweat and arousal. Throaty, breathy sounds from her; guttural, primal from me. And then the relief, the satisfaction, the pleasure of release. Release. Release.

Afterwards, Eleanor wrapped her arms around me and buried her face in my arm. "Aren't you excited to begin our life together, George?"

* * *

I dreamt that night of black flies. I was in an unfamiliar market. Bins overflowed with strangely shaped, brightly colored fruits. People overwhelmed the narrow space between the rows of produce, jostled me. I was trying to reach the end of the aisle where a young man, a stranger beckoned. My need to reach him was urgent, but the more I tried to walk to him, the more people blocked my way. All of a sudden, the bins of fruit were black, blanketed in black flies. The flies buzzed and buzzed and buzzed until the noise of the crowd was nothing. I pushed the people around me, but I was no closer to the man at the end of the aisle, and I began to realize the flies were watching me. They had red eyes that glowed like embers. The strange man yelled, "Come on!" but I couldn't reach him. Just as I began to suffocate in bodies and insects, I woke with a jolt.

Eleanor was sound asleep. But I was standing by the open window of the hotel, naked, sweating, with the steamer trunk next to me, tipped over and opened, the contents a tangle on the floor.

PART II
THE WANDERER

Beirut, Lebanon
July 1953

CHAPTER FOURTEEN

The sun danced gilt-faced over the Mediterranean Sea. The view from our hotel room in St. George's was inclusive: immutable blue water, pale light tangled in the fronds of palm trees, a balustrade-lined corniche filled with well-dressed people, some in the Western tradition and others in checkered kaffiyehs and wide-legged trousers called sherwals. Reposing on the white iron-ringed terrace and smoking a cigarette, I looked out into the Bay of St. George dimpled with swaying boats, boats that moved in tandem with shaking palms. A foreign silence was punctured occasionally by the sound of car horns, and I inhaled the salt-tinged air as smoke threads unraveled around me.

Eleanor was sick; she had been enjoying the food with me, but much of it was prepared with mountain water, water that, for some reason, was not kind to her stomach. We were scheduled to dine with her uncle, Saad Rizkallah, and his wife Leila at their home in the little mountain village of Aarbaniyee.

"Sweetheart, we're going to be late," I called from the terrace.

"Almost ready." The disembodied voice drifted from the room, reached me, and then vanished in the ocean's breath.

Minutes later, my young wife, painted and perfumed, was blotting beads of perspiration from her upper lip in the backseat of a taxicab. We stagnated in Beirut traffic, a mire of European cars and Arabic service cabs. Driving along Rue Maarad, we passed through Place de l'Etoile, Star Square, with its tall clock tower that pierced Beirut's heart, the city's financial, commercial, administrative district. The tower stood as if a sentry, proud and watchful, guarding the Parliament and complimentary buildings that fanned out around the four-faced clock. Cathedrals, cafés, and restaurants nestled among Art Deco buildings, the identical faces of which were ivory but blushed gold in the streetlamps. A tapestry of gray pigeons rippled through the square as pedestrians moved perfunctorily around them. Arabic music, percussive cymbals, and wailing ouds from a nearby cab made their way through our open window in frenetic drifts. Red awnings hooded windows and outdoor café tables where old men in suits smoked shisha and polished women with shopping bags drank steaming beverages. I sucked in the fresh mountain air, ubiquitous in this country despite urban surroundings and interrupted only by pockets of sweet, paprika-infused shawarma, emanating from one of several cafés.

City streets choked on vehicles, but eventually, Beirut opened into wider roads, roads that led upwards into Mt. Lebanon. The cab jerked and wheezed but continued ascending higher along dirt pathways that cut through groves of ancient trees. Black cedars twisted against the gilded dusk like broken silhouettes. Lemon trees leaned over roads, limbs heavy with fruit. Pale stone houses with roofs in shades of burning orange lined the scant-used roads. A little girl read a book on the steps of a simple stone church which occupied the center of

Aarbaniyee. An old woman with skin of weathered ivory, much like the houses surrounding us, balanced a cigarette between long, bony fingers. She leaned against the dark body of a cedar and watched the movements of the folks around her: the children's bonhomie, the two neighbor men engaged in animated conversation, passing a cigarette back and forth, taking turns inhaling the nicotine.

As we passed in the wheezing cab, the townspeople stopped whatever they were doing to notice us. Some smiled and waved. The old woman, stoic in her simple garb and wiry white bulb of hair, smiled, too, an act which multiplied the lines embedded in the landscape of her face. Two little boys began to run alongside the car, laughing and shouting, "Hamdellah assalamah!" *Thank God for your safety!* The village, Aarbaniyee, was welcoming us home. Yes, I thought, this was Lebanon, land of ancestors and Ummi's stories.

An old man with skin like the bark of the cedar tree and hair as white as the snow-capped mountains around us, hung nimbly from the top of a tree, plucking the pine cones and placing them in what appeared to be a burlap sack. The old man looked down at us as we exited the cab, and he smiled a toothless grin.

Saad Rizkallah's house was pale stone like the ones surrounding it. The house was nestled among trees—tall cedars, some could easily have been one hundred twenty feet or more, with clusters of pine-like needles erupting at the crowns. Shorter lemon trees teemed with fruit next to olive trees, squat with sliver green leaves and twisted bark. Just beyond the house, a panoramic view of distant, snow-capped mountains and green valleys sprinkled with houses far below. An open terrace revealed freshly laundered clothes rippling on a clothes-line in the wind. The dirt road crunched beneath our feet as we walked towards Saad Rizkallah's front door.

"Habibis, welcome home!" Leila greeted us with kisses on each check and a tight embrace. A thickset, olive-skinned woman in her late forties, Leila was elegantly dressed, ebony hair perfectly coiffed. Her large nose did not dominate her face, but it sat nicely in the soft folds of her skin and full cheeks. A cluster of lines framed her dark eyes.

"Amma Leila!" Eleanor hugged her aunt. The dim light in the foyer betrayed tears in her eyes. Eleanor was only a baby when her mother died and for the first years of her life, Leila came to Connecticut to care for her and her older brother.

"And you must be George!" She hugged me just as tightly. "We're so disappointed we didn't make it for the wedding, habibi." Leila cupped my face in her soft, fleshy hands and smiled into me, kind, maternal tears smudging her cheeks. "Come inside, children." She took us each by the hand. "Saad!" Leila shouted. "They're here!"

As we made our way into the Rizkallah home, passing richly colored furniture and Persian rugs, stone walls draped in incarnadine and royal blue tapestries and religious pictures, the room we entered opened into a good-sized kitchen. Saad had just set down a bowl of olives next to a colorful surfeit of Middle Eastern dishes decorating the long oak table.

"Habibis!" He almost shouted as he opened his arms and moved towards us.

"Ami!" Eleanor rushed to embrace her uncle, a tall, broad-shouldered man who made his niece look like a small girl beside him.

"You are home now, children. Come eat. Your bellies must be crying." Saad shook his head with concern. Though his hair-line was receding, he had thick, white hair that was carefully pomaded. "Satinah!"

Before we sat down, Saad and Leila began piling our plates with food: tabbouleh, hummus, olives and cheese, pita bread, grape leaves. They performed this task with enthusiasm and pride, beaming as they arranged the plates in front of us.

"We are your parents while you are here. Anything you need, just ask." Saad slapped me on the back before taking his own seat at the head of the table. Leila sat across from him and immediately raised a glass of arak, indicating that we should do the same.

Saad mimicked his wife and, in a loud, sonorous voice, said, "To our children, Eleanor and George. May God bless you with happiness and many sons. May you come to know Lebanon as she knows you, and may this be the first of many visits. Welcome home, habibis. Cheers!" He emptied his glass in a single gulp and reached for the dark green bottle in the center of the table.

I took a sip from my glass and let the liquor burn my throat. Although it was partially diluted with water, arak seemed to be more potent here than in Connecticut, a fact evidenced by the blush spreading across Eleanor's cheeks. The addition of the water caused the liquid to assume milky-white translucence.

"It's good, no? We make the arak from our own grapes. Aarbaniyee's soil is better than anywhere in the world!" Saad explained in a loud, passionate voice, gesticulating and sending flecks of spit into the air.

"It's perfect," I assured. And it was perfect. Everything in Lebanon was perfect: the cloudless sky, the city atmosphere— an amalgamation of Old World Eastern and modern Western traditions, the spices, the history, the people.

After dinner, Saad, with a bottle of arak tucked under his arm and two glasses in his hand, asked me to accompany him for a stroll outside. As he moved, his large belly swayed. It had become darker but remained light enough to take in our surroundings. The sky, a dark blue, was starless, the moon not quite risen. We walked along the dirt road, rendered more walkway than actual street by the absence of vehicles. I followed Saad as he crossed the road and made his way towards a garden. Brightly colored flowers and fruit trees filled the bucolic area. Saad led us to a round table surrounded by white wicker chairs set on a stone patio in the midst of the garden. An ashtray heaped with cigarette shells and ash was the centerpiece.

"Sit, my son. I've had enough exercise for the evening." He laughed, sat, pulled out a pack of cigarettes, and handed me one. He placed the twin glasses on the table and filled them generously with liquor. Around us, distant pieces of conversation, glimpses into other worlds and lives, floated between blossoms. The older man, avuncular in his smile and the way he pushed the glass towards me, lifted his drink as if to toast me.

"I have long awaited this moment." He drank nearly all the contents in a gulp.

"What do you mean?" I asked, perplexed as I sipped from my drink.

"God didn't bless us with any children of our own, and we have always thought of Eleanor as our daughter." He finished the last sip and poured himself another glass. "I have waited a long time to share a drink with a son." Before imbibing more, he brushed away a tear from his eye with beefy fingers. The gold rings on his fingers twinkled like night stars.

"That means a lot. Thank you." The words felt insufficient, trivial in the face of such genuine emotion. Something like affection curled in my gut, but I didn't know how to express it. I thought, then, of Bayee, of his distance, his serious mannerisms. I thought of his drunken outbursts and his last painful days. I thought, too, of his cedar tree thriving in our backyard.

Saad and I chain-smoked and laughed and drank arak as the night wrapped itself around us like a blanket made of sweet-smelling air. Long after the dark blue sky had deepened to black, Saad drove us back to the hotel in his rundown car. He sped down roads and nearly took out several other cars before reaching St. George. My stomach, which was much stronger than Eleanor's, was turning a bit from the emphatic turns, acceleration, and sudden jolting stops. And probably the bottle of arak we had shared. Eleanor, clutching her belly, politely hugged her uncle and ran up to our room before I had exited the car.

"If you need anything, habibis, we will take care of you." Saad smiled from the driver's seat.

I thanked him and followed Eleanor's lead. We readied for bed and Eleanor relieved her stomach.

When she exited the bathroom, her hair set in rollers, she lay down next to me. My wife was so close the dampness from her eyes, a relic of the recent voiding of her stomach, leaked onto my arm. Despite the sickness, she was amorous, grazing my arm with the tips of her fingers and in her best sensual tone, "I'm not sleepy yet."

"Try to rest. It's been a long day." I turned away, towards the window, beyond which lay a black, starless sky.

CHAPTER FIFTEEN

Lebanese women seemed to have a fanatical obsession with trendy European fashion. Dressed in Western garb, they swarmed European clothing stores like flies on fruit-filled wooden bins. Eleanor, who was one of these women, had been seduced by Chloe, a recently opened Beirut fashion house founded by Gaby Aghion, an Egyptian-born Parisian.

"Luxury prêt-a-porter clothing, George. I've wanted to buy one of her designs since I read about Aghion last year. She's the toast of Paris right now." Eleanor explained her exigent need to visit the upscale, downtown store over breakfast.

"Leaving me so soon!" I feigned hurt and then smiled. By all means. I wanted to visit the souk on Rue Weygand anyway.

Eleanor laughed and bit her bottom lip, looking at me over a cup of thick, black Turkish coffee. It was her attempt at coy.

Visions of fresh, exotic persimmons, figs, tangerines, oranges, and melons, the kinds that would have made Bayee jealous, filled my thoughts as I ate a last crispy bite of menushe, toasted bread coated with a blend of dried sumac and sesame seeds. A few spoonfuls of creamy laban topped it off.

Eleanor and I parted ways after breakfast. The telephone on the nightstand table rang notifying Eleanor of her Aunt Leila's arrival in the lobby. She was to accompany Eleanor on her sartorial adventure while I made my way into the streets of downtown Beirut.

* * *

The souk on Rue Weygand bustled with morning congestion. A dark green cable car called a tramway, or as the Lebanese referred it in their distorted French way, "trum-why," chugged along the street. Pale, stone-faced buildings and awning-hooded sidewalks were home to bins of produce and street vendors hawking hand-woven scarves. Others peddled statues of the Blessed Mother and crucifixes, cheap bracelets, freshly made sajj with hummus, shawarma, and other Middle Eastern delicacies. I walked along the sidewalk brushing past porters waiting for work who sought relief from the beating sun under blonde, hand-woven baskets. From the wicker sanctuaries, the sleeping porters' legs protruded, their worn shoes coated in yellow dust, inches from the glistening footwear of businessmen. A middle-aged Muslim woman selling her scarves caught my attention. A deep purple scarf called out to me from her display. The color was reminiscent of the long, curling eggplant skins that would litter the counter as Ummi and I made baba ghannouj together. As I decided to purchase the scarf as a gift for my mother, I nearly collided with a man crouched low over a cache of old books.

"Aasif!" I exclaimed. "Sorry."

The man stood up and laughed. In English laced with a Levantine accent, he said, "How American of you to apologize to me though I was the one blocking your way." Full, fleshy lips curled upwards into a smile. Rebellious black curls fell loose, framing a tanned, roguish face. A dark goatee gave him a refined air. But it was his eyes that struck me. They were blue-gray, the color of the sky in winter. I almost didn't notice that he stood with the help of a cane. He looked like he was in his late twenties, maybe early thirties.

I couldn't remember how to be witty or clever so I settled for smiling and extending my hand. "George Lahoud."

"Andros. Andros Seleukos." Somewhere in the distance, marketplace sounds crashed against the street like the Mediterranean waves outside St. George's Hotel. "George Lahoud? Lebanese-American, then?"

I nodded. "Andros Seleukos? Only Greeks have that many vowels in their names."

He laughed, revealing a set of perfectly white teeth.

"You have good taste." The book in his hand was familiar, the almost ethereal portrait of the author staring from the cover.

"I couldn't call myself an artist if I didn't adore Gibran." Andros leaned heavily on his cane, the copy of *The Prophet* clutched in his other hand.

"You're a local artist?"

"A student. At American University." The stranger dug his gaze into me. The rapid beat of the Muslim woman's Arabic filled the space around us as she tried to convince an elderly gentleman in a turban and a suit to purchase one of her scarves.

He offered nothing further. Tucking the book under his arm, he continued to peruse the makeshift shelves, pulling an incarnadine, leather-bound book with an Arabic inscription from its place. I wondered what the title translated into in English. While I could speak fluently, I couldn't read or write the language.

"I'm visiting family in Beirut." For some reason, I didn't

want to share that I was on my honeymoon. I also didn't want to walk away.

He smiled politely, hardly looking up from the new book in his hand. The moments that comprised an acceptable, casual exchange were almost spent, but my eyes begged to linger just a moment longer.

"I've heard AUB's campus is something to see."

Andros began walking in a stilted way towards the merchant. "It is."

I stood with the eggplant scarf in my hand. I silently pleaded with him, this Greek stranger, to say more, to encourage more. I lowered the scarf to conceal the visceral imploring that grew below. Perhaps I felt emboldened by this new environment: I was in Lebanon. Here, I was not George the butcher, George the son of George Lahoud Sr. Here, in the souk on Rue Weygand amid Middle Eastern delicacies and bric-a-brac, I was just a man intrigued by a stranger.

Andros handed money to the woman and turned to leave the stand, to resume his place among the foreign mass throbbing in the marketplace. But a second before becoming just another inconsequential encounter, he turned towards me.

"I can give you a tour sometime."

"Three o'clock?"

* * *

Eleanor was not amenable to continuing her day solo.

"I don't understand why I can't come with you. I want to see Hamra, too." My wife sat on the edge of the bed having just finished painting her nails red. A navy-blue dress clung to her curvaceous frame.

We had returned to our hotel around lunch to freshen up

and relax before late-afternoon activities. In a fresh oxford shirt and slacks, I wrapped a checkered kaffiyeh around my neck and put on a new pair of sunglasses. I ran fingers through my pomaded hair, parting it to the side.

"You'll be bored. I want to spend time in the library on AUB's campus." I thought back to the premature end of my collegiate career at Georgetown. I would have graduated this past May. I'd be starting medical school at the end of the summer. Probably living in DC.

"And what? I don't like books?" Eleanor held up her left hand, curled her fingers, and brought them to her lips where she gently blew on the fresh coat of lacquer.

"That's not what I'm saying, my love."

She dabbed at her thumbnail with her right pointer finger, testing the durability of the paint. Apparently satisfied, she reached into her purse on the bedside table, pulled out her gold tube of lipstick and painted her lips a shade of pink. She blotted them with a tissue from the dresser. The gold bracelets on her wrists jangled like an off-key song.

"What's so special about this campus anyway?" She appraised herself in the mirror before walking towards the door. "I'm sure it looks like any college."

"Don't be dense. That's like saying every dress looks the same because it's qualified as a dress. Do whatever you want." I could feel my heart overreacting in rapid beats as I moved in front of her and almost ran to the elevator.

Eleanor, right on my heels, shouted so the elderly British couple in the room next to us could most likely hear. "Are you suggesting that I go out into Beirut all on my own? A young woman by herself in a strange city? What kind of husband are you, George?" She stopped and folded her arms as I entered the elevator. The elevator operator, a young tan boy in a white uniform, asked in English, "The lobby, sir?"

Before the gilded door shut, I looked directly into my wife's round face and said, "You'll find something to do." My tone was sharper than I intended, and I could see it cut her deeply enough to wound. Her eyes became pools deep enough to swim in.

* * *

Andros Seleukos, my Greek stranger, leaned against the pale stone of the main entrance to the campus on Rue Bliss in Hamra. A cigarette in one hand and walking stick in the other, he was well dressed in pressed collared shirt and slacks. As I approached him, I noticed he was not wearing socks with his loafers and the top two buttons of his shirt were unfastened, revealing an explosion of fine black chest hair.

"Keefak," I managed to articulate, difficult because of a sudden dryness in my throat. "How are you?"

The Greek stranger answered with a smile. Without a word, he tossed the cigarette and started walking in his stunted way through the wrought iron gate. I followed, appreciating the light limestone face of the entrance. The other side of the gate opened into a green oasis, a hill overlooking the vast expanse of Mediterranean Sea which surrounded the campus. Limestone buildings and sweeping palm trees filled the pastoral setting as feral cats scampered across walkways like the squirrels in Connecticut. I looked back at the entrance, just beyond which cars and people hurried by, relics of a distant metropolis. The words, a verse from the Bible, *that they may have life and have it more abundantly,* was etched on either side of the gate, one side in Arabic, the other English. Turning around, I saw Andros had not waited for me but had continued moving in the direction of the sea. I caught up to the surprisingly quick man and waited in vain for him to begin some kind of tour. Instead, he continued and paused only to light a cigarette.

"Want one?"

Andros handed me the one he'd just lit and took another for himself. I took the cigarette and put it in my mouth, acutely aware of its recent placement between his lips.

"Thanks."

Andros resumed walking. The sound of his cane against the walkway matched the beating in my chest, steady palpitations. Distant city sounds and the laughter and chatter of students coalesced in sweet Mediterranean air. A few men on bicycles rode past us. They wore sports jackets and sweater vests with shorts and laughed as they sped by. One of the men wore a brimless, rounded cap called a kufi, emblematic of his Islamic religion.

We made our way to an elegant building of reinforced concrete faced with dusky white limestone. We proceeded into the Jafet Memorial Library and a capacious entrance hall paneled with the same polished stone of the exterior. Andros moved like dust, fleeting, unnoticed by the students walking in groups and speaking in hushed voices throughout the oak-paneled central hall. The smell of old books grounded me, took me back to my two years at Georgetown.

We moved beyond the main desk and past a bust of Nami Jafet. The sculpture immortalized the well-known businessman and scholar's largesse and explicated the eponymous building which had been dedicated only a few months earlier. I took a moment to appreciate the marble floors before I realized Andros was already making his way up a flight of polished limestone steps. I caught up to him just as he reached a doorway at the end of the third floor.

He opened the door to a rooftop terrace.

"Now see your Lebanon."

Beyond the crown of a palm tree, sun-blanched mountains, limestone buildings, and infinite sea unfurled below us. Palms and cedars and olive trees among other flora decorated the view. The white face of the sun smiled on the beautiful country below it. And just as beautiful, just as moving, a stubble-framed smile barely removed from the brightness of the Mediterranean sun.

I couldn't remember any other particular sites I had wanted to visit on AUB's campus. In those moments, it seemed to me that nothing in all of Lebanon could be a more worthwhile site than this terrace-view. Andros leaned against the doorway smoking another cigarette. His arms folded across his chest, he seemed neither rushed nor relaxed. He watched me from the shade of the door. I pretended to admire the city below. The air smelled of salt.

"Beautiful, isn't it, George?" I knew he was referring to the view, but I couldn't help but apply the comment to the way he said my name. I always thought of it as a rough-sounding name, filling the mouth like course sandpaper. But the way Andros said "George" was soft, almost like silk sliding off his tongue.

We returned in silence to the main gate on Rue Bliss.

"Are you thirsty?" An excuse to remain in his company.

"I could drink."

"Any cafés close by?"

"We're on a university campus."

I could feel a film of perspiration christen my brow. Andros walked out of the gate, turning after a moment to be sure I was following.

"There's a place a few blocks away." He crossed the street, weaved among the traffic. Arabic songs sneaked in between static on the car radios. The city sounds pricked like whispers. I walked as close to Andros as social decorum permitted, feeling the waves of summer between us as his fingers teased mine. I pulled my hand away and dug it into my pocket. He continued to limp beside me, seemingly unfazed by the rejection. We didn't speak but made our way down a narrow cobblestone street at the end of which was a large limestone restaurant where the street ended and the dining area began with outdoor tables and chairs scattered like the pigeons pecking around them. A web of flowering green and purple clematis covered the uppermost part of the small building. We passed under an arch of bougainvillea blushing pink. We were seated at a corner table. Andros ordered a glass of arak; I followed his lead.

The space between sips was filled by my imagination. I thought of him smoking cigarettes at a kitchen table, reading the morning paper while a lovely raven-haired woman served him breakfast in a ruffled apron and heels. I pictured him alone, in a kitschy studio, unleashing his soul upon a submissive canvas. I saw him at day's end, skin crusted with dried pastel paints and expired sweat, hair damp but still reckless, stretching his sore leg as he sat on the edge of his bed, cane resting against the good appendage. I wondered what it must feel like to be the cane brushing against his leg.

Sitting at the tiled table, allowing heat to swell in my gut as I drank copiously a first then second glass of liquor, I noticed his belly spilled just so over the constraint of his belt. A perfectly sculpted body but a stomach soft and rounded, incongruous, inconsistent, intriguing. Like a woman's, like my wife's. In that moment, I longed to experience the softness of his belly.

The air was thick with the nearby sea. The conversation between us was nothing more than disconnected words dangling in the atmosphere. Andros's gaze was thick with arak, his eyes cloudy, reluctant to meet mine. Those eyes, his eyes were the sea I could fall into and drown. We were separated by a table filled with half-eaten relics, plates smudged with baba ghannouj and humus, green olives and pita bread, and ashtrays heaped in a growing mound of black-gray ash. After another round, or maybe two, our eyes finally ran into each other at the center of the table and lingered. In that moment, completely and all at once, I was overwhelmed. He was like the city of Beirut to me: illusive, enigmatic, broken, but full of infinite possibility and suggestion. The veins of the city flowed with complicated history, intoxicating nightlife, and an enchanting blend of Eastern and Western culture. It was familiar, it was strange, it was a memory and a dream. It was real, it was fantasy, it was home. I had been waiting for Beirut all my life, waiting to visit my parent's country, my country. And here it was sitting across the table chain-smoking and swigging licorice-flavored liquor.

"People will think we're together," he said, his tone slippery, smooth like the liquor.

I turned my thoughts to Eleanor, imagined what it would be like to leave her, what it would be like to spend afternoons with this Greek stranger sharing drinks like secrets. A tall, dark-haired waiter came over with another round. The new glass was cold in my hand. It made me realize holding onto this afternoon would be like holding onto water.

I didn't say anything, just looked. I wanted to jump into the blue-gray water of his eyes, let it drip in rivulets down my skin. I should have turned my eyes away, sought refuge in the glass bowl of hummus between us on the table: neutral territory. But I gave into transgression and they lingered, taking in the conviction of his gaze. Heavy black lashes fanned from the lids. A small, round mole christened the corner of his left eye, a starting point on a map, a suggestion: *Begin your adventure here.*

Minutes passed in beads of condensation forming on our glasses. I savored the cool moisture as it ran down my fingers. A softer, unrecognizable version of my voice broke the atmosphere with a question. "So, what's your story?"

"My story? I don't know. It's still being written." He smiled.

I noticed I was chewing the corner of my lower lip. "Tell me the beginning. How did it start?"

"Like most stories do, I suppose. It starts with a boy. He grows into a man. The man wants things that most people want: contentment, success, love." Andros stopped speaking to put a cigarette in his mouth. With a gold lighter, he lit it and sucked in. He exhaled. "Mostly he wants one great love. The kind of love poetry and novels and songs are written about." He leaned back in the chair.

"Your story doesn't have that yet?"

"It seems the plotline is moving in that direction. A new character has been introduced in the most recent chapter." He looked off into the distance. The sun lit his features, but a mysterious darkness persisted behind his gaze. I wanted to inhale the edges of his face, to trace every secret, every detail of his life written in the lines of his skin. I ached to belong to the parting of his lips, a place I imagined could feel like home.

"And what's this character like?" My skin crawled in unfamiliar ways.

He looked across the street and continued smoking. A couple of older, gray-haired men stood smoking cigarettes in a doorway. He seemed to regard them with casual interest.

"He's a stranger. Lost, I think."

"Lost?"

"Yes." He offered nothing further in the way of an explanation. He just sat smoking, watching, drifting. I picked up my glass, swigged, and placed it too loudly back on the table.

"And?"

His gaze returned to mine, and he smiled. "Sometimes you must get lost to find yourself." He leaned back further in the chair and turned his face skyward, letting the sunlight dance across the tanned bridge of his nose. His eyes were closed as if he was alone or simply in a somnambulist state. Perhaps this all was just a dream.

CHAPTER SIXTEEN

L etting Andros inside my world for a moment was like cracking the window for a little air during a hurricane. He was a gust of wind that blew into my life with destructive force, uprooting everything in his wake. I did not know if I would ever recover, ever rebuild the safe, conventional scaffolding of my existence.

The Sunday after our initial meeting, we arranged to have afternoon cocktails by the pool at St. George. My wife was attending mass with Leila, and after brief protestations, she acquiesced in allowing me to remain behind. She left me in the hotel room with a parting mumbled comment about my soul.

Tall lamps with black cast iron bodies crowned in white shades resembling little cedar trees lined the ringed terrace. Short, squat shrubs comprised the poolside flora. Long white tables shaded by flat, royal blue umbrellas with white tassels were scattered along the pool deck. They were occupied by men dressed in their finest suits and dark sunglasses and elegant women in sundresses and wide-brimmed hats. White boats with sails, men in black swim trunks, dark glasses, and cigarettes, oxford shirts open exposing fine torsos and dark chest hair comprised the panoramic view of beach, ocean, and poolside bacchanalia. An Olympic-size swimming pool marked the epicenter of the deck.

In aviator sunglasses, Andros was waiting for me in a reclining chair by the pool. I sat in the vacant chair beside him and skipped any greeting or small talk.

I blurted in a hushed tone, "I'm married."

He half-smiled, lifting the left corner of his mouth, which dimpled the cheek. "You say it like it's a secret."

"It's not. I'm telling you now."

He remained recumbent. "I suddenly feel as if we are doing something dirty. Of course, that would only be the case if you were attracted to me. Are you attracted to me, George?"

His question was the tip of a butcher knife, glinting in the sunlight of the shop window.

"Don't be ridiculous. Do you think I'm queer?"

"Do you have a problem with queers?"

"No, no. Not at all. I'm just not funny like that. I'm married. Like I told you a minute ago." My skin had gone cold despite the heat. *It's not the secrets we keep that haunt us. It's the ones we tell that take on life, that find us sleeping in our wife's arms in the middle of the night. Sweet Eleanor.*

He didn't say much after that. He smiled like he was privy to a story I had not yet heard, like he knew something I didn't. We spent the afternoon imbibing cocktails and laying in the hot Mediterranean sun. Our conversation was a bowl of lentil soup on a winter afternoon: hearty and satiating. We made plans to lunch at the hotel restaurant the next day.

* * *

Eleanor's mood was light, and she dressed entirely in white. I told her I had met an artist on AUB's campus and he was fascinating and more than a suitable guide and companion. Perhaps I oversold him, but she seemed content and unsuspicious. We walked, arms linked like any fashionable young couple on a honeymoon. We made our way downstairs to the restaurant and were seated at a table outside. A semicircular terrace overlooked the pool and beach below. A white railing enclosed the terrace, but the view remained unrestricted. I focused on the elaborate filigree of the railing as we waited for Andros's arrival. Eleanor lit a cigarette and adjusted her large, round sunglasses.

A handsome man in white linen pants and familiar sunglasses was led to our table by a server in a white tuxedo. His unruly curls were tamed, slicked back with pomade. The top few buttons of his shirt were unfastened revealing black tufts of chest hair.

"The illustrious Andros, I presume?" Eleanor's pink-painted lips curled into a mellifluous smile. She tapped the ash of her cigarette into the ceramic ashtray beside her, returned it to her mouth, and extended her hand to Andros.

"And you must be the ravishing Mrs. Lahoud." He took her hand and brought it to his lips, kissing it ever so gently. *Oh, to be that hand.* Eleanor squealed. "Aren't you delightful? Please, sit. We waited to order drinks. Honey, get the waiter's attention, won't you?" Andros sat beside my wife, opposite me. Around us the tables were filled with an amalgamation of European and American tourists and wealthy Middle Eastern locals. A pair of fair men in suits, European based on their British accents, argued loudly over twin cocktails and a bowl of olives. On the other side, a long table filled with women in expensive dresses and hats and men equally well dressed perpetuated a contagious bonhomie: bottles of wine, plates of hummus, Arabic bread, assorted cheeses, and olives littered the table. Music played from inside the bar as the ocean sang in waves outside.

Eleanor was enchanted; Andros had her laughing between bites of pita bread and hummus. The afternoon was hot; the air stuck to our skin and the alcohol went to our heads. Andros the raconteur told of growing up in Ashrafieh, mostly tales of a mischievous child with a strict Lebanese Christian mother and Greek Orthodox father. Daylight turned to nighttime and Eleanor was tired. Reluctantly, I retired with her to our room for the evening but not before planning an evening out with our new friend.

As we made our way back to our suite, a polished man, middle-aged with a prominent handle-bar mustache who worked the front desk called, "Mr. Lahoud, sir, a letter has arrived for you. Shall I bring it up to your room?" His English was flawless, Arabic barely perceptible in his words.

"I can take it with me now. Thank you." I walked up to the man and handed him a few cents. Ummi's familiar cursive marked the envelope. Her penmanship distinct, letters small, pinched, constructed into tightly wound sentences surely admonishing me for something even while on my honeymoon.

"From your mother?" Eleanor asked as we entered the elevator. She removed her hat and blotted the back of her neck with a white handkerchief she'd pulled from her purse.

"Of course."

Eleanor readied for bed while I took the letter to the terrace. Lights danced on the water below like fireflies. A whisper of music and laughter was almost indistinguishable from the brisk breeze. I pulled out my lighter and lit a candle on the small table beside the reclining chair.

My Habibi,

I can't believe it has been a month since your departure, in some ways it feels like ten. Your brother is doing a wonderful job running the store in your absence although sometimes I question his business acumen. He gives so many things away for free! I know you and your father did the same thing, but at least you both had the good sense to be discreet about it!

Tell me son, how is our Lebanon? Have you visited the souk in Byblos? Please be sure to visit St. Joseph's. There you will find the shrine of the Blessed Rafka. I would like you to light a candle for me. If you time it right, perhaps you will hear the Sisters chant in prayer. It is one of the most beautiful sounds in all the world.

Habibi, I want you to keep the words of Kahlil Gibran close: "He told us many a tale that night but also the next day, but what I record was born out of the bitterness of his days though he himself kindly, and these tales are of the dust and patience of his road."

Identity is forged through the dust, the bitterness, and the sun of our days; I know that you yearn to wander, my son. But please, be true to the Bedouin in your soul: never travel alone but with your family. Always we are with you in your heart, in the bites of fresh sajj you will surely eat from a roadside stand. I am with you, my son.

I hope you are eating enough.

Your Ummi

I reread my mother's letter until the candle burned out, Eleanor had retired to bed, and the only light came from buildings below. Ummi was a laconic woman, but in writing, her words were as lovely and passionate as the dishes she created. Her reference to Gibran seemed strange, misplaced, and it sat heavy on my chest. I pressed the letter to my heart and shut my eyes.

* * *

Uncle Saad happily agreed to drive us to St. Joseph's. In his rundown car, we drove winding roads that pierced the bosom of Mt. Lebanon. We passed through copses of fruit trees, towering cedars, and by small stone churches and larger, ornate basilicas that housed the remains of venerated priests and Catholic saints. Deep in the mountain, we made our way through the Maronite Catholic villages with their roadside shrines to the Blessed Mother. After an hour or more, we pulled into a long stone driveway.

Pastoral settings like this existed only in paintings and Ummi's stories. I was immediately moved by the beauty—the green hills bathed in golden sunlight, a limestone chapel, marble steps. The Sisters of St. Joseph's were chanting in Arabic, a sound which filled the stillness and was interrupted only by the mantra of crickets. A young boy around eight or nine skipped down the marble steps, away from the chapel.

Saad leaned against his car, choosing to remain at a distance in what he called with a wink his "private meditation." A hand-rolled cigarette lingered between his thick, nicotine-stained fingers like an unspoken promise. He wore large, dark aviator sunglasses, and his white hair was hidden by a dark gray fedora. A gold chain hung from his thick neck. His gray suit looked expensive, but he did not wear a necktie nor did he button the top few buttons of his dress shirt. Saad was vaguely gangster-like in his apparel and demeanor. He certainly did not resemble the pious, simple country folk who visited the shrine or the Sisters who tended her chapel.

Eleanor and I walked into the chapel. I was reminded in that moment of a conversation I'd had with Father Hayek not very long ago. I told him I was the visitor. And now, here, I was an actual visitor, feeling at home in a place I'd never been. I followed my wife to the front of the small chapel, taking in the sweet-smelling incense and the quiet. Men and women sat or kneeled, some with rosaries, some with closed eyes and folded hands. Eleanor genuflected and sat in the oak pew towards the front. I sat beside her, listening to the nearly silent Lord's Prayer she whispered in Aramaic. Instead of joining her in prayer, I thought of my parents. This was where they came from; the place they never stopped loving.

The thought of Ummi mobilized me. I left Eleanor in prayer, genuflected again in front of the altar, and made my way towards the marble basin at the back of the chapel. I pulled a small glass vial I had purchased earlier from my pocket and filled it with Holy Water. This gift would mean more to my mother than a purple scarf or replies on postcards. *Purple Scarves. Andros.*

My breathing quickened, and I suddenly felt the urge to leave this sacred place. I pocketed the Holy Water and dashed out of the chapel where I joined Saad by the car.

"Finished your prayers already, my boy?" He tried to stifle a laugh and exhaled spicy-sweet smoke. "You look like you saw the face of God in there." He again attempted to laugh quietly as our interaction was the only sound for what seemed like miles.

"It was very hot. I needed air." I leaned against the car next to him.

"We'll get some food when we leave here. There's a roadside stand that sells the best sajj around. But don't tell Leila I said that. She thinks everything she cooks is the best."

Eleanor came out of the chapel, adjusting her black veil and smoothing the folds of her dress. "Did you pray at all?" She asked as she approached.

"Sure. Not that it's any of your business." I shot her an irritated glance.

Before she could respond, her uncle interrupted. "Who's hungry?"

* * *

When the day ended and we had returned to our honeymoon suite at St. George, we laid in bed as a fan hummed from the corner of the room. Eleanor rested her head on my arm and picked the lint that had collected like sweat from my naval. Such an intimate, affectionate gesture. I kissed the top of her head, smelling something floral and just a hint of cigarette smoke. She looked up at me, her husband, like I was her world, her everything, and I had never felt as terrible as I did in that moment.

CHAPTER SEVENTEEN

The labyrinthine streets of Byblos were decked in velvet cushions and divans, oriental carpets spread across the cobblestone floors of outdoor patios, and ornate glass hookah pipes could be found at nearly every table. The notes of the oud caught in the sultry Lebanese night. The inky blackness of the sky seemed to go on forever. Eleanor's red-painted nails stood out against a glass of arak, the beads of condensation ran down the glass and onto her fingers. Her other hand found my leg. She held tightly—more demanding than seductive.

Liquor-fueled heat caused flushed cheeks and slick, tanned skin. The air was heavy with the nearby sea and too much perfume. Leila and Saad met Andros, Eleanor, and me at one of the many trendy bars in Byblos. Beside me, they were but silhouettes, corporeal extensions of the night. Distraction assumed the form of the man across the table. Andros's gaze was thick with arak and something akin to hunger.

Between unctuous bites of hummus and pita, Saad related a story about some corrupt politician or other. I could not digest the tale or the sentiments. He rubbed his thick, bejeweled fingers together, flicking pita crumbs onto the table like cigarette ash.

I couldn't sit any longer. I stubbed out a half-finished cigarette in a glass ashtray, took a swig of my drink, and left the table to ostensibly relieve myself. This action was met with a protesting look from my wife.

"You'll be right back, dear?"

I responded by turning around and walking away.

I didn't have to see him to know that Andros had also left his seat. As I walked away from the bonhomie of the restaurant, away from the beating heart of Byblos and towards the sea, towards the ruins, towards the vacant stands that comprised the Old Souk, towards the quiet of the harbor, I could feel him behind me. The music and laughter faded into the night like a forgotten memory. His walking stick beat against the uneven cobblestone in tandem with my chest. I quickened my pace, begging him in silent speed to slow down, stop, go back, go home, go away! I started running, turning with the narrow street, navigating by the slivers of silver moonlight, which threaded the stone path. I imagined his cane catching on a sharp stone edge, his body lunging forward as I disappeared around a corner, losing him to the darkness. The thought stopped me with the force of its probability, and, abruptly, I stopped running.

Andros couldn't stop as quickly. He crashed hard into my back and we both stumbled forward into the cold gray face of a stone wall. I could feel his soaked shirt against my back. The scent of alcohol and cigarettes tangled with the sharp citrus spice of his cologne. I remained pinned against the wall while the heat between our bodies swelled like the sea in a storm. The only sound was the faint echo of a world somewhere and the hard breathing of two trembling men. I couldn't tell the difference between his breath and the sweat on the back of my neck, but his arms wrapping around my waist were undeniable. He turned me around to face him. His dark curls had their own rhythm, some clung in dampness to the side of his face, others moved in the breeze. I reached my shaking hand up and touched the soft stubble on his cheek.

"Stop running." Andros said breathlessly as he pulled me to him and brought his mouth to mine. I took in the shape of his lips and the energy of his tongue working against mine. He pushed me hard against the wall as my body shook with such force, I thought I would break apart in his embrace. Muscles tightened, the amalgamation of our breath and bodies made me dizzy. In the gilded light of a streetlamp, in some dark corner of Byblos, kisses passed between us like a new secret. I met his strength with equal force, the certainty of his movements steadying mine. I began kissing the nape of his neck, taking in the smell of aftershave. A soft moan escaped as he found the hard place between my legs. He unfastened my pants and took me in his hand as the other grasped his cane. Up and down, up and down, face against his neck, the beating sound of husky voice, up and down, up and down, the prickling of hair against my tongue as it found his throat, up and down, skin against skin. The knot in my stomach coming undone.

When I was finished, he fell forward softly against my trembling body. I wrapped my arms around him and pulled him to my chest where his head found my shoulder.

The dull buzz of arak in my head began to clear. "We should go back."

"Yes. Your lovely wife might start to worry." Andros moved away from me and turned to walk back to the restaurant. He took my hand in his and held it firmly.

We walked only a minute or two along the cobblestone path when I released his hand and quickened my pace.

"God forbid someone sees." Andros's words had teeth. He

added, "Why don't I just hang back. We don't want anyone to think we took a walk in the dark together."

He didn't wait for me to respond. I paused for a moment to watch him in silence as he disappeared around a corner. I stood alone in the dark street, quiet save for the hum of the sea and distant sounds of music and people. I studied the bend of a palm tree leaning over the wall, the fronds sliver in the moonlight.

I resumed my spot at the table long before Andros returned. Eleanor, pink with arak and worry, took my hand in hers and brought it to her lips as soon as I was seated next to her. I pulled my hand away as quickly as I could, but I was certain she detected the distinct sent of man on me. I pulled out a cigarette and lit it to steady myself.

"Where's your friend?" Saad asked as he nibbled a pastry.

I felt my face grow hot. "He probably had too much to drink. I'm sure he's fine."

Leila exhaled smoke and stubbed out her cigarette in the ashtray. "You two weren't together?"

"I said I don't know where the hell he is!" I spit the answer at Leila like it was all her fault. Like she was to blame for everything.

"Jesus, George. What's wrong with you?" Eleanor nearly whispered beside me.

"I'm sorry, Leila. I'm sorry." Before Saad and Leila could shake their surprise, I got up from the table. "I've had too much to drink. I need some air."

I didn't give anyone the opportunity to follow me. I took off running. Eleanor or Leila called out something unintelligible. Retracing steps through the winding streets, I ran and ran and ran. My heart ran and my thoughts ran and my body ran. I ran from Eleanor and her family. I ran from expectation. And, for the first time in my life, I ran to. I ran to the place where the sea met the land. I could see a man sitting in the swath of sand, gentle waves kissing the soles of his feet.

"This seat taken?" I kicked off my shoes, rolled up the bottom of my pants to my knees and sat beside Andros in the sand. A tapestry of yellow and white lights filled the dark. Byblos surrounded us in a soft u-shaped curve, Andros and I the epicenter. Small white boats rocked in the harbor ahead, pulling taught the ropes that kept them from drifting away. Limestone buildings and tall palms looked surreal in the gilded light. The stars were silver shards of glass lodged in the blackness. I dug my feet into the warm, wet sand as the water lapped at my toes.

"Aren't you worried someone will see us sitting together?" the words curled from his mouth in a sarcastic tone.

I hoped his angry comment would redress the situation, and I ignored it. Beads of sand peppered the black tufts of hair on his legs. He leaned back, his hands in the sand keeping him erect. Andros stared up at the night sky.

I said, "I don't know what's going to happen tomorrow. I don't care. I only know this: tonight, I want you. I want you and I've never been more certain of anything in my life. If my life is only made of a single truth, it's you. You are my truth." I fixed my gaze on the dark, infinite sea.

"I'm not sure what that even means." His voice was softer than a minute ago.

At that moment, we turned to each other and without another word I cupped his cheek and pulled his face to mine. I let my lips brush his, taking in the scent of arak on the soft fleshy mouth, took in the soft hair on his chin and the pleasurable way it tickled mine. My heart was pounding so loud it deafened everything but the sound of our rapid, hard breathing. I would never forget the way his skin raised to greet the brush of my fingertips. Lebanon and Connecticut and Eleanor

and Laila and Saad and Ummi and Bayee and Michael and
Jacob and Georgetown and the store faded away, disappeared
into the darkness and dampness, lost in the sound of two men
finding something in the night.

* * *

I don't recall the details of the walk from the beach, the cab ride
to Ashrafieh, or even how we made it to the small room in the
pension that served as both living quarters and art studio to
Andros. While the surroundings were hazy, the specific
gestures and actions of the night will forever be branded in my
memory.

I had longed to experience the poetry of his lips, the
rhythm of his tongue working against mine, the beat of his
breath in my ear. He was the song my heart sang when no one
was listening.

Nails pulled at the skin of his back. I buried my face in his
neck and bit down, hard, sucking up the pulsing skin, inhaling
it, devouring it like air, like life. This was air. This was life. This
was the perpetual knot in my stomach coming undone.

I explored where lint had collected in the small hollow of
his belly. Sweat cloyed in thick tufts of chest hair. The heat of
buzzing particles, particles of being alive, of being in heat. The
heat was overwhelming. I licked beads of sweat off his back like
drops of honey, savoring the sweet taste of perspiration on my
tongue, a taste sweeter than Ummi's baklawa. He took me in
his mouth. I brought him back up to me and kissed him, tasting
myself. Our animal sounds scraped the wooden floors and
crawled up the walls. My hands searched every inch of his tan
skin, taking in the soft prickle of chest hair, stomach, thighs. His
thigh muscles tensed beneath the embrace of my fingers. I gave
short, rapid kisses along his belly, slowly made my way down. I

buried my face in his nether region. The course black hair smelled of sweat and soap. His erection pushed and pulsed towards me, finding my mouth. I wrapped my lips around his hard place. Andros's hands pulled at my hair and pushed down, guiding my head in pleasurable rhythm. Minutes passed. The wet salty sweet taste coated my tongue. He pulled me to rest in his arms. A cigarette in the ashtray on the bedside table sparked in its death throes.

"What now?" I asked as I buried my nose in his shoulder.

"How about this?" Andros reached across to the bedside table and grabbed a half-empty glass. He took an ice cube and put it in his mouth. He pulled the cube from between his pouty lips with a quiet sucking sound. He smiled. Black curls feel wild and messy, framing his face. The hair on his face was trimmed and neat although it had already begun to grow since the last time he had shaved, probably earlier that morning. Or yesterday. Yesterday was a lifetime ago. His dark eyes glinted with mischievousness.

"Lay back on the pillow," he instructed.

I obliged. When he smiled into me like that, I had no free will. I was his.

Andros touched the ice to my lips. A shock of cold not unpleasant. "Close your eyes."

The icy sensation moved down my face and neck. Cold drops of water began to trickle from the ice and run down the sides of my neck, mixing with sweat. The heat from my skin met the cold kiss of the ice eliciting goosebumps. The contrast of temperatures was strangely arousing. The sensation continued south towards my privates; I guessed the ultimate destination. He paused the ice cube at the center of my belly. All at once the cold skin of the ice was joined with a rougher, warmer, equally wet feeling. Andros's tongue was licking in circular movements, following the path of the ice as it continued down to the throbbing, hard member. The competing temperatures, the icy touch of melting water and caress of his warm, wet tongue moving in ways and rhythms erotic and stimulating beyond the fantasy.

Fingers laced, the strong, thicker hands of the butcher's son and the thinner, dexterous paint-stained hands of the artist. Our hearts beat hard and fast as if this was madness or danger, as if death was setting in. But it was madness that set in when eyes locked, when gazes and breathing and bodies tangled in bed sheets that smelled of detergent and faded cologne. Glasses half-filled on the table beside the bed along with a sundry of expired pleasures: discarded cigarettes in an ashtray and a plate of uneaten, presumably, stale Arabic bread. Our bodies bumped and crashed on the white sheeted mattress. The shape of the shadows along the wall, jagged like kisses, sharp like the breathing of lovers in heat. Rounded and smooth, sometimes, the shape of his body in ecstasy. The shadow was long, trailing, unfinished, indefinite—the shape of our affair, the shape of the shadow that we made.

We must have fallen asleep at some point between pleasing caresses and liquor-soaked kisses. The sun had risen, scattering the darkness like pieces of paper, ending our night together and beginning an uncertain day. Dust danced in slanted light coming in through the one window in the spartan room. Dawn meant day and day meant consequences. I would tell Eleanor I passed out in the street. I had had too much to drink, I was sorry. She would cry and yell and forgive me. A picture of Jesus Christ on the cross hung above the four-post bed.

Andros stirred beside me. He stretched his arms high over his head and smiled at me from the pillow. The sunlight brightened his face. The shadow of beard had darkened overnight, but his eyes looked rested as if he had slept the entire evening.

"Good morning." He pulled me to his chest. "Sleep, ok?"

"Like I haven't slept in years." I paused. "Can I ask something?"

Andros reached over to the bedside table and pulled out a pack of cigarettes. He placed one in his mouth and lit it. Exhaling smoke and reply, he said, "Go ahead."

"Are you religious?"

He smirked. "I've got God in my heart and you in my bed, what more do I need of religion?" He blew smoke towards the open window. "This talk is too serious before breakfast." He threw the blanket off and stood up. Somewhere in the back of my mind thoughts of God and morality lingered, but they were nothing more than tenuous concerns with the more present Andros, the aftertaste of his body still fresh in my mouth. Walking with a limp in search of clothes and cane, Andros moved about the room in beautiful nakedness. Who was this man before me that made me forget everything else but the quiet masculinity of his stunted gait? He ran his hand through his unruly curls all without removing the cigarette from his mouth. I studied the sickle-shaped birthmark on the inside of his left thigh, winking at me as he moved. I remembered brushing the slightly raised mark with my fingertips the night before. This was a secret knowledge intimacy afforded me. I felt as though I had privilege over strangers and mere kin. Only I had gazed upon this birthmark like a single, glistening star, the echo of our private night sky.

He found his linen pants, kicked under the bed in the frenzy of movement belonging to the previous night. He sat on the bed and slipped his bad leg into the pants. With his lower body covered, he stood with assistance from his cane, which was beside the discarded clothes. Smoke bloomed from the cigarette in his mouth. Andros moved towards the end of the bed, it seemed with extra effort, perhaps stiff from the love-making or a hangover. My belly began to rumble. I remembered then that I did feel other things like hunger. I was, after all, only a man.

"You are hungry." It wasn't a question. "Come. Let's see what Sarea has prepared this morning."

Sarea? Last night's events began to untangle. The visceral memory still felt so lucid, the montage of his lips on me played with the clarity of a favorite song, but the specifics, the details of place, the where and how, were blurred. I had a vague recollection of a boarding house in Ashrafieh, and a story about a Greek Orthodox family farm.

"Who's Sarea?" I tried to act casually as I dressed.

"You don't remember?" Andros chuckled. Instead of answering the question, he continued walking out of the room and down a flight of wooden stairs. I followed closely behind, now more acutely aware of my surroundings: the flight of stairs opening into a capacious room filled with richly colored couches and divans and an older man reading the paper. I suddenly felt self-conscious of my presence with Andros, this beautiful half-naked man smoking a cigarette. Even as a wave of Turkish coffee tickled my senses, I smoothed out my linen shirt and pants, self-conscious of the wrinkles and what they suggested. What questions would my presence raise? A familiar knot took up in my throat, and I swallowed hard. For a moment, I felt unclean. Or as an animal might before slaughter.

"Morning, habibis." The old man greeted us from the couch, barely looking up from *El Nashara*, a local Lebanese paper. The man was bald, round, and his skin was decorated in a constellation of age spots. What hair he had covered his arms and chest, white shoots protruding from beneath his nicely pressed white shirt. He wore thick, black-framed glasses, which gave his eyes a bulging appearance. Before either Andros or I could respond to his salutation, the old man erupted in a fit of coughing.

An older woman whose thick white hair was elegantly fastened in a chignon came from another room with a glass of water. "What excitable news is it this morning, hayati?" The woman was pleasantly round, much like her husband. Her dress was simple, clean, rustic, but she carried herself with inherent class.

"Corruption, Sarea! Corruption!" Shaking his head and coughing in apparent disgust, the old man looked up at Andros and me. "Welcome to Beirut where even God can be bought for the right price!"

"Michele, please! Don't bother these young men so early in the morning with your diatribes!" Sarea rolled her eyes, threw her hands up in the air, and turned to us. "Please, Andros, habibi, excuse my husband. He is so grumpy in the morning! I've just pulled some manoushe out of the oven. Sit down, sit down. I'll bring some labneh too." She scurried off to a back room, presumably the kitchen, while Andros sat on the dark green couch across from Michele. I followed his lead and sat beside him, deliberately leaving space enough between us for a third person. Sarea returned quickly with the freshly baked manoushe. The warm scent of dried zatar herbs, sumac, olive oil, and bubbling bread as it was placed in front of me was irresistible. The familiar smell elicited a rumbling from my gut. I didn't even realize how hungry I was until I put the soft yet crisp bread with a dollop of the white labneh, or yogurt, in my mouth. It was a ravenousness I had never before experienced. I breathed in the warm, perfectly spiced bread with the smooth balance of creamy labneh, denying my taste buds the privilege of tasting the divine flavors for a moment.

"My child, you are so hungry! Have you not eaten in days?" Sarea laughed good-naturedly, the softly aging edges of her face brightening. She was seated beside her husband, who had resumed reading his newspaper, occasionally punctuating the atmosphere with a clucking sound.

"Your cooking is some of the best I've had since arriving." This reply was not untrue. Sarea's cooking was very similar to Ummi's, and I enjoyed the familiar taste of home.

"You think her breakfast is good, you should try her kaak. Her sweet bread is otherworldly, and I don't even like sweets," Andros added, sliding several inches closer to me as he spoke.

His movement startled me, and I slid away and closer to the end of the couch. While the ache to be close to him, to let our legs brush gently against each other, was as visceral as my hunger, I was mindful of the older couple sitting across from us. I distracted myself by taking a long sip of thick coffee. The hot brew complimented the savory breakfast.

From the far corner of the room, a clock struck eleven. The melodic chime triggered a return to reality. Eleanor. How many hours had I been gone? Was she terrified? Worried? Angry? I looked out the window.

"Thank you, Mrs...?" As I stood and outstretched my hand, I realized we hadn't yet been formally introduced.

"Murad. But call me Sarea." She shook my hand firmly, but I detected the faintest hesitation in the gesture. Did she know? My stomach fell, and I was fairly certain the menushe I had just devoured was about to make its way back up.

My lack of response, or perhaps my coloring, was enough indication for Mrs. Murad to add, "The bathroom is down the hall and around the corner on the left, habibi."

Andros moved to follow me, but I shot him a fierce look.

The following ten minutes or so were spent on the cool, white tile of the bathroom floor, hunched over the toilet bowl. All the wine and arak from the night before came up with a vengeance. My gut curled and tightened and unraveled in painful bursts of nausea. This must be punishment. Punishment for drinking too much, for wanting and taking too much. I took Andros. I had him and he had me.

A quiet knock on the door interrupted my sickness and self-recriminations.

"Come in," I croaked.

Andros peeked his head around the door. "Did someone have too much to drink last night?" He smiled and came inside the small bathroom, shutting the door behind him. He seemed to be relying more on his cane for support today. In one hand he held a glass of water.

"Whatever would give you that idea?" I smiled in spite of myself.

"Lucky guess." He reached down and handed me the glass.

"Thanks." Before I could take a sip, I felt another wave of nausea swell inside me. I leaned over toilet. "You should probably leave. I'm going to be sick again."

He left without a word, granting me privacy to be sick. Another fifteen minutes or so passed before I felt well enough to return to the living room.

Michele hadn't left his spot on the couch. Andros sat directly across from him, reading a section of *El Nashara*. For a moment, I stopped and allowed myself to imagine what a life with Andros would look like. He would sit at the kitchen table, reading the morning paper over a steaming cup of freshly brewed coffee. I would prepare eggs and toast or menushe and join him at the table. We would smoke cigarettes, the nicotine eradicating the traces of alcohol lingering in our system from the night before. Cigarettes and coffee over the morning news, such a simple, perfunctory, beautiful existence. Michele's sudden fit of coughing interrupted my fantasy, and I came back to life in the present tense.

"I'd like to thank you, Mr. Murad, for your hospitality." I

walked towards the old man, wiping his eyes with a handkerchief as his lungs seemed to clear.

He nodded.

"You must return to your lovely bride." Andros said with a tenuous note of emotion: jealousy, anger, disappointment? He kept his blue-gray eyes on the paper in front of him. If he looked up to meet my gaze, I imagined they would be a shade resembling the ocean in winter.

I didn't say anything else. I found my way to the door and let myself out. Once in the narrow, winding street and out of view of Andros and the Murads, I let the sharp pang of departure hit me, the pain splintering, filling my being, piercing even my bones. He wouldn't look at me as I was leaving. I needed to look into his eyes again. When would we see each other next? We never made plans. What if he was done with me? A series of images: abandonment, Andros with another man, evenings in bed with Eleanor. I wanted to go back to the house, to Andros, but I knew I had to return to the hotel. As I waved down a cab, I took in the coffee shops and congestion of large apartment and office buildings of Ashrafieh. Clouds smudged the blue sky. Trees with long, thin trunks topped with a wide, flat canopy of green filled the neighborhood. People moving about in Western and Eastern sartorial blends, business suits and dresses, turbans and hijabs, little children with their mothers and groups of men smoking cigarettes.

"St. George Hotel, please," I said as I got into a cab, narrowly missing a frantic Pontiac in the process. The headlights of the car flashed and swerved, the driver blasting his horn and throwing up his hands as he passed. *You are the light of an oncoming car. You crash into me and I am destroyed, Andros. I ache to tell you this. Minutes have passed like years. I only want to return to your bed, the racing of my heart unbearable until your touch calms it.*

"You're Lebanese?" the cabbie asked, adjusting the mirror to look back at me. I noticed his face was pock-marked, but his eyes were stunningly blue.

I nodded. My reticence prevented more questions.

Too soon we pulled to the end of the Zeitouna Bay complex and were in Ain el Mreisseh and in front of St. George. Ain el-Mreisseh occupied the space between the Corniche and the Port of Beirut. This quarter of the city sat at the bottom of a hill overlooking the city proper to the north. With small bays to the east and west, it was almost isolated from the rest of Beirut. Old Lebanese houses and mansions overlooked the sea to the west. A two-tiered arcade of pointed arches framed balconies of two-storied buildings. Pedestrian walkways and flights of stairs connected the neighborhood.

I paid the driver and made my way into the reception area. Thoughts of Andros temporarily abated, replaced with trepidation as I entered the elevator and gave the attendant my floor. We creaked upwards and, too soon, the elevator stopped, the doors opened, and I got out.

I swallowed hard, smoothed the wrinkles in my shirt, and knocked hesitantly on the door of room 407 despite the key in my left pocket. For some reason, as I stood before the door to our elegant suite, I became painfully aware of who had paid for these accommodations. This whole trip was financed by Eleanor, or rather, Eleanor's father. Somehow this realization made me feel dirty.

"Yes?" a diminutive voice beyond answered.

"It's me."

The door swung open. Eleanor's eye makeup was running in every direction, smudged and tear-streaked along her eyes, cheeks, and even her chin. She was wearing the same white chiffon dress from the previous night. Her hair was mostly loose, sticking in waves to her damp face.

Without a word, my tender, understanding wife slapped me hard across the face. She turned away and marched into the bedroom where her suitcase was open and her clothes were folded beside it on the bed. I savored the burn prickling across my skin. I deserved this and so, so much worse.

"Where the hell have you been?" She wasn't yelling. Her voice was straining against emotion, quivering, almost quiet.

"I—I must have passed out in the street. I woke up in a doorway next to a puddle of vomit. I didn't realize how much I drank last night." I gave a chuckle, but its spurious sound only made her more upset and me more uncomfortable.

She responded by silently throwing her clothes half-folded into her suitcase.

"Sweetheart, what're you doing?" I stood in the doorway of the bedroom afraid to cross the threshold. *Was she leaving me? There's no way she'd leave me. She wouldn't. Would she? God, please don't leave me.* The thought of being alone—truly and utterly alone—no Andros, no Eleanor, made me feel nauseous for the second time that morning.

She still didn't say a word. The sky outside had turned gray, the smudges of clouds had overtaken the perfect blue of just an hour earlier. The picturesque view obscured by an impending storm. A crack of lightning snapped somewhere outside and then the rumble of thunder. "Eleanor? Please say something." A crack of nausea snapped somewhere inside. Then paranoia. *Did she know? God, did she know what I had done?*

She stopped tossing her clothes and turned toward me. "I didn't know what happened to you! You son of a bitch! I didn't know what happened!" She had grabbed my shirt and pulled it towards her, looking directly into my eyes. "I didn't know!" Eleanor started sniffling and sobbing and pushing me away from her all at the same time.

Praise, God. She didn't know. "I'm sorry, my love. I really am. I just had too much to drink is all. It won't happen again, I swear!" I tried to put my hands on her shoulders to calm her, but she swatted them away.

"You son of a bitch! This is all your fault! I didn't know!" Eleanor crumpled onto the floor. She put her hands over her face and sobbed a hard, guttural sound.

"Honey, I said I was sorry. Don't you think you're overreacting?" I joined her on the floor, trying once again to pull her into a comforting embrace.

"Aunt Leila phoned the hotel this morning. Dad had a heart attack." She stopped resisting me and laid her head in my lap as she continued heaving loud, unfamiliar sounds.

The shock of her words struck me in the gut, compounded the guilt already weighing heavily upon me. "When?"

"Few days ago." Her sobs were reduced to hiccups. "He's stable, but obviously we have to cut our trip short." I processed this sentence in two parts. First, Kamil was okay. Immense relief, even gratitude. Second, going back home meant leaving Andros. A tightness took up in my throat. I couldn't breathe or swallow. Rain began to beat against the window. Eleanor got up and found a pack of Old Golds. She took out a cigarette and lighter and, with shaking hands and dripping eyes, put a smoke in her mouth. She inhaled deeply and seemed to steady herself.

"But he's okay." I reached out for a cigarette, which she handed to me wordlessly. I continued, "So we can stay."

She stopped trembling and crying and her eyes narrowed to slits. "What did you just say?" Her voice was as sharp as my butcher knife. She extinguished the new cigarette in the ashtray on the nightstand.

"He's okay. We can finish the trip. We still have four months left." I breathed in the nicotine. I could hear the desperation in the words.

I felt the vase before I saw it. All at once the thunder and lightning was inside my head. Thoughts and memories cracked and splintered and pierced the skull that insulated them. A sharp burst and then throbbing. She had grabbed the closest thing to her, an antique porcelain vase on the nightstand table, and chucked it at my head with a strength I didn't know she possessed. Fortunately, her aim wasn't aligned with her force and she only clipped the side of my head. The impact was enough to knock me down and daze me momentarily though the pain would probably not go away too soon.

"Jesus, Eleanor! Are you trying to kill me?" I rubbed the side of my head and stood up facing her, meeting her belligerence with my own even though I knew she had every right to be upset with me. Somehow the cigarette remained in my mouth so I added it—still lit and smoking—to the collection of shells in the tray. "Just because you're upset doesn't give you the right to assault me, God damn it!" The anger, the frustration, the repression was flooding all my senses, amplified by the pain threading through the right side of my head. As she began throwing her clothing in my direction, I grabbed her suitcase from the bed and threw it across the room, a trail of multicolored dresses fluttered and fell in its wake, like a skein of broken-winged butterflies.

Eleanor practically leapt across the bed in pursuit of the suitcase. "You son of a bitch! Those are from *Chloe!*"

"You just threw a vase at me!"

"These are brand new Aghion designs!" She began picking up the dresses, one at a time, and folding them carefully on the bed.

"Who the hell cares?" I kicked the side of the bed.

The gesture seemed to remind her of her fury. Eleanor went for the closet, on the floor of which was my steamer trunk. Locating a pump from the mess, I saw her aim the sharp point of the heel at the leather flat-top of the decades-old trunk that followed my father from the old country to Connecticut, and back. The rage inside me sprouted appendages and darted towards her, reaching out for the shoe before she could land a blow.

I ripped the black pump from her fingers, one of which was curled so tightly around the inside of the shoe it made a snapping sound when I finally yanked it free.

A sound somewhere between animal and unreal filled the hotel room. Eleanor began whimpering like some injured creature. She crumpled to the floor of the closet and cradled her hand, rocking it back and forth like she held an infant. "Son of a bitch!"

The sudden injury stunned and released me from the rage. "Are you okay? I'm sorry I didn't mean to hurt you, sweetheart!" I knelt beside her placing my hand on her shoulder, which she shook away. "I'll call downstairs for a doctor."

"Finish your god damned honeymoon without me." Eleanor remained seated, leaned against the wall, and rested her head on the pastel wallpaper. She closed her eyes. She added in a whisper, "That's what you want anyway, isn't it?"

I reached for the unfinished cigarette still burning in the heap of ash in the tray on the nightstand table. I sat with my back to her on the edge of the bed. Taking a long inhale, another crack of thunder whipped against the sky as the storm twisted outside. I picked up the phone on the bedside table and called the front desk.

CHAPTER EIGHTEEN

I sat beneath a wide umbrella with tasseled fringe by the pool. Andros was sleeping on a white beach chair beside mine. Our cocktails rested on the small table between us. Eleanor had left Lebanon. We didn't speak before her departure, and I wondered what she had told her father about my absence. Each day I expected to receive word that he would no longer be paying for my room at the St. George, that the money was cut off, but it had been three months, and I had not been asked to leave the hotel. In fact, the only repercussion came in the form of a very angry letter from Ummi shortly after Eleanor returned home. One line in particular played in my head over and over again: *You have brought shame upon our family*. If she only knew how true these words were. I couldn't bear her maternal repudiation, and I ignored all subsequent correspondence. Saad and Lelia phoned the hotel several times. I didn't know what they might say or how angry they might be so I ignored them. After several weeks, their attempts to reach me finally stopped. I felt sick with guilt, but I concentrated on Andros and chilled glasses of gin. Plump green olives and slices of cheese pocked white porcelain plates. Olive oil pooled in matching bowls as apricots and figs bridged the threshold of lunch and dinner.

* * *

There was a café on Hamra Street that Andros and I visited for the coffee as much as for the company. Politicians, intellectuals, and artists of all kinds frequented the many cafés and bars that comprised the Ras Beirut Quarter of the city. The streets of this quarter were also the home of galleries, banks, upscale residences, cinemas, theatres and world-renowned hotels like the Mayflower and Commodore Hotel, which offered suites with a 360-degree view of the city skyline.

The Muslim proprietor, Shahbaz, prepared elegant pastries that filled glass cases in the front of the small, brightly colored space. Taking in the scent of freshly baked filo pastry, pistachios, honey, and rosewater, I thought of Raina, of cooking on Sundays, and ordered a piece of baklawa.

"You like those sweets?" Andros asked as he took a seat at a table by the open window.

"They're divine. Proof God exists," I responded as I grabbed the pastry and two Turkish coffees, paid Shahbaz, and sat across from a scowling Andros.

"Disgusting." He made a dramatic expression, turned up his nose and waved his hand. "Proof God has a sense of humor, maybe." He took the steaming cup. "There's nothing better than black coffee. Except arak. Or gin." He laughed and blew on the hot beverage. "I only need three things to live: coffee, alcohol, and cigarettes."

"Well, this changes everything. I don't believe I can spend time with someone who does not appreciate the exquisite nuances of baklawa." I smiled at him and took a large bite of the dessert, flakes of golden pastry and crushed nuts fell onto the porcelain dish.

He smiled and shook his head. Looking out the window into the bustling street, he commented, "Qabbani is about to walk inside."

I looked up just as the Syrian politician and poet entered. Everyone knew the story of Nizar Qabbani. He worked at the Syrian Embassy in Beirut as a diplomat, but it was for his poetry that the man was famous. I remember devouring *The Brunette Told Me* when I was studying at Georgetown. Armed with pen and page, the man was a crusader for feminism and progressive ideals. The story went that Qabbani's sister committed suicide rather than marry a man she did not love. He was fifteen years old at the time, and it was her death that inspired his first collection—a collection of poems that celebrated romantic love and urged women to fight against the traditional expectations placed upon them by society.

The well-dressed man, clean-shaven and black hair carefully pomaded, was handsome. He smiled at Shahbaz, ordered a coffee, and took a seat at a table filled with other Arab men in suits, presumably other politicians.

"When you laugh, I too, forget about the sky," I whisper the allusion to Qabbani's "When My Lover Asks Me."

Andros heard the reference and smiled.

Qabbani's voice floated above those of his companions. Snippets of current events and political debate made its way to our table. "We are dragging Lebanon into the light of modernity," Qabbani said loudly to his companions. "At least women can finally vote!"

"Is it really a step in the right direction? What can they add to the political landscape with their silly ideas and opinions?" A gentleman with a full beard laughed and was met with a scowl from Qabbani.

"Your East, dear sir, weaves of women's skulls a crown of refined honorability."

He spoke with such passion even Andros turned to me and commented, "He really is more poet than politician, isn't he?"

The gentlemen at Qabbani's table shook their heads, some chuckled. Their response reminded me of the way we sometimes dismissed Uncle Taffy. Andros and I couldn't help but continue eavesdropping on the inspirational man as we sipped coffee and chain-smoked cigarettes. I also savored every bite of Arabic pastry almost as much as the overheard diatribe of the renowned Syrian progressive diplomat.

* * *

We readied ourselves for an evening on the town after spending the day reposing by the pool. In the evening, the St. George hotel was made of hooded lights and cigarette smoke, a glittering beacon in the heart of Zeitouna Bay. Strands of white lights festooned from palms reflected on the surrounding marina and were indistinguishable from stars. Expensive cars parked along the street in front of the hotel under the protective covering of white awnings.

The Corniche at night was a spectacle. People moved and laughed and smoked in the western coastal neighborhood of Manara, along Luna Park. Each night was equally enjoyed by the natives, the tourists, the expatriates, as if it was the celebration to end all celebrations. In the midst of the boardwalk, the grand, brightly colored gold, green, and red revolving wheel called Safinet Nouh, or Noah's Ark, spun recklessly, like a spinning traffic light perpetually indicating "go." Go out into the night, give yourself to her and to your appetites. The spinning heart of Manara.

We ventured into Rue de Phenicie, Phoenicia Street,

specifically to the infamous Les Caves du Roy. The new nightclub was housed in one of Beirut's most exclusive hotels, the
Hotel Excelsior. A sign at the entrance boasted of the most
glamourous night club in the Mediterranean and was owned by
Lebanese entrepreneur Jean Prosper Gay-Para. Three life-
sized iron statues evocative of some ancient past, relics perhaps
of its Roman history, stood beneath the sign as if sentries of the
night. The center statue, a soldier with a dagger in his belt,
stood with each arm on the back of a companion. The statue on
the left held his arms at his side and the right kept his hands
folded as if in prayer. Pray for us sinners, watch over us. Religion even in a den of sinners. Designed by Serge Sassouni, the
interior was decorated in varying shades of rust. White lights
filled the ceiling, glistening like the room itself was celestial.
Wooden pillars mounted with crystal tops like miniature fountains were affixed to the ceiling. Gold railings lined steps
leading to tables set with small globes containing a single
candle. At the center of the room, a circular red and gold bar, a
ring of white lights hung from above, ethereal, church-like.
Except God couldn't be found here; here, nocturnal virtues
belonged to the flesh, and the people of Beirut had come to
feast.

I followed glances at Andros back to their source. Men and
women alike gazed upon the man who wore the evening like a
three-piece suit. Andros was dressed entirely in black—black
shirt, suit, slacks. His eyes—a shade between cobalt and silver
—smiled at the entire room. I stood close, the sleeve of my
jacket brushed his. Although I was beside my lover, we might
as well have been in different buildings. The realization that
all I'd ever be able to brush against in public was his jacket,
discretely, was a gut punch. These strangers would never
know this man belonged to me. For a moment, I considered
grabbing his hand, holding it as if we were just like any other

couple. Perhaps no one would notice? Perhaps no one would care?

Polished men and women, painted and perfumed, flitted about the room, laughed at tables as they smoked and sipped trendy cocktails. A group of young couples stood out at a table in the corner, the man at the center of the crowd was unmistakably Egyptian-born actor Omar Sharif. The remaining coterie was equally handsome and fashionable, almost certainly American or European elites. The adrenaline pulsed as thickly as the smoke. The music fostered the frenzy, pounding beats and hearts and dancing bodies. Andros grazed his pointer finger against the top of my left hand. Such a slight touch, but my breath lodged somewhere between diaphragm and throat. He smiled, sipped a glass of gin, and winked at a raven-haired woman seated at a table across from us with another woman who could have been her sister.

"What thoughts are dancing in that handsome head of yours?" Andros took out a cigarette.

"Very bad ones. You wouldn't be interested." I smiled, balancing a gin between slippery fingers. *Straight up, with a twist.*

Smoke curled over his lips. "Coy now, are we?"

The pair of raven-haired beauties, eyes painted and lips red as the sunset after a storm, approached us with matching smiles. One woman was a few inches shorter and slightly rounder then the other, the only distinguishing characteristics.

"You boys leave your sweethearts at home?" the taller, trimmer woman spoke, noticeably eyeing Andros. Her gaze lingered two seconds too long on his plump lips gently sucking on a half-spent cigarette. She spoke in English though her lips protested the unnatural movement of the words against her tongue. The choice of English, not Arabic, indicated that Andros and I stood out as foreigners somehow.

"That depends on who's asking?" Andros responded in a saccharine voice, too inviting, too familiar.

The dark-haired woman smiled, continuing what she assumed was a flirtation. "Lena is asking." She extended a tanned hand bejeweled in a gaudy assortment of gold rings. Gold bracelets clanked in accompaniment. Her kinky dark curls fell to her shoulders, frenzied, unhindered like the music.

"And Nadia." The shorter woman was equally done up in gold jewelry with the same curls shorn in a pageboy cut.

"And what are the lovely Lena and Nadia drinking on this fine evening?" He kept his eyes on Lena, never breaking gaze even for a moment and signaled the bartender to bring drinks.

Nadia, apparently the only one interested in my presence, looked at me and asked. "And you are?"

"George." I accepted her outstretched hand and brought it to my lips placing a long kiss on the warm, moist hand. She giggled.

I looked over at Andros to see his reaction, but he was still making eyes at Lena.

A band called The Wilson Girls made up of three English women played on the raised platform at the front of the room. With blonde bouffant dos and adorned in Middle Eastern belly dancing garb, the trio embodied quintessential American beauty veiled in oriental elegance. The beating drums and the powerful voices of the attractive women filled the air. A swirl of lights blazed in the dark room like the stars over the corniche. The gin accelerated the rush of the environment; I dared steal a look at Andros; it was too much.

The ladies excused themselves to the powder room. Andros seemed once again to become aware of my existence. "Something bothering you?" He put his drink on the table and leaned in.

I pulled away, leaned back as far as I could in my chair. "Of course not."

"What's wrong?" I thought I detected a genuine note of concern in his cool, even words. Arabic rhythm was creeping into his English, indicative of his level of intoxication. He leaned closer to me. "You're jealous." He smirked. It wasn't a question.

"I don't give a damn who you flirt with!" I stood up rather abruptly and moved towards the returning ladies. I took Nadia by the arm and instructed her to place her drink on the table. We were going to join the mass of people dancing in the center of the room. Andros followed my lead and led Lena to the floor.

The effect of the candlelight and canvas of white lights covering the ceiling created the illusion of dancing under the night sky. The three-tiered crystal mounts resembled fountains in the waves of light. Well-dressed men in suits and women in their finest dresses, engaged in conversations around the circle of tables surrounding the dance floor. The Arabic music filled our bodies; alcohol and attraction filled our souls. The beat was frenetic. Bodies moved with energy; hips moved back and forth, hands lifted high above as in prayer. This ritual was religious in a way, wasn't it? Nadia had quick feet and quicker hips. She moved as if she was made of musical notes. Although the gin had weighed heavily upon my limbs merely moments earlier, the cloud of drunkenness had dissipated, and I kept up with her. She clapped her hands and laughed, or I imagined she laughed as she smiled and threw her head backwards. I couldn't actually hear the sound above the loud music. Without realizing it, I, too, was laughing. For a moment, I forgot. I forgot that I had a wife halfway across the world, a lover flirting with a stranger, or that I was dancing with a woman I probably wouldn't recognize the next morning. I forgot the feeling of crashing and breaking against Andros. I gave myself to Les Caves du Roy, to the sultry Beirut night.

The set ended in raucous applause. Sweating bodies glistened in the dim lights like the faux stars above. Clouds of cigarette smoke blanketed the room. Pockets of multilingual dialogue punctuated the atmosphere. We made our way back to the table, Lena and Andros not far behind. Leaning more heavily upon his cane, Andros seemed to have difficulty resuming his seat. For those few moments, I had forgotten that for Andros, dancing would prove difficult. Searching the small collection of memories, I realized I had never actually seen him attempt the physical act. The fact that he had just tried, and apparently poorly by the expression on Lena's face, was telling. Of what, I wasn't entirely sure.

"Enough of that nonsense." Andros's tenor had become sour, a departure from his earlier amorous one.

"You alright?" Lena helped him sit in the bench seat.

"Dandy." He was seated with his cane next to him. I sat across next to Nadia. "George you were certainly cutting up the floor." A note of resentment? Jealousy?

"Sure." I smiled, smug with myself. I put my arm around Nadia. "Sweetheart, you were great out there."

She took a cigarette from a ruby-crusted gold case, placed it in her mouth, and laughed. "Just trying to keep up with you! You have a light?" She leaned in close enough so I could smell some earthy scent. Like leaves or grass. Her cheeks were flushed a shade darker than her rouge. I imagined Andros's face paling with anger at our close proximity. When I turned to look at him, he was asking a server for some narghile and looking at neither Lena nor myself.

Within minutes, a glass-based hookah pipe was placed in the center of the table. Andros lit the coals on the top part, sputtering a few sparks before catching as he sucked from the mouthpiece of the serpentine tube connecting to the base. He inhaled profoundly and exhaled a dense cloud of smoke. Passing the narghile to Lena, she made a show of taking the piece between her plump, red lips and sucking in a suggestive way.

Andros did not notice. He did not look at her or Nadia or even me. He leaned his head back against the russet velvet booth and stared up at the tapestry of white lights. Perhaps he was letting the calmness of the narghile wash over him, quell the fire of liquor that had been raging in his blood since this afternoon. I noticed in that moment that his eyes were pink-rimmed and watery, emblematic of little sleep and too much drinking. The blue-gray color lacked its usual vibrancy, more a silhouette, the color of a gray winter aching for the blue of spring. I ached for him that way. I sat there, looking at him, and the world blurred and melted away in swirl of revelry and cigarette smoke. Human conditions ceased; it was only Andros and I, a first kiss, and the sanctuary of the Byblos harbor.

My rumination was ended when Andros left the table. Where was he going? Why didn't he say anything to me? Had I gone too far? He must have been angry with me. He hated me and was done, we were done. I panicked and left Nadia and Lena at the table without a second thought. They must have called after us, perhaps Nadia moved to follow and Lena, sensing our need for privacy, stopped her.

Despite his stunted gait and the difficulty of moving through the mob, Andros walked quickly towards the exit. I followed him outside. Crowds of stylish folks, an amalgamation of Western and Eastern trends, were still making their way into the nightclub even though it was probably around three in the morning. The night air was humid and stuck to our skin like the tension between us. We hadn't even reached an acceptable distance from people when Andros stopped and slammed me against the side of the Hotel Excelsior.

"What the hell is going on?" He shouted in my face. He kept his hands firmly pressed against my shoulders pinning me against the cool stone. Thoughts unraveled and spun into memories of warm, moist lips pressing against each other.

"You tell me." My voice was calm.

"What in God's name do you want me to say? Do you want me to say that I haven't eaten or slept in days? That the thought of you with someone else makes my insides crawl?" He had removed his hands from me and stood, nearly erect, hand shaking on his cane. A high-pitched laugh sounded and men's inchoate voices rumbled like thunder about a block or so beyond us, somewhere between Hotel Excelsior and the Palm Beach Hotel.

"You were all over Lena in there like you wanted to make it with her!" I spat the accusation that had been brewing all evening.

"So? Pretense, George. You should know that better than anyone. You know, since you're going home to your wife in a few weeks." The illusion shattered, another shard in a growing collection.

"That's what this is all about?" I moved towards him. "So what if I stay?" The question had been burning the back of my throat, stuck there unsaid these last few months. It was the desire sleeping in my gut, awakened with this jealousy and anger, at once surprising and intoxicating. I pushed him down into the narrow street between the two grand hotels. There were no people, no signs of life. I pressed my mouth against his, a force he returned equally electric. In that moment, I knew that his kiss would forever brand my lips; they could never belong to anyone else. I needed to remain here with Andros. How could I return to Connecticut, to Eleanor now? I let myself imagine a life with him, here in Lebanon. We'd buy an apartment in Beirut, maybe in the Ras Beirut Quarter. He'd spend his days painting in a brightly colored studio while I studied at American University. I'd cook elaborate meals in the evening, which we'd eat on the terrace even in the rain. As the distant sounds of the Beirut night echoed in the humidity, the blasting horns and pockets of music and conversation, I let hope swell inside me like the sea. I would hold onto it like water, desperately trying to keep it in my hands only to have it spill slowly, but inevitably, everywhere.

"You won't." His breath was hot and smoky. He spoke the accusation against my face, his mouth only inches from mine.

"I need you."

"And your wife? What of her?" His forehead against mine, eyes shut tightly, as if opening them made this conversation too good to be true. If he opened them, I'd disappear.

"What of her?" I found his mouth and kissed him hard. I stopped only to breathe the directive, "Take me somewhere."

* * *

The sound of his screaming woke me in the middle of the night. Andros was shaking violently, sweat knotted his hair.

"Wake up!"

His eyes were open, but they stared blankly passed me, passed recognition. They focused, wide, on some tenuous object or remembrance in the back of his mind. The blue-gray of his eyes was cloudy, overcast, threatening; the sky before a storm. The pupils were dilated; the fear was real as if whatever vision he fixed his sight on was immediate and unstoppable. He breathed and gasped and yelled unintelligible things. It was as if my attempt at waking him was nothing more than a whisper caught in the back of my throat.

"Please wake up!"

Minutes or maybe only seconds had passed before Andros was awake, cognizant of his surroundings. He wasn't able to speak, but he had stopped thrashing and making terrifying primordial sounds. His breathing slowed to rapid.

"I didn't mean to wake you." He ran his hands over his drenched face and hair and laid back on his pillow. His voice strained in an unfamiliar way.

"You okay? Bad dream?"

"Something like that." His body remained tense, but he reached out and brushed my arm with his fingertips.

"Do you want to talk about it?" I used to have bad dreams as a young boy. Even now, from time to time, dark shadows and unknown threats lurked in my dreams, ephemeral but still disorienting. I remembered Ummi's stories of Lebanon and her childhood. There was a kind of fairy tale quality to her stories, narratives laced with exotic places and eccentric characters. Andros probably wouldn't find the same kind of comfort in fairy tales.

"Combat exhaustion, the docs call it. Night terrors can be a symptom." He laid there rubbing his temples as if the movement would unfasten the unpleasant images locked in his mind.

I wasn't sure how to respond. Andros had never mentioned his time in the war. I had wondered if his limp had not been a relic of combat. Many men his age, probably most, in fact, had fought in Europe or the Pacific.

As if in response to my thought, he added, "Not my only souvenir from North Africa. Did you never wonder about my very charming limp?" He laughed a weak, strained sound.

"What's there to wonder about? It's irresistible." I wasn't being coy. I found his imperfections intriguing, attractive even.

His laugh resumed its natural cadence. He lowered his

hand from his temples and pulled me to his chest. I could feel his heart pounding, the rapid pulsing was soothing, almost like the ticking of a clock. I didn't say anything, and neither did he for a few minutes. We just lay in each other's arms, savoring the warm touch of skin against skin, breath against breath, heart against heart.

He would tell me later of his time in the war. Always drunk, always apologetic for bringing it up. He needed to tell someone. I was honored to be his someone. He would describe the North African frontier, a gray desert veiled in the broken and bloodied bodies of men and the hard, void faces of weapons. Tanks, guns, blasts eliciting pink mist filled the battle-field of the past and the present landscape of his dreams. The shape of his mind at night was a leg, once familiar, mottled with black tar and incarnadine blood.

"I remember not knowing why my eyes were so wet. Explosions of light and smoke were everywhere. And the sounds. You don't want to know the kind of sounds men are capable of making. I saw the blood on my leg before I felt the pain. Black dirt and dust and grime and blood, so much blood, and smoke. It falls from the sky and covers me, still. But it's the sound that war makes that haunts me in the night. The sound of man killing each other is the knot in my mind. I had wanted to die. Thought about ending it. And then I got shot and suddenly I wanted desperately to live, to be alive, to go home." Andros stopped talking. I laid in his arms, absorbing his story. I wanted to soak up his pain, leave him with nothing but peaceful slumber and beautiful memories. In that moment, I knew that I would do anything for this man. I would swallow his emotional and physical pain and bear it ten times over if it meant he'd be happy. I settled for kissing his shoulder.

He stretched his leg beneath the sheets and winced before continuing. "I had wanted to do something, make a difference, you know? After Beirut fell in '41, I volunteered to fight with the Free French forces and ended up in North Africa. I was injured in the first few weeks of combat and returned to Lebanon in time for the big snows of '42. And that was it. My brief, ineffectual stint as a soldier. Honestly, I was happy to exchange my gun for a paint brush." His breathing had returned to an even pattern, a comforting, mellifluous sound. The quiet ticking of a clock on the nightstand was the only other noise. A breeze infiltrated the room, evidenced by the dancing white sheer curtain hanging from the window. I waited for him to continue the narrative, soothed by the room's soft lullaby. I wondered *is this what contentment is?* I realized that he had fallen back to sleep. I was left awake, filled with questions and new knowledge. Was this but a dream? Were we nothing more than two somnambulists engaged in meaningless conversation in the middle of the night? Would morning erase our nocturnal intimacy? No, I thought. Impossible. This was contentment.

He told me once of another, less visible injury.

"The mud was so thick it pulled the thin soles of our boots into the ground. The tent was dark. The commander had a cough, a wheezing sound that caught violently in his throat every few minutes. He smoked hand-rolled cigarettes faithfully, almost without pause. We could never figure out how he had such an infinite supply. His skin was sallow and wrinkled and hung from his frame like loose clothing. The cot in the center of the tent had no sheets but a threadbare blanket strewn across an exposed mattress. It was so dark inside. A gas lamp on a table was nothing more than a single flame, yielding no light, no warmth. Only darkness as thick as the mud on the ground." Andros paused and lit a cigarette before continuing. "Commander called me into his tent. I didn't know what I had done. I racked my brain trying to think of something. I was fastidious in maintaining my bunk, my rifle, my uniform. I was as clean and put together as a man in battle could possibly be. I was obedient." A visible film of perspiration decorated his forehead, his cheeks flushed. "I could smell antiseptic and cigarettes, but I could barely make out the tall, narrow shape of the aged commander. My eyes adjusted to the lack of light, and I saw him sitting on the cot. He coughed for a minute or two then asked me if I had a sweetheart back home. *Sir?* I couldn't understand why I had been summoned to the commander's tent to talk about my personal life. *Sit beside me, Seleukos.* He commanded. I did. I was confused and it was so dark. *It's so lonely here, Seleukos. So lonely. You're almost dainty. Like a woman, no?* When I realized what was happening it was too late. I tried to stand up, but he pinned me down to the mattress. The rusted springs creaked and punched my stomach. I called for help. He didn't look strong, but he was. I begged him to stop. I cried. I screamed. It didn't stop until he was done. When it was over, he dismissed me with *disgusting faggot.* I wanted to die. It was so dark outside."

Andros was shaking. I held him. We wept together. He vomited beside the bed. I cleaned it up and brought him a glass of water, but he had fallen sleep.

CHAPTER NINETEEN

L ife at the center of Hurricane Andros was incomplete contentment. When we were together, life felt blissful. When we were apart, I questioned everything: the authenticity of our relationship, his affection, my affection, my marriage, our affair, where I lived, where I wanted to live. But when Andros walked into a room, any room, his skin slick with Mediterranean sun, hair as reckless and indifferent as the blue-gray of his eyes, there were no questions, only certainty. I was certain that he, that Andros, was the answer to every question I had ever had and would ever have again.

We were princes and gods. Beirut was our Olympus, our Eden, our Elysium. We embraced bacchanalia like we were entitled to it. Long nights were memories made of liquor and music and kisses stolen in dark corners of darker rooms. The sound of his laugh was a song all its own, a forgotten childhood bedtime story, a bowl of Ummi's warm lentil soup on a cold winter's eve.

He was the secret quivering on my lips, waiting to be told. I watched the way the morning sun softened the lines that fanned his eyes. He slept, breathing long, heavy breaths punctuated by an occasional snore. Wanting nothing more than to prolong this moment, I savored the warmth of his breath on my chest as he slept. His head rested on my arm, which I could no longer feel. I wondered what it would be like to watch him grow old. The softening of his skin, the deepening of lines around his eyes. There were no words in English or Arabic or any extant language that could articulate how much love I felt in that moment.

City noise—indistinguishable chatter, a rush of traffic—drifted in from the open window. I noticed an easel with an unfinished canvas at the opposite corner of the room, away from the light. Shades of dark grays, blues, and black swirled in an abstract way, though a silhouette of a face seemed to float disembodied at the center of the mass of dark colors. I yearned to get up and study the painting in progress more closely, to trace my finger along the bends and curves of the dried paint, to imagine the energy and movements of his hands as he transferred his emotions onto canvas. I longed to study his work as it seemed to me then that this was an artifact of his soul, a glimpse into the innermost workings of his heart. I craved the opportunity to experience him this way, and it occurred to me that I had yet to even see a single painting done by my artist. I thought of him in that possessive way; Andros was *my* lover, *my* artist, *my* secret.

As if hearing my obsessive thoughts, Andros stirred.

And then groaned. "My head is pounding." He sat up quickly and reached for the pack of Old Golds on the bedside table. A glass half-filled with black, cloudy water was beside it, filled with an assortment of used paint brushes.

As soon as my arm was free and the tingling subsided, I got out of bed and walked over to the painting. A darkness evocative of a night sky exuded from the canvas. The head or shadow of a man, perhaps, seemed trapped in the center of the artwork. I was mesmerized by this painting. My heart raced as I studied it. Yes, this was, I thought, a man trapped in a prison made of shadows.

My rumination was interrupted by Andros, who had grabbed his cane and walked up behind me. He rested it against a stool which was beside the easel. By the way his breath caught in his throat as he leaned forward and wrapped his arms around me, I could tell he was in pain this morning.

"What do you think of it? It's not finished." It was the first time I'd ever detected a note of nervousness in his invariably even, assured voice. He cared what I thought.

"Terrifying." I paused, focusing on the dark shade of a man. "Honest." For the first time, I related to an image depicted in paint, my own isolation and denial translated into a work of art. I didn't know how to convey these thoughts without trivializing them, but I tried. "I've never felt so moved by a painting before." I turned to face him.

He didn't say anything. He brought his hand to my cheek so gently it was hard to feel its warmth against my face.

"My whole life I've been stuck in darkness," he said. "Then you bumped into me at the souk, and from that moment on I've felt as if I'm fighting to get out of this prison, I've built for myself. It's constructed of shadows, and I'm clawing my way out, slowly, into your light, but chasing you is like chasing the ground. It's infinite until it isn't, until we reach a precipice and there is nothing left to do but fall. Do we fall into the sea and drown, hayati? What becomes of us shadows?"

"We fall into the sea and swim to a boat. The boat takes us far away, to a place where shadows dance in the sunlight." The day invaded the room, filling it with light and the honking of cars below.

"You must fade into the day now, mustn't you, my love?"

He didn't wait for a response but ran a hand through his hair. His eyes were tired, a faded sky before the rain comes. He stood shirtless, loose-fitting pants seemed hardly to stay on. He found his cane and moved with difficulty to the stool in front of his easel. He reached for a crystal snifter filled with day-old gin, tepid but surely still potent, which sat beside a rickety table filled with assorted paints and stained rags. A dark green ceramic ashtray with a mound of cigarettes piled and nearly overflowing occupied the remaining space on the table. Andros took the second to last cigarette from a pack and lit it. He inhaled, held in the smoke, and slowly exhaled. He took a sip of the gin, returned the glass, and grabbed a rogue rubber band. Running his fingers through his hair, he swept capricious curls into a ponytail and fastened it with the band at the back of his neck. A shadow of facial hair had darkened into the beginnings of a beard. I imagined that he would spend the rest of the day at his canvas, drinking lukewarm gin and chain-smoking between frenzied strokes of dark-hued paint.

I could have spent the rest of my life standing beside the unmade bed watching my artist, my Andros at his easel.

Andros didn't look away from his work or from the cigarette burning in his hand. His voice aged a thousand years in a single moment as he said, "You have the restlessness of the ocean in you; you'll never be satisfied, you'll spend a lifetime crashing on shores, coming and going like the tide. No beach will ever have the pleasure of keeping your kiss forever. I know this. Your weakness is that you don't. You will spend your days trying to be something you are not. You are not a river, flowing in a single direction with purpose and precision. You will spend your days lying to yourself, crying over the receding tides of an ocean not meant to stay still." He sighed and lowered his voice to a barely audible tone. "And I will spend mine trying to catch you, trying to keep the tide from receding. This will be our story."

"Whatever you say, my love. I'm heading to the telegraph office now." I bristled, for a moment, at his pessimism. How could he doubt us, doubt me? My life was here in this room, with Andros, and I was more certain of this then I had ever been of anything else. I was done with Danbury, with the store, with Eleanor. Michael had been managing fine without me for months. And my wife would be all right eventually. Perhaps one day she'd even marry again.

I picked up my crumpled trousers from the floor and shook them out. I put them on, grabbed my oxford shirt and sandals, and walked over to Andros. I kissed him on the cheek, the smell of faded aftershave and fresh smoke stuck to his skin. He looked at me, into me, through me. The sun itself was never so magnificent. Andros was my sun; my world would die without his life-giving light. And I would not be Icarus; my wings were not made of wax. I could reach the sun. I would not drown in the sea below.

* * *

I really had planned on sending Eleanor a telegram. I had written it out in my head, articulated my remorse, reassured her of my love. I was going to express my deepest affection, convince her that my unhappiness would contaminate her life like the chemicals from the hat factories that tainted the Still River. When it came to the point in my message where I was going to give a reason, expound upon our final denouement, my words were clear, effective, precise. *I am in love with a man.* It seemed so simple in my head. But then again, things always seemed effortless without the consequence of human action.

When I sat down at the roll top desk in the hotel room to write out the note, my pen would not shape the ink into intelligible letters. Thoughts of Ummi and Michael, of the grocery store, my father's legacy, my wife percolated in my head and prevented my hand from writing. Ummi's words, *You have brought shame upon our family,* looped in my head. I glanced at the stack of unopened letters that had collected on the desk. What other castigation filled those pages?

I couldn't leave Eleanor. What would happen to her without a husband? What would folks think? She would be so ashamed, so embarrassed. How could I tell her I was in love with someone else and that someone else was a man? Doesn't she deserve her own Andros? I needed to return to Danbury. For her. Of course, there was also the money. My marriage provided financial security that I was beginning to like. I looked around at the posh hotel suite: the king-sized bed, the ornate carpets and gold light fixtures, the marble-tiled bathroom. The wastebasket filled with empty liquor bottles, brands and vintages I could never have afforded before my marriage. And, then, what would Ummi do without me? Michael would need my help running the store. Connecticut was my home, wasn't it? I had thought it was. But then, I had never before felt such a strong a sense of place, of belonging as I did tangled in bedsheets with my lover. He was my home. Would leaving him condemn me to a lifetime of homelessness? Was this what Andros was talking about this morning? I thought back to the evening of Les Caves du Roy. How cruel would it be to spend a lifetime in restaurants and clubs together but separate? Never a couple, always a couple of friends. Two men don't live happily ever after—in America, in Lebanon, or any corner of the earth. To be together would be to exist as a world of two. But, then, how lonely is alone together?

* * *

I needed air. I needed to be free of this room. I needed to think. I floated as if disembodied to the promenade with its cliff-side cafés and the seaside sidewalk of the Avenue de Paris. I was met with the Raouché, or Pigeons' Rock, golden-brown arches of stone protruding from the still blue of the Mediterranean. I walked the stretch of the Corniche in front of the Raouché but drifted down a path leading to the lower cliffs. The two gigantic rocks beckoned, imperial gravestones, delineating the aquatic ossuary of so many others who'd come here before to relieve aching minds and hearts.

People below in swimsuits splashed in the water, oblivious perhaps to the corpses decomposing far below them. They swam around and under Pigeons' Rock, one youngish Lebanese couple paddling together on a hasakeh. This attractive couple, perhaps newlyweds themselves, were perfect. A handsome man, beautiful woman, laughing together in the sea where everyone could see them. I would never have that with Andros. I would never be able to hold his hand in public, kiss his cheek when others were around. We'd be relegated to dark bedrooms and hidden corners. I would never be willing to be true to myself with him, with anyone. I watched the couple, but my mind continued splintering into thoughts of Andros, Eleanor, Lebanon, Connecticut, sex, marriage. Eleanor dancing off-beat, laughing and careless. The sickle-shaped birthmark on Andros' inner thigh. Stars bursting, reckless over Byblos. The store in the morning, fully stocked shelves and smelling of freshly baked pita and Turkish coffee. Preparing kibbeh with Ummi. His mouth, the parting of the sea, the place I went to learn the secrets of his body. The couple played and laughed, oblivious of everything and everyone around them. I choked back tears and the swelling desire to throw myself off the cliff and into the embrace of the water below.

I thought of a newspaper clipping from *The Hoya* hidden

beneath old black-and-white photos in a shoebox under my bed on Elm Street. An article I wanted to forget and nearly did. Jacob. My friend. I remembered the words I had said to him once, a lifetime ago. *I'm not nearly unstable or drunk enough to be a poet.* He must have been laughing at me then, full of prescience. Jacob knew so much more than I did about so many things. He knew the pain to come, knew it would be unbearable. I couldn't understand why he had killed himself then. So many years ago. I wish I could say that I didn't understand now.

* * *

Andros—

I find myself retreating into the dark. You will live forever in my dreams, but the daylight will inevitably return us to dust. I'm yours, now, always. Forgive me. I'll look for you in the shapes and shades of the moon and take comfort knowing you will be looking into the same pale-faced star.

—George

That was not the note I had intended to write, but these were the words that flowed organically from my ballpoint pen. In black cursive, the words curled into an elegy of our all-too-brief affair. I hated myself for writing this missive. I rested my head on top of the desk, my hands clasped at the back of my neck. A sharp pain began beating in my temples. I knew I wouldn't have the guts to deliver this letter myself. I slipped a few American cents to a Muslim bellboy to make the delivery for me.

I began packing my Saratoga trunk. Neatly pressed shirts and trousers, a watch made in Byblos for Michael, a scarf for Ummi. Books, ballpoint pens, photographs and unsent postcards filled with eloquent apologies to Eleanor. Scars and souvenirs, artifacts and artwork. I couldn't fit everything in my trunk. Some things had to stay behind.

I went through the items in the bathroom: soaps, glass bottle of cologne, a straight-edge razor, a box of twenty-five cent Ace rubber combs. Little black hairs had collected in the crevice of the porcelain soap dish resting in a pool of water on the corner of the sink. A radio in the bedroom crooned Ella Fitzgerald, her ballad about love echoed in the silence of the room. I stood before the mirror, a cigarette sputtering in an ashtray and a glass of half-drank arak beside it had accompanied me into the bathroom. I stood in a white undershirt. My hair appeared disheveled without pomade, and I hadn't shaved in nearly two days. The dark shadow of beard matched the dark shadows cradling my eyes. Even with traffic, the bellboy would have delivered my message to Andros by now; the clock ticking on the windowsill indicated this by the five o'clock hour. I imagined he was cursing me between sips of arak and waves of nausea. That was what I was doing.

* * *

I must have imbibed an entire bottle of arak. Memories played in my head, stuck on repeat. The four months together, stuck on repeat. The lightness set in and then thoughts, spinning like a carousel, like the Safinet Nouh. Bodies and lips tangled in bedsheets, smelling of salt and licorice. His tongue sliding along the hard place between my legs, eliciting pleasure. The way he pressed his body against the back of mine, the rhythm of his muscles moving against mine. Pain. Such pain. Then pleasure. Such pleasure. Nausea. The urge to void my stomach. Voiding my stomach on the oriental carpet. His smile more beautiful than the Mediterranean sun.

The morning exposed itself in the gold and pink that

played on the dark blue carpet that had served as my bed. The cruel night had come to an end, but the pain still overwhelmed. My head pounded as if it was a tambourine in the hands of a zealous musician. A half-packed suitcase lay open on the bed. Assorted shirts, pants, jackets, socks were strewn about the room, emblematic of my reckless intoxication. This was it. The final day in Beirut. My driver was scheduled to pick me up at 5 p.m. I could not move against my protesting limbs and remained on the floor.

And then a loud knock sounded at the door. And another. And it continued loudly, ferociously. Housekeeping wasn't scheduled to clean the room until this afternoon. I looked at the clock on the bedside table. Nine a.m. I resolved to ignore it though I did get up off the floor and sat on the edge of the bed. And then I heard the familiar voice.

"George! Open the door!" Andros shouted through the wooden barrier between us as if it was the only thing that stood in our way. His voice mobilized me, but I froze in front of the door. I pressed my face to the cool, hard surface, my hand against the knob.

"I know you're there! You coward! Open the door!" His voice was loud, distressed, angry. The older British couple down the hall on holiday would certainly hear him. So would the young American couple with their two-year-old son in the next room. And probably the handsome Muslim thirty-something who worked the front desk floors below us.

"Coward!" The entire city of Beirut shook. My hands shook with the force of the word. Or perhaps they just shook. I didn't say anything.

Andros was no longer knocking; he was pounding the door with his fists and screaming one word over and over again.

"Coward!"

I turned so my back was against the door and slid to the

floor, covering my head with my hands. Andros yelled so loudly, so profoundly that God in Heaven must have heard him and damned me while the devil waited to claim my soul.

Andros finally stopped beating the door. The echo of his footsteps trailed the hallway. I listened until I could no longer hear the kiss of soles against the wooden floor.

And then I cried.

PART III
THE MAN

Danbury, CT
June 1954

CHAPTER TWENTY

Trying not to think of Andros was like walking in the rain and not getting wet. Thoughts of him filled my head at the most inopportune times. Cheeks flushed and hardness implored from below. Often, I was seized with paranoia; was he mourning me by taking comfort in some other man's bed? The image of his lips brushing the muscular torso of a stranger blinded me with nausea and rage. My hands shook so hard I couldn't light my cigarette.

I couldn't leave him without saying goodbye. I had stopped at the pension on my way to the airport. He was home, and he was angry, but he saw me anyway.

"Filthy coward." He wouldn't look away from the canvas in front of him. He was unable to keep the brush in his hand steady. He had graduated from a glass to the bottle. It was easier to drink from the bottle then stopping to pour its contents into a glass.

"I have to go back," I said softly, more to myself then to Andros.

"Why are you here? I got your letter."

"I had to see you one more time."

"What makes you think you have the right to?"

I didn't know what to do. I only knew that my stomach felt as if a thousand butterflies had died and their broken wings were lodged in my gut.

"Would I have the right to stand here before the man I love if I was telling him I'd come back to him?" Yes. Yes, was the answer.

He finally permitted himself to look at me. "What're you saying?" He brought the bottle of arak to his dry, cracked lips. Spit clung to the mouth of the bottle as it retreated.

"I'm saying I'll come back."

He snorted. "I would like nothing more to believe you. Maybe, for the sake of my sanity, I just might."

This was the memory that played in my mind as I sat to write Andros three months later. How was I supposed to tell him that I hadn't lied, but circumstances had changed? How could I make him believe that I had every intention of returning to him? I could only manage to write a single line, realizing the futility of either eloquence or elegy; the curve of my script rose cruelly from the crisp white paper.

Andros,

I have a son.

* * *

June in Danbury. My days were measured in moments away from Andros. I drank to drown the beat of his heart pounding in my head. My endless lament interrupted by occasional glimpses of happiness: cradling my infant son in my arms. Baby Georgie was plump and rosy-cheeked. His little fingers curled tightly around my finger, and he'd refuse to let go. I'd wipe the drivel from his mouth as he brought my finger to his lips and suckled it. His nonsensical sounds were a song my heart sang, a song it didn't even know it had in it.

Eleanor and I fought almost incessantly. I had returned to Connecticut to a six-months-pregnant wife. She had never told me we were expecting. Or, rather, Ummi had relayed the news in one of the letters I had ignored. She had not forgiven me for our fight before her premature departure from Lebanon or for the fact that I didn't call her or follow her home. I had, after all, finished our honeymoon solo. When I learned that she was carrying my son, my treatment of her, my abandonment seemed all the more cruel. Ummi had been right. My actions were so shameful. But Ummi, as mothers tend to do, forgave me.

Eleanor's father did not forgive me. How could I blame Kamil? As a new father, I was only beginning to comprehend the role and all the complex emotions it encompassed. The need to protect my son from anything and everything was overwhelming. I understood and did not begrudge him his hostility: I had hurt his daughter. I had embarrassed her. There was nothing I could ever do to make up for this in Kamil Rizkallah's eyes. He saw me as a mercenary husband; I had married his daughter simply for the wealth and status such a union afforded me. And while I resented the insinuations about my avarice that he made at the social encounters we shared, perhaps a part of me believed it to be true.

The tension between my father-in-law and I was short-lived, however. Kamil suffered another heart attack not long after my return. This time, he did not survive. The day we buried Kamil in St. Peter's cemetery, I think we buried Eleanor, too. We returned to the house, her father's house, now ours, the most elegant residence on Elm Street, in silence.

* * *

She moved about the house in a mauve housedress and matching headscarf. Her cheeks still rouged and lips painted pink despite the sallow appearance of her once salubrious complexion. Eleanor cared for our son, nursed him, bathed him, washed his little cloth diapers with precision and maternal affection. Eventually, she even regarded me with wifely affection, too, snuggling next to me in our bed at night, sometimes brushing her cool lips against my neck and leaving a trail of soft kisses along my skin. I would dismiss her with complaints of exhaustion.

Days at the store resumed as if I had never left, never fell in love, never suffered immeasurably. The store was indifferent to the emotional goings-on of human existence. It was uncompromising in its pragmatic needs: order inventory, stock shelves, sweep and dust, attend to the customers, stock the shelves, cut the meats, select the produce, count the money, lock up in the evening. Life continued.

Half-filled bottles of gin, relics of Bayee's proclivity, provided the embrace I longed for at the day's end. Until that embrace was no longer satisfying, and I grew lonely waiting for ghosts. I couldn't help but wonder if this is why my father drank. Was something inside his chest broken? Was he pining for something or someone else? Did alcohol conjure up some lost love or missing piece of his soul? Perhaps he, too, had loftier aspirations, dreams of bigger accomplishments and elegant adventures. Pain fractured most things in my life during this time except for my reflections on Bayee: I saw him with newfound clarity. I thought, maybe, I finally even understood him.

The cloudless sky was absence; it was the infinite space between us. Most folks regarded the day as beautiful. They saw the flawless blue, not a cloud in sight, as quintessentially seasonal. I saw nothing but emptiness, pain. I saw the space beside me at night where my wife slept, the space where the man I loved should be. This was summer after Andros.

When the loneliness and suffering became unbearable, I sought other outlets. I looked for him in the beds of strangers, in the hollow darkness of the nights without him, the hollow darkness inside me where love used to be. The hollow darkness of drunken men. The clumsy tangle of limbs and shadows and phalluses. The only place I came close to him was the bottom of a bottle. I laid awake in bed most nights with the window open. A breeze slipped through the branches of the elms outside. I listened to the leaves whispering their secrets to the trees. My secret was lodged inside my gut, macerating in the gin that surely pooled there.

I found myself wanting to write to him every week. I would lock myself in the office with a drink and stationery. Sitting at the roll top desk, pushing aside bills and inventory and unopened mail, I sat to pen a missive to the man I loved who lived on the other side of the world. I fiddled with the dial of the radio, trying to find the right song for my ruminations. Pockets of white noise, a rapid succession of disparate music, the perfect song. Perry Como. "No Other Love." I lit a cigarette and grabbed a ballpoint pen.

Andros,

My lips mourn the absence of your kiss. I lay awake at night, cursed insomnia. I am trying to live my life as if I had never met you, but nothing is the same. The very simple perfunctory tasks of the day—stocking the shelves of the grocery store with fresh pita bread, greeting an old friend on the street, cooking with Ummi, even holding my infant son—nothing has meaning anymore. There is only emptiness. Words are vapid expressions and movement is by rote. Why can't I let you go? As much as I long for you, I long to forget you. Life would at least be tolerable without the ubiquity of your memory. I see the shape of you in everything; I read your letters compulsively, but your words have become blisters on the bottom of my feet, and I try to walk away, but it hurts. The memory of your fingertips brushing my stomach is the flight of birds in winter, to be beautiful elsewhere. The sound of your voice in my head is tachycardia, I can hardly catch my breath. The way you smiled, God, your smile, is the light of an oncoming car—it crashes into me, and I'm destroyed. Your skin is an invitation lost in the mail that I'm still waiting to arrive, hoping, dreading. This is the misery you've left me with. Then again, I suppose I left you. And most would call this misery love.

   Yours,

   George

I looked over my writing and sighed. I had inscribed my words onto a greeting card from Woolworth's. The card itself felt trifling, weighed down by the effusive letter inside. I thought about taking my lighter to it, but the thought of incinerating communication between Andros and myself made me more miserable. I swigged from the glass beside my stationery, choosing instead to play with the edges of the paper, bending, unbending, then bending again the corner of the cheap card. I would send it, of course. And I would hear back. And our correspondence, our very affair, would become nothing more than epistolary. Furtive glances were exchanged in words on a page, kisses were tears punctuating assurances of devotion. Lovemaking was reduced to letters traveling across weeks and countries to impatiently waiting hands and hearts. This was what our love story became.

In the world beyond our discursive affair, I was unhappy. I ached infinitely. I began a series of abortive affairs, a string of one-night-stands in dirty hotel rooms on the edge of a neighborhood called Greenwich Village in New York City. Sometimes I stayed with the men for an hour or two, sneaking out of the room as they slept off the liquor-infused romp. In the begin-ning, I showered immediately afterwards, an attempt at rinsing off the sheets crusted with expired fluids and the apathy of the hotel staff and the smell of a strange man. And then I didn't bother anymore. Let the stink of sweat and booze linger on my skin; I was contaminated anyhow. I slinked in and out of rooms in the darkest corners of my existence, an intruder in my own life.

The self-loathing escalated as I began to enjoy, even if only for a moment, the release that came with spilling my semen inside another man's anus. Sometimes they squirmed, their buttocks shaking back and forth. Others were perfectly still in supplication, an almost obsequious display of intercourse. The only constant was my dominant position above and behind them. I pulled myself out, wiped myself on the already stained sheets, and fell into the cold embrace of the bed. I would light a cigarette and exhale as each man engaged in some version of post-coital ritual, which ended with me alone in a by-the-hour dirty hotel room. These episodes were not special or significant enough to differentiate; each just a meaningless, gin-laced haze, hardly even its own memory.

"That was amazing," a man named James, or maybe Jack, exclaimed as he tried to cuddle after one rendezvous. His mop of black hair was sculpted with so much mousse it had remained perfect despite rough foreplay.

I didn't dignify his comment with a response. Instead, I fixed my gaze on the mirror across from the bed. The frame was painted black and chipped. Paint was peeling from it in curls like the skins of an eggplant. James or Jack took my reticence as an invitation to continue trying to tease conversation out of me.

"Aren't you the strong, silent type?" He laughed sugges-tively. "You've certainly proven your strength. Guess we have to prove the silent part now." He laughed in a sing-song way.

I turned to look him in the eye as he was crawling towards me on the bed. Just as he was about to rest his head on my shoulder, I intercepted him with a shove that knocked him completely off the bed.

"What the hell?" He spat at me, no longer coy. "You're crazy, man!" James or Jack or whatever the hell his name was grabbed his clothes from the chair next to the bed. His skin hung from his body like a loose-fitting dress. It was sallow and lacked muscle tone. He had red-rimmed eyes that watered. Maybe he was crying, I couldn't be certain. The man stormed out of the room, slamming the door behind him. I stubbed out my cigarette in a tray already filled to the brim with half-smoked shells and ash belonging to the men who'd used the room before me, perhaps the only remaining artifacts of their secrets and sins. I picked up the glass of gin beside the bed and drank from it until I could no longer feel the burning sensation in my gut. All the while the ghost of a familiar man watched me from the mirror across from the bed. The handsome man, no longer clean-shaven but still attractive, whose hair fell recklessly in short waves no longer carefully pomaded, who sat tangled in post-coital sheets with drops of dry spittle and gin crusting at the corner of his mouth, stared a long, blank stare. I grabbed the now empty glass and flung it with all the strength I could muster at the mirror and screamed at the top of my lungs as it shattered into countless glass splinters. No one knocked at the door.

I walked over to a small window, looked into the nighttime. There was something about a city skyline at night. The buildings glittered like they were made of a thousand imprisoned stars. The night sky contained in tall concrete structures. Perhaps I was a lost star, captured and held hostage in some grand skyscraper, one building among many in a phantasmagoria.

I didn't stay in the city overnight. I returned to my house on Elm Street, to my sleeping wife. I crawled into bed, trying not to wake her. Eleanor heard me or sensed my presence beside her, and she wrapped her arms around my body. I shivered, afraid she might detect the scent of strange men on my skin. The amalgamation of foreign sweat and cologne and a hint of sex were most certainly oozing from my pores despite the attempt at concealment with a pair of freshly laundered flannel pajamas.

"You're back so late," more an observation than question, spoken in a tone heavy with sleep or worry.

I didn't try to concoct some bogus excuse but offered simply a not insincere apology. Eleanor buried her face in my shoulder and tightened her embrace. She must have smelled them on me, I worried with mounting terror. Just as I was about to pull away, cast aside the bedsheets and run from the room, to where I wasn't sure, I felt dampness on my neck. Eleanor was crying. Silently her tears painted trails down the side of my neck, eliciting goose pimples as they retreated inside my nightshirt and down my shoulder. I turned over to face my wife. Her eyes were shells, empty but for the dampness spilling from them. I wiped her cheeks slowly, affectionately. The moon's silver shadow illuminated her pale face, invoking some sort of celestial beauty I had never noticed before. We didn't say anything but stared as if we were looking at each other for the very first time. It was only in that moment that I realized I wasn't the only one in pain. I had broken Andros, I had broken myself, and I had broken, perhaps the most innocent of all of us, my sweet Eleanor.

I wrapped my arms around her tightly, wanting, needing to make love to her. Determined to be a man, to be a husband, to love and to be loved, I pulled her silk nightgown up over her hips. Determination pumped through my body. My heart beat hard. Eleanor didn't need coaxing. Her lips were on top of mine, pressing, damp. I couldn't help the thoughts threading through my mind. Could she taste the salt of another man inside my mouth, on my lips? I pressed against her in what I imagined were pleasurable movements, rubbing my erection rhythmically inside her. A soft sound, like a purr, emerged from her parted lips. His lips. His lips were the parting of the sea, the place I went to be myself. I thought of his open mouth, his tongue licking the upper lip slightly, back and forth, rapid, a little dance that teased me so. Her lips weren't so thick. Narrow, the stone jetty jutting like the land's arm towards the sea, the strip of land I followed towards the sea, to the place I went to be alone, with him. She bit down on her bottom lip as the purring continued.

I was inside of her, on top of her. She pulled at my pajama shirt; I worried it would tear. He had torn my shirt, sending buttons flying in all directions, hitting, snapping against the floor. Waves of warmth undulated from below; I retreated, the wave retreating from the shore. The shadow of black hair decorating his chin, the prickle against the palm of my hand. I took myself in my hand, thinking of Andros, thinking of the edge of his tongue gliding upwards, pleasure, pleasure. Release. I spilled the sticky white on the inside of her thick white thigh. She lay panting a few moments before getting out of bed and leaving the room to clean herself off. When she returned, climbing beside me, throwing her arms around me and nuzzling her face in my shoulder, I was asleep. At least, I pretended to be.

The next morning it was as if the night was nothing but a dream. Neither of us spoke of it, and Eleanor went about the perfunctory details of her day as if nothing had changed. It was Saturday and Michael was opening the store. I sat at the kitchen table drinking a cup of black coffee as I read *The News-*

Times. The morning headline told of Danbury-local Marian Anderson becoming the first African American singer to perform at the New York City Met. I perused the subsequent article, wanting to care more about her success and what it meant for African Americans but falling inevitably and self-ishly into a bout of discontent. The bacon hissed from the frying pan as Eleanor let it crisp. Her paisley dress was pressed and her apron was ruffled. Her hair coiffed and makeup erased any trace of tears. Georgie cooed from his highchair as he drank from his warmed bottle. He stopped from time to time to look at his mother at the stove, and, reassured by her presence, resumed suckling the rubber nipple of his bottle. Outside the window, the rose of sharon bush had lost its leaves, and I found myself missing its late summer lavender flowers. The only sounds that came from the kitchen were sips, sizzling, and the turning of the newspaper pages. We were the picture of bour-geois contentment.

CHAPTER TWENTY-ONE

Andros—My Heart,
        The memory of you burns like the breath of strangers.
I look in the bedsheets hoping you are hiding in the stained mess,
but, alas, there is only me and drunken degenerates.

I pray that you are less miserable, but, and articulating this
makes me a selfish person (but we both already know this to be
true), I also hope that you are just as unhappy as I am. I confess I
would be insane with jealousy if I were to find out that you had
moved on, found someone else to fill your nights and to share
your dreams. I know I have no right to ask you to wait for me.
We would be old and gray by then, anyhow.

Would it be wrong of me to ask you to visit us in Connecticut? Eleanor cared for your company and would be delighted,
I'm sure. Please consider it. I cannot stand the absence any
longer.

Your Forever Love

* * *

Dearest George,

Your recent letter was met with a lightness I haven't experienced since you left Lebanon. Your fears are my fears. I spend my days and nights drinking, sometimes painting. I have a show in Beirut in a few weeks. An elderly gentlemen named Boutros, you may remember him from one of our nights at Les Caves du Roy, has become my patron. I am to have a showing of my work in a gallery. This newfound success (if you can call one show after a decade of painting success) may complicate a trip to the States. Let us not dismiss the idea, merely put it aside for now.

Paul Guiragossian has become a close friend. He invites me to dinner sometimes with his wife Juliette. If not for his mentorship, I believe I would give in to the bottle. Paul says painting is his first language and a true artist should only speak through his craft. I speak fluently with a brush in one hand, a glass of arak in the other, and a cigarette dangling from my lips. This is expression. This is language. You took my already limited ability to communicate with you when you left; Greek, Arabic, English—it is all meaningless. Images are my only words now. With that, I leave you with this...

A canvas unrolled into a raw painting, dark smudges of color blurred into a shadowy image. Two distinct figures twisted at the center, in ecstasy? In wrath? In redemption? Surrounding the figures were black mountains and a gray sea. Silhouettes of buildings filled the panorama. I could not help but think this was our story, two ill-fated lovers tangled in each other, set against the backdrop of a dark Lebanon.

* * *

Winter assumed a shade of blue-gray that reminded me of Andros's eyes when he was angry. I stopped traveling into the city as often, reducing my visits to monthly or bi-monthly trips.

Eleanor stopped visiting with her friends. Her coterie of female companions, many of whom she'd known since childhood, had taken to calling on me at the store to check on the well-being of their dear El.

"She hasn't met us for lunch for three weeks now," Mona Thomas whined in her high-pitched voice. Hands on her wide hips and black rhinestone-crusted cat-eye glasses sliding down her tiny nose, Mona continued, "We *always* have lunch and then do our shopping Tuesday afternoons. She won't even phone me back, George." She emphasized my name in an accusatory tone while pushing her glasses closer to her beady eyes.

"Mona, I'm sorry, but I don't know what to tell you. She's been under the weather." I focused on the inventory in front of me.

"Is it the baby? Is Georgie, okay?" She kept her hands on her hips and began tapping her patent-leather heel. Apparently, Mona was not leaving without what she deemed a satisfactory response.

"It's the influenza. She didn't want you to worry or try to come by. She's afraid you'll catch it."

Her hands dropped to her side. "Oh gee, George. Influenza? Oh gee." She adjusted her glasses and pulled her wool coat tighter as if she might catch the flu simply by saying the word.

After Mona's visit, her friends stopped visiting the store. Even when Eleanor didn't resume her weekly rituals, the girls didn't bother inquiring with me. But when I asked my wife why she wasn't socializing, she responded with "no reason." It was then that I became concerned. And it was then that I started to take stock of all the little things I hadn't cared enough about to notice during the last few months.

Eleanor was typically scrupulous in her housekeeping.

Dishes crusted with old food were now piling in the sink, some-times for days, until I washed them myself. Laundered clothes lay unfolded on the bed. Piles of ash overwhelmed trays of mostly smoked cigarettes. During the day, Eleanor had started wearing her light pink damask satin house coat fastened with two buttons at the waist. She liked to dig her hands deep in the wide pockets. She kept her brown curls swept up in a matching pink scarf. She chain-smoked between washing diapers and playing with Georgie—the only responsibility she hadn't shirked. She even stopped painting her nails.

Eleanor had curled up inside herself and disappeared. I reached out, touched her cheek, but she didn't move. She was lost somewhere behind the skin, beneath the gray half-moons cradling her eyes. I wondered how long they had been there. The capricious spirit of my wife had jumped off a bridge. This woman beside me was a breathing corpse, a ghost. She had been filled with joie de vivre once, but that had been pulled from her like unwanted hair, plucked and yanked until she was smooth and lifeless. I had done this to her. I couldn't help but wonder what her life would be like had she never met me, never loved me. I imagined Eleanor, radiant in a new dress, fussing over a husband who adored her, making silly faces at their own infant son. I imagined Eleanor laughing. She used to laugh once.

* * *

"Honey, why don't you see your friends today?" I said to her one morning after she burned two slices of toast and poured me a cup of lukewarm coffee. "It might be good for you."

"You care about what's good for me now?" Though her voice was flat, drained, a familiar flicker sparked in her question.

"That's not fair."

"Isn't it though?"

"What's with this petulance?" I shook the pages of the newspaper, straightening out the creases that bisected the local news.

Eleanor huffed. "Despite what you think of me, I'm not an idiot." She turned away and walked out of the kitchen, leaving a pot of boiling squash for koosa spitting at the stove. Her eyes looked like muddy puddles.

What did she mean? Did she know about the affairs? Did she think I was with other women or, God forbid, did she know the truth? I wanted to vomit but settled for a few bites of burnt toast.

The spat escalated into a full-fledged brawl moments later. I had resumed my breakfast only to be disturbed by the edge of a heel flying past my face.

"Tell me, George, was it always about the money? Did you ever really love me?" Tears leaked from already puffy eyes.

"What are you talking about? Of course. How could you think such a thing?"

"How could I not?" Her shoulders slumped, her tone almost quiet, Eleanor walked towards the doorway.

I sat in silence, no longer willing to lie to this poor woman, this woman who really did love me.

And then all at once she yelled, "Jerk!" Wiry wisps of brown hair escaped from the restraint of her light pink head scarf. The canvas of her face was painted vitriolic hues. Her red cheeks puffed out with her words. Spittle stretched in the corners of her mouth like spider webs in the corner of a windowsill. She shouted a skein of insults at me all while standing with her arms fixed on her wide hips.

"Jesus, Eleanor!" I got up so hard from my seat that I

knocked over the wicker-back chair. The crash slapped the air and disrupted Georgie from his morning nap.

The squeal of the baby drew Eleanor away from me and provided a welcome egress. After lowering the gas so the kossa simmered softly, I grabbed my bowler hat and coat from the coat rack by the door in the kitchen and dashed into the biting cold of the January day.

The sunshine itself seemed to freeze on the sidewalk. The sky was blanched, gray clouds wove through it like the veins in marble. The air had teeth; it gnashed and nibbled at faces indiscriminately. Week-old snow lining the sidewalk more closely resembled the brownish muck found on the bank of the Still River. I pulled my wool coat tighter and dipped my head against the aggressive kiss of the wind.

Michael was already at the store. He was cashing out an older woman with a white bulb of hair at the counter. A few other patrons decorated the aisles, some said "good morning" and "hey George," the salutations offering much-needed warmth missing from my day. *None of you really know me. Friends, cousins, brother, mother, wife. You don't know who I am. I tell you "I'm well," a pleasant shade of pale blue. But really, I'm the color of a midnight rainstorm. Aberrant winds rage inside my gut daily. My mind is occupied by a dense black haze. Most of you have known me my whole life and yet none of you know who I really am.*

The old woman left the store with a single bag of groceries and a pleasant, tight-lipped smile accented in red lipstick.

"You and Eleanor have another row?" Michael walked around from behind the counter and straightened his black necktie.

"How'd you know?" I took off my coat and grabbed a freshly pressed apron from the hook behind the counter.

"Your face, brother. How you're so good at poker is beyond me." He flashed a bright smile.

"I don't know what I'm doing wrong." I ran my hand through my slicked-back hair and placed my hat on the counter. *More lies. I'm doing everything wrong. Everything. She has every right to be angry with me.*

Before Michael could provide any advice, Ummi came from around the back of the store.

"George, habibi, I need you to teach me to drive today."

Michael and I exchanged looks, and then I asked, "Why do you need to know how to drive, Um? Michael and I take you where you need to go." Teaching a fifty-something woman who had never so much as sat in the driver's seat of a vehicle before was definitely not on my list of things to do.

"It is important. I need to go to Mimi Shadeed's house," she said matter-of-factly as she fastened and unfastened the top button of her brown wool coat. A matching fur hat christened her fair head. Once, her hair had been the color of the sun. Now, it had faded to the color of a January day.

"Why do you need to go to Mimi Shadeed's and why can't one of us take you?" I was losing patience. I walked around her towards the back of the store.

"Because I want to watch the Danny Thomas Show. She has a television." She left the top button unfastened and brushed her hair softly behind the curve of her ear. Her expression never changed from serious. "I don't want to rely on you boys forever."

"Fine, Ummi. I'll teach you after lunch." I shook my head and slammed the door to the shop kitchen behind me.

I imagined that Ummi nodded her head in triumph and walked out the back door and upstairs to her apartment. I sat on the worn wooden stool, the seat of which was chipped and dented in places from years of constant use. The radio sat in the windowsill beside the stool. I wiped a smudge of dust from the top and turned the dial to the news. A British man with a tight, polished voice that had the consistency of pudding pontificated on the importance of taking the proper precautions in severe winter weather.

"Deep snow and freezing temperature continue across Britain, leaving much of the country cut off from essential supplies." He continued espousing the value of preparedness, which seemed to me irrelevant if many parts of the country were already deprived of supplies.

I pulled a cut of meat from the freezer. Though wrapped in coarse white paper and bound with twine, the crimson loin was crusted in ice. I brushed the flecks away as if they were frozen tears stuck to nothing more than a chapped, raw cheek in winter. My knives were already arranged from the night before. I had washed and disinfected them so that they glinted and reflected clear images. I could still smell the bleach and blood, but they were familiar, comforting scents, much like the spices associated with favorite childhood dishes. Bleach, blood, and the warm nuances of allspice and ground cumin. Once upon a time, I resented the smells of the butcher's kitchen. Now, among them was the only place I felt calm.

* * *

Uncle Taffy came into the store later that afternoon.

"I'm going to teach your mother how to drive today." While the old man was dressed in pressed trousers, a camel-hair jacket, and a gray bowler hat, he was wearing a pair of tan slippers.

Before I could say anything about his choice of footwear, Michael interjected. "Uncle Taf, you don't drive."

"Right you are! George is going to show me. It's nothing."

227

He dug his hands deep in his pockets and stood in front of the counter, grinning at me. "Celia has the right idea, and I can't have my sister driving all around town while her brother walks like a damn hobo. And besides, I'm her brother. It's my responsibility to teach her."

Michael chuckled and shot me a devilish look.

"When did I become the resident driving instructor?" I shoved the stack of inventory across the counter.

"You know how to drive," Uncle Taffy stated and shrugged his shoulders.

"So does Michael." I returned the glance and smiled.

"Michael drives like a demon! I won't have him putting my life in danger!" Uncle Taffy walked backwards as if he was afraid of me for simply offering the alternative.

I knew I couldn't argue with that logic; Michael was a notoriously reckless driver. When we were in high school, he had borrowed Bayee's Lincoln to take some girl he was sweet on to the fair. Somehow, and to this day he claims not to know how it happened, Michael nearly took out a hot dog vendor, crashing the Lincoln into the purveyor's stand and crushing the steaming dogs with the tires. The damage to the car wasn't all that bad, but the hot dog vendor was quite angry and the beating Michael got from Bayee reflected that. My brother had to pay the man every week until the following summer when his debt had been repaid. Unfortunately, the incident didn't impact his driving habits.

"Do you really need to learn how to drive today?" I asked in a final attempt to free myself of this untenable situation.

Uncle Taffy smiled. "I'll meet you in front of the store at close." The sound of his slippers flapping on the linoleum floor as he exited stuck in my head like a bad song for the remainder of the day.

A punctual man, Uncle Taffy was in front of the store, still donning slippers, exactly ten minutes before I switched the sign to "closed" and locked the doors. It was a Saturday, and we closed early so it was still light. The day was the kind of cold that weighed down your skin, flattened it, and wrung the warmth from your bones. The sky was dull, a gray-white shadow of its usual complexion. Muddy snow had collected in piles, bifurcated by the mostly clear sidewalk.

"I'm ready to drive, buddy boy. Look at my special driving gloves." He modeled a pair of green woolen mittens that were so thick they would probably interfere with gripping the steering wheel.

"Uncle Taffy, do you think you should wear more practical shoes?" I tried to be as kind as possible in my criticism of his footwear.

"Can't get more practical than these slippers. It's like wearing pillows on your feet." He bragged, "I've started a new trend, George. Taffy Salame is an innovator of fashion."

When Uncle Taffy began referring to himself in the third person, any point that contradicted his was automatically moot. "Well then, let's go, Cristobal Balenciaga," I smirked as I opened the driver's side door of the Lincoln for Uncle Taffy.

I sat next to my uncle on the bench seat. Before I could even begin to instruct, Uncle Taffy pulled a handkerchief from his coat pocket and wiped the dashboard and steering wheel in a vigorous, circular motion. I chuckled quietly, suddenly grateful for my senile uncle. He was genuinely oblivious to the car-wreck of my life. It was a much-needed break from the questions, stares, and concern of every other member of the family.

"Germs, Georgie, germs," he muttered as he cleaned.

I rolled my eyes, sat back, and braced myself for the longest five-mile drive of my life.

After starting the ignition and pulling out of the spot, a

process that took nearly a half hour, Uncle Taffy managed to get the car in a stop-and-go sort of cruising. He stalled repeatedly in rather inconvenient spots since he refused to drive on empty side streets and insisted on driving on Main Street. Cars blasted their horns and drove around him, to which he responded by waving and smiling. When I thought the experience couldn't get much worse, we got to a hill. Instead of avoiding it, he chugged upwards with surprising ease, only stalling once. When we began to drive downhill in what should have been the least stressful portion of the ride, Uncle Taffy decided that it was time for a cigarette. Taking his hands off the wheel, he reached in his pocket for his pack of Old Golds and lighter.

"Don't let go!" I grabbed the wheel just as it veered towards the curb at a rather fast speed.

"Law of momentum, Georgie, boy."

"That makes no sense. Stop the car. Now." I had guided the vehicle off the road and along the curb into a parking position. Uncle Taffy sat in the driver's seat puffing away at his cigarette.

"It's okay, Georgie boy. I needed some nicotine. This driving thing is a bit stressful."

"You're done driving. I'm taking us home." I got out of the car and walked around to the driver's side.

"Wasn't that fun?" he asked as he slid over to the passenger's seat.

"Delightful."

I suppose there was something delightful in the fact that even when life was a car speeding out-of-control down a hill, my family was unchanged.

CHAPTER TWENTY-TWO

A ndros,

    I have suffered the memory of a perfect sunrise, spent with your head on my chest. I reached for you in my sleep last night. I searched for your hard body, to pull you close to me in the deepest sea of dreams only to wake to the realization that you were not there. The shape of the person next to me was soft in ways that you are not soft, curved in places you don't curve. I woke to the unsettling absence of your snoring. I had only wanted to bury my face in the nest of your chest hair, to inhale the salty sweet dew of your skin. Last night I reached for you only to drift into a familiar abyss, the unwelcome embrace of someone else. The worst kind of waking dream. I closed my eyes again to float back to you, to the sea, to the beach that night in Byblos. I hope tomorrow night our dreams will cross, and I'll find you there, curled beside me in bed as I nuzzle the little hairs on your arms; they will tickle my lips and the inside of my nose and I'll smile as I fall back to sleep.

    Yours Forever,

George

* * *

When I remember the day I left Eleanor, I tell myself she wasn't crying into a pot of boiling grape leaves as I carried my trunk into the kitchen. I pretend she yelled and threw a shoe at me. The quiet shame in her tears was unbearable to recall. When I remember that afternoon in July, I imagine my son was not sitting in his highchair, arms extended towards me, as I turned around and walked out the door. I pretend he was taking a nap or playing with his worn stuffed duck.

That morning began as many other mornings had. I woke up tired, having suffered another night of interrupted sleep, dreams all-too real yet not real enough. I went downstairs where Eleanor was making breakfast. Toasted Arabic bread with zatar and creamy labneh. I savored the demanding zatar spices dominating the flavor of the breakfast, the punch of aggression but with the caress of a lover's good morning kiss. Delicious. Georgie was chewing on the nose of his stuffed duck and cooing some unintelligible baby speak. The windows were open, but no cool breeze moved the white lace curtains. The air was so thick and still that movements or conversation would leave an indelible print upon it. Eleanor was silent; the only sound she made came from the clanking of dishes in the sink or on the stove. The most recent letter from Andros was concealed beneath the morning paper I was feigning interest in. He would not be visiting. I knew this already. Had known this. When I remember this morning, I blame my impetuousness on the heat. It was too hot to be miserable. But it could have been the gin I was imbibing in my porcelain coffee mug. When I think back, I didn't just get up from the table, go to my room, pack my essential belongings in my trunk, kiss Georgie, and tell Eleanor I was moving out without another word. When I remember the day I left her, I tell her something she can keep with her, something she can curl up with in the middle of the long night.

When I remember the day I left my wife, I am not a coward.

* * *

The store on the corner of Beaver and Elm greeted me with indifference, as if we had no shared history. It did not know me then. I was strange. I was different. I was liberated. I was alone. The cedar tree in the yard, separate, dissimilar from the native elms and birches surrounding it, was all at once familiar. It offered me kinship; we had a tangled past, but our future was one and the same. I lugged my trunk up the steps to our apartment, it never stopped, after all, being mine. I was born there. I grew up there. We were one. The creak of the door hinge confronted me. I was at this threshold again.

Ummi hardly looked up from her magazine. An issue of *Mademoiselle*. When did she start reading that? A cigarette balanced between her thin fingers, threads of smoke curled towards the ceiling fan. The ashtray beside her contained a smattering of shells and ash. A breakfast plate held the remnants of a half a grapefruit, the soft citrus bulb scraped clean, just the blushing hint of flesh still detectable. The radio played Beethoven and the stove bubbled and sang a familiar song.

"Why do you have your trunk?" She didn't look at me. She sensed something wasn't quite right just as she knew when a dish or bowl was returned to an incorrect place in the cabinet.

"I'm moving back home."

She looked up from her magazine and brought the cigarette to her painted lips. Before replying, she inhaled deeply and blew out a cloud of smoke. She flicked ash into the tray beside her on the table. "With Eleanor and the baby?"

"No." I stood, immovable in the threshold. Stagnating in the heat.

"I don't understand."

"You understand perfectly."

"Why?"

"I don't love her. I'm miserable."

"Those things don't matter. You're a husband."

The conversation was stagnating in the heat. She was not going to give in. There was only one thing left to say.

"I'm attracted to men." The heat was unbearable, crawling up my limbs and clawing at my skin, eliciting pools of sweat with its talons.

She stared, directly, forcefully. At first, she didn't move. She sat and stared. A thousand summers came and went. And then, mercifully, terrifyingly, she got up from the table. Ummi walked slowly towards me. Without a word, she slapped me hard across the face. My cheek burned with its rebuke. She turned around and walked out of the kitchen. She didn't say a word.

* * *

Ummi was not speaking to me. Eleanor was not speaking to me. Michael was confused. Uncle Taffy was wearing pajamas around town to match his slippers. People looked differently at me. Side glances and hushed voices seemed to follow me like my own shadow. I knew I was the rapidly beating heart of a fresh scandal in Danbury. This was, after all, 1955. Men do not leave their wives and children. Mostly, they don't love other men.

"Just because a man loves another man, it doesn't make him less of one."

I tried to explain to Ummi one night as she sat in silence reading a letter from Raina as I attempted to peruse the newspaper. She wouldn't speak to me. She had allowed me to move back home, although the only indicators that this was even acceptable was the fact that she didn't throw my things into the yard and she fed me. While she permitted me to eat her cooking, I did notice the lack of tenderness in preparing the dishes she typically presented with her brand of affection. Meals were cold, bland. Spices—signs of maternal love—were missing from all the food she made for me upon my return.

I had hoped Michael would be supportive. I told him I was unhappy, that I didn't love Eleanor anymore, that I actually never had.

"I love you brother, you know that, but you don't leave your wife and kid. You just don't do that." His tone was missing its joviality, its horseplay. He was serious. He was worried for me.

The bottle of gin on my bedside table did not judge or rebuke me. I was safe in the fiery embrace of my favorite drink. It reinforced my decision. It whispered bitterly, sweetly in my ear that I had done the right thing, that I had to do it. My only sanctuary was in the arms of a bottle. Such a cold, empty place. But it was safe. Here, it didn't matter who I loved.

I had been gone for three months before I tried to visit Georgie. I wanted, needed, to hold my year-old son in my arms. I missed the way he scrunched his face for no reason, a fan of wrinkles overtaking his tiny nose. When I left, he had started saying "Dada." How many new words had he learned in the intervening weeks? Sometimes, when he was sleepy, he'd sigh a long sound that reminded me of an old, frustrated man. It was beautiful.

I showed up at the house when I knew Georgie would still be awake. He would have finished his supper, Eleanor would have just bathed him, his brownish-blond curls damp but still wispy, crowning his little head like rays of sunshine. I walked up the brick steps to the front porch and knocked on the door. It was a cool evening, a reprieve from the heat of a long summer. Would I be granted reprieve, too? I waited a few minutes, but there was no answer. I could see the lamp alight in the living room window and hear the faint hum of the radio. A soft rain began to fall.

I started pounding on the door. "Eleanor!" I shouted between the knocks. There was no doubt in my mind she could hear me.

After several more minutes, she answered the door in her light pink housecoat. Georgie was wearing his blue cotton pajamas with the ducks on them. His red stuffed duck was tucked under his chubby arm while he rubbed his eyes with the other hand.

"I would like to see my son."

"No." She moved to shut the door in my face, but I put my shoe inside the door before she could.

"You can't do that. He's my son!"

"You're not a father just like you're not a husband! That's what you wanted, isn't it?" Eleanor stepped backwards. Her eyes had faded, drained of purpose, of contentment. She had a face full of life once—lines fanned from her eyes when she smiled, a smile that dominated her face, rendering all other features light and full. This was not the face that greeted me. This face was empty; it was a face full of pain. The smile had broken, laugh lines had splintered into a web of wrinkles and puffy, bloodshot eyes, emblematic of sleeplessness. This was

the face I had created, a face that reflected the pain and emptiness inside my own soul. It belonged to me as much as the baby
in her arms.

"Honey, please." I moved inside the foyer. I brought my
hands to her forearms gently. "Please. He's my son." I looked
past her into the kitchen that lay just beyond the dark hallway.
I could see the calendar hanging on the wall above the cabinet
of spices. I noticed it had remained on the month of July, stuck,
immovable as if the act of not turning the page prevented the
passage of time itself. If she didn't turn the page, August would
never come, and she would have never been left alone. Instead,
she had become the month of July, sweating, burning, isolated,
stubbornly refusing to move forward. Eleanor must have felt as
if no other woman in the world had ever been abandoned by
her husband. She wanted to pretend July 15th had never
happened, her life stood still on that day. Her small protesta-
tion, her refusal to change the calendar, was the only agency
she had in an untenable situation.

Eleanor stared blankly at me. She didn't respond even to
the sincerity of my plea. The last thing she said as the door
closed behind me, "You left me. You left."

I was left outside in the now hard-pouring rain. I had
created this new world, this new place where I stood alone on
dark steps as rain fell all around me.

I made it to the sidewalk before the tightness in my throat
was too much. I swallowed hard the lump rising from my gut.
Warmth, all at once, leaked from my eyes. I fell to my knees in
the middle of the sidewalk on Elm Street. The elm trees were
wrapped in gray solitude. The familiar houses of my youth
looked on in reproach. The lights winked in windows, sanctuaries. The inside of my mouth was empty, dry. My hands grabbed
the back of my head and pulled down or fell forward, forehead
meeting the hard ground, rain dancing, slanted, frenzied in the

streetlight. The sky was darker than it was only moments ago but blurred, distorted by the tears. Life was darker, distorted. Sounds came up from some depth inside me I didn't know existed, a flood of pain, insides twisted and writhing. Snot trailed in rivers down a new landscape of face, a fractured landscape. Despite the cold rain, my cheeks burned, a mottled pink, a botched blush. I experienced the urge to wretch right there on the sidewalk, in front of the white colonial with the front porch, the house I called home once, the house where my son lived. I couldn't breathe; I could only sob. My entire body shook with the force of a grown man's tears.

The light in the living room window turned off and the white house on Elm Street was dark, indistinguishable from the stormy atmosphere. The only sound was a man crying like a boy in the nighttime and the boy he wept for crying inside the dark house behind him.

* * *

I was sure the blood in my veins had dried up and turned to dust. The gin didn't even burn anymore. It was difficult to discern sober thoughts from drunk ones. Everything hurt = ringing out a customer, small talk, smiling at my brother's jokes. The knowing glances of strangers and friends pricked like icy rain on naked skin. I drank more gin. Winter came again.

"You're starting to smell like your father," Ummi said one night after another silent dinner. She was scraping the remnants of stuffed eggplant into the garbage can.

"What's that supposed to mean?" I closed the book of Khalil Gibran poetry, not concerned about losing my place in a book I'd read a thousand or so times.

"You stink." She wouldn't look at me. "Like booze."

I didn't know how to respond to the accusation.

"God is punishing you." The sound of the fork clanking against the plate struck nerves as well as scraps of food.

I kept my mouth shut, choosing to stare out the window. The night was thick beyond the glass panes. There seemed to be traces of light, a smattering of stars, a shell of moon. The cold temperature left a film of frost on the inside of the window. I remembered when I was a young boy I used to trace my finger in the frost on the window pane, scraping it so it crumpled soft like wet dust. The warmth of my skin melted it and left shapes and designs in the glass.

It would be days before we'd speak again.

* * *

I curled up in bed with ghosts and shadows. The night was made of gin and shadows. Blackbird wings fluttered outside. The sky was made of repressed dreams and lost memories. And blackbird wings. The bottle was almost empty. How many had I gone through in a day? In a week? How did I still function at work? Did I function? People complained yesterday. Michael said I didn't order enough bread. We ran out. Damn the pita bread! Let them make their own bread! Michael asked if I was okay. I stormed into the back room and took a bottle from behind a stack of old, yellowing cookbooks. A blackbird tapped at the window. No one else saw it. No one else was there.

I woke up in the morning. Dust mites floated in the sunlight peeking through the diaphanous white curtains. The day itself was sunny, but my mind was unclear, foggy with half-remembered images and desires. My head was heavy, but another part was energized and erect. I dragged myself to the bathroom for relief. A teapot screamed from the kitchen. The distant mumbling of the morning news came from the radio. I believed it was Sunday.

"You're coming to church." Ummi placed a bowl of labneh next to a plate of toasted Arabic bread seasoned with *zatar* spices. I hadn't been inside St. Anthony's since my wedding day.

"Wasn't planning on it." I helped myself to some hot water and tea leaves from the silver canister. Ummi's pack of Old Golds was laying on the counter beside the canister, and I took a cigarette as I sat at the kitchen table. While the tea steeped in a ceramic mug, I lit and inhaled deeply.

She pursed her lips and narrowed her eyes. "That's part of your problem." She was sitting across from me and helping herself to some bread and a dollop of thick yogurt.

I chose not to respond to her comment. We ate breakfast in silence except for the radio chatter coming from the corner of the kitchen.

As Ummi readied herself for mass, fixing her white-blonde coif and tracing her lips in pink, I, too decided to dress in my Sunday best. Perhaps in the hope of getting back in Ummi's good graces, I spritzed some cologne, adjusted a necktie, and pulled on a jacket. When my mother was opening the door to walk outside, I was behind her, ready to accompany her on the ten-minute walk. She didn't look satisfied as she noticed my presence beside her.

The brisk morning air was soothing. My head cleared as we walked, but my hands were shaking and my joints were stiff. My body was not in good condition for an hour of sitting on hard wooden pews, kneeling, and standing on command. As we quickened our pace, we were a few minutes past ten, I thought back to a conversation with Andros, his words sticking in my head. *I've got God in my heart and you in my bed. What more do I need of religion?*

Father Hayek droned on about the Gospel of Mark. I didn't really listen. It was strange to be sitting in St. Anthony's again. My brother and his family beside me. Jesus on the cross above the altar. The altar filled with pink and white carnations, defiant, as if it wasn't winter. Light illuminating stained-glass windows like vivid paintings. The priest in his garb, the smell of burning incense, the vapid pedantic sound of his voice. The organ played all the familiar songs. All familiar faces, as if no one had left, as if life hadn't happened in the intervening years. Everything was the same. But nothing was the same either.

I noticed Eleanor was not sitting with her brother and his wife. Perhaps my intentions were not simply to please Ummi. I was selfishly hoping to capture a moment, surreptitious, precious, where I could see my baby boy, even if only at a distance. That would have satisfied my soul in a way the sermon was failing to do.

Mass let out. Michael would be coming over for Sunday supper with Marlene and their two sons. Uncle Taffy would also be joining—he had dressed in his best slippers and robe today, thankfully wearing a long black camel-hair coat that mostly concealed his bizarre sartorial choices. We all walked home together after mass.

"How you holding up, brother?" Michael asked as we sauntered behind the womenfolk.

"Fine."

"You see Eleanor or the baby at all?"

"Tried. And failed."

"That's it? You tried and failed? So don't fail." His tone cut in an unfamiliar way.

"You have no idea." A new edge to my voice. "Where do you get off telling me what to do? Huh? You have no idea." I could feel my words shaking inside my mouth before I spit them out.

Michael stopped walking and grabbed my arm. He looked

at me, eye to eye, brother to brother, man to man. "You're a father, God damn it. You don't have the right to fail."

I stared at him and let his words prick at my skin and turn me inside-out. I couldn't respond and was grateful when Michael started walking again. Marlene and Ummi were a block ahead of us, indifferent or unaware of the exchange that had just taken place.

I could think of nothing else for the rest of the day. I did not have the right to fail. I was a father.

* * *

Winter became the tear stains on my pillow. Spring was warmer but no less cold. I drank just as much and felt just as much. I went to Eleanor's house on Elm Street and waited for her to leave after countless unanswered commotions at the front door. She never left. She never went outside. The only person who came and went from the house was her brother, Kamil. He didn't acknowledge me either. I was the dirt on the bottom of his shoe. The house began to change. It seemed unused. Curtains were never moved, never opened or closed for morning light or evening privacy. The porch furniture remained in storage even as the days grew longer and warmer. Sometimes I could hear Georgie's sounds from their insular world. People said his uncle took him outside and to the store and the park. There were sightings mentioned to me in passing comments, offering me kaleidoscopic snapshots of his life. He was walking now. His hair was curly, brown ringlets with a golden hue, like his tita. He had teeth. He liked the slide at Rogers Park. He screamed and cried until his uncle let him repeat the activity again and again and again. He clapped when he reached his uncle's waiting arms at the end of the long yellow slide.

One evening, many evenings, I drank. The apartment was dark; Ummi was out. I shut my eyes and the world exploded around me, leaving me shaking and alone. Lights came from somewhere. Stars? The light in his eyes was a star to wish upon. If I still believed in wishes. A flood rose from below and then out, onto the floor. I was swimming, swimming to him. I swore I was almost to shore, his little chubby arms outstretched, waiting. *Wait just a little longer, my son.*

Ummi took me in her arms. I didn't know when she returned. Maybe she was home all along? I knew her by her hair: yellow and white. Stars, planets, celestial. I thought maybe she was crying as she pulled me to her breast, but I was weeping and drunk and the dampness on my shoulder was probably my own tears. I was a child, a young boy. Night terrors seized me and she fought them off. But these weren't terrors contained in the nighttime. They were real. They were drunken mirages washing over me, and I was drowning. I could have sworn I saw dampness on her cheek, her eyes, unfocused, red not blue. The last thing I remember before passing out: Ummi's soft words in my ear. *Everything will be okay, habibi.*

* * *

My Heart,

Some days it feels that it was only yesterday I bumped into you in the souk on Rue Weygand. Today, I want so badly to forget. To forget you. I want to stop traveling on roads that assume the shape of your body tangled in bedsheets, but there would be no roads remaining. I want to rip your image from my memory and burn it. I wish the sun would burn the sky black so I would no longer be reminded of the blue-gray color of your eyes. I long to purge my heart of you the way I purge my body of too much alcohol. The heaviness inside my head is unrelenting. I give up. And yet just as I pull away from the memory of you, some days I push towards it. Just yesterday I needed to remember, to cling to thoughts of you like life breaths. I wanted nothing more than to trace the edges of your most recent canvas with my fingers, inhale the edges of your face. Create a new memory of you only to rip it to pieces once again. And then I wondered if the hair on your chest would still prickle my back if I pressed into you. In some moments, these thoughts are life blood. In others, they kill me slowly, deliberately. Drinking them is drinking poison. Once, you killed me with a simple hello. Today, I'm dead.

Restraint breaks beneath my skin. I give in to the dirty, primal cravings. If I can't be with you then I find others. Your touch is the flight of birds in winter, to be beautiful elsewhere. I needed to go, to be beautiful elsewhere. Forgive me. I have to confess to you, unburden myself. There have been so many other bodies, but yours is the only face I'll ever see. The sounds of other men in the night fill the space between us. And it is so much space, my love. My Andros.

I know that I will not grow old in your arms. But we will live forever in broken shadows and memories laced with liquor and cigarettes. I will grow old with my eyes fixed on the moon, taking comfort only in knowing that your eyes see the same pale-faced star. My love for you is as faithful as the passage of time; it will endure surely as today becomes tomorrow.

I will live in this shadow, our shadow. And though I would fight a hundred wars for you, I surrender you now. I surrender to begin another fight. I will fight for love. A love that will pull me from the shadows and rest in my arms. I will keep your love inside me, but I fight now for the love of my son.

This story, our story, my story is not written in words but in tears on pillows. It is written in the savory bites of my mother's grape leaves, in the dusty air of my family's grocery store. It endures

in the hollow of my gut, in the ever-diminishing puddle of gin at the bottom of my glass. My story lives in the branches of a cedar tree, in the scar tissue insulating my heart. And it all began with an ending.

Yours Forever,

George

CHAPTER TWENTY-THREE

I called Eleanor every single day until, at last, she acquiesced to occasional visits, mostly lunches and afternoons playing in the apartment with Ummi and me. Ummi longed for her grandson perhaps almost as much as I did. She knit him blankets and hats and mittens and bought him stuffed animals. When he stopped coming over, these items mostly remained in unopened packages on the floor of her sewing room. But she continued buying gifts and sewing clothing, as if doing so would ensure her grandson's eventual and complete return. She always believed her grandson would come home one day.

When he was about five years old, I brought him back to the house after an afternoon in the park. Eleanor had retreated quickly inside with Georgie, but, before I left, I opened the door to leave a bag of tomatoes on the table in the foyer. Eleanor must have thought I'd already gone because from the kitchen I witnessed her yelling at our little boy, grabbing him by the shirt as he looked up at her with tears in his eyes.

"You're just like your father, aren't you? Aren't' you?" she screamed in his face, her cheeks flushed and eyes watery.

Without waiting for them to notice, I shut the door quietly behind me and walked down the porch steps. The image of my boy shaking and crying as his mother cursed him for being my son made my insides constrict and throat dry.

While my nightly perambulations would continue through the years, because I was a coward and also because I loved him more than anything, I would no longer attempt to visit with my son.

Twenty years passed in surreptitious observations and drunken strolls in the middle of the night. He was a man now. I learned about him from customers who came into the store and folks at St. Anthony's who kept in touch with Eleanor— Eleanor, who had become a recluse. He was in medical school in the city although he still lived at home with his mother on the weekends and during breaks. I never filed paperwork to legally separate from my wife. She'd already been through so much at my hands. It didn't seem necessary to put her through anything else. Certainly not the indignity of a divorce.

Under my proprietorship, the store expanded. I saved enough money to update and renovate the dated space. The new addition was a small café where patrons could enjoy our freshly baked Lebanese pastries. Ummi, adorned in fashionable white bob and lipstick, began to more closely resemble her dear cousin Raina than the simple, rustic woman from my youth. This new Ummi wore the same modest dresses she always did, but with lace apron and red-lacquered nails, she was different. She sold knafeh and mafrokeh among other pastries. She brewed pots of Turkish coffee, which she served in elegant white cups. She pressed her red-painted lips together often, which to those of us who knew her, we recognized as Ummi's almost-smile.

I had been too consumed with my own life to recognize the dainty steps my mother took towards independence. I surmised it began after Bayee's death. Slow, timid changes at first—a darker shade of lipstick, Women's Magazines in addition to newspapers and Bible verses. Then, as she became emboldened with these tiny victories—over whom or what I never could be certain—she jumped. I taught her to drive, and she loved it. In fact, neither of us would ever admit it to anyone, but it was the act of driving that ultimately restored our fractured relationship. I took her for driving lessons every Friday after I closed the store. At first, they were tense. She was nervous doing something so far out of her comfort zone. And I was still uneasy around her. She was one of only a few people in the world who knew the absolute truth about me, and I wasn't entirely certain that she accepted it.

The first time she drove Bayee's old Lincoln without stalling, Ummi laughed. She really, truly laughed—a sound like music, like the seabreeze in Byblos. After that success, we went driving every Sunday afternoon after mass. We'd drive to the shops in Westport or to Candlewood Lake in the summer. Ummi couldn't get enough, and I couldn't get enough of my mother's joy.

We didn't speak of my affection for men. She preferred it that way. And maybe I did, too. It was easier sometimes to simply exist in a world where I was the dutiful son—running my family's store, taking care of my aging mother. I was also the favorite uncle—Michael's four children adored visiting me at work. It almost didn't matter that I was the failed husband and father.

Michael remained a steadfast friend. I eventually told him the truth about everything—about my marriage, about Andros. He was shocked but supportive.

"Whatever makes you happy brother," he smiled behind the counter during a slow afternoon. "Ha! I knew you weren't better than me with the ladies back in the day. You had an unfair advantage. They were more comfortable with you." We chuckled, and he lit a cigarette. Then added, "Still, you need to understand that none of what you just told me changes the fact that you have a responsibility to be a good and decent father."

"I know, Michael. I know." When had my younger brother become so wise?

* * *

Raina visited Danbury from time to time. I made a habit of reciprocating with trips a few times a year to DC. We finally did travel home together, to Lebanon. The two of us, cousins, almost like mother and son. She even met Andros, and, as I predicted, they adored each other from the moment they said hello. Raina pushed me to remain with him in Lebanon.

"Let your brother manage the store. He'll be fine," she suggested.

"And you'll leave Joe?"

The question effectively ended the conversation.

As if it was their destiny to remain contradictory though inseparable forces, as Ummi bloomed, Raina faded. Her beauty was unchanged, but her spirit diminished as the years wore on her. Her husband's affairs, the death of her oldest son, her increasing loneliness, left her sad. But she buried this sadness deep inside her, and she only ever let it out when she was drunk. She was also maternal in her affection for me, and this tenderness increased after her son passed. She spoiled me with hugs, kisses, and compliments each time we were together. She'd cup my face in her small, warm hands, smile adoringly into my eyes, and smooch both cheeks. "Habibi, you are so handsome. Just like your father. Come, let's sit and talk. I have some new records you must listen to!" Even in her sadness, Raina Jowdy was radiant.

* * *

I filled the walls of my little café with all kinds of artwork. Mostly paintings by local amateur artists—housewives cultivating a hobby, teenagers who excelled in their art classes, and even my own paintings. Early watercolors were crude at best, but in the weeks and sometimes months that I could go without a drink, I'd temper the loneliness, the desire to reach for the bottle, by reaching for a paintbrush. During one lengthy dry spell, I painted a set of three trays. Each one had a different floral pattern, and, admittedly, they were quite beautiful. I hung these pieces on the wall behind the counter in the café. I liked to keep the artwork new and on rotation, but, besides these trays, one other piece was a permanent part of the décor. A canvas with two dark figures twisted at the center surrounded by black mountains, a gray sea, and the silhouetted skyline of Beirut. I waited a lifetime for this place and probably would wait another one. But it didn't really matter any longer. I had this artifact, this memory, this story—my story—hanging in the store that raised me, in the town that was and always would be mine. Home, no longer an impasse; my only constant.

Time changed things for men like me, but they did not change me. I preferred to watch the progress unfold from a safe distance. I admired the bravery, the action these people took. They marched. They held signs. They knew who and what they were, and they did not care. Some even held hands and kissed in public places. I envied these men.

I had casual relationships through the years, but my heart would only ever belong to one man. Andros and I remained in contact. We exchanged letters and visited each other every few years. These were the weeks I lived for, the moments that made life beautiful. And these days, although all-too brief, made everything worthwhile. If my life could only consist of a handful of perfect moments spent with the one man I'd ever love, then I would consider myself lucky. Maybe even blessed. But Andros knew I would never move to Lebanon to be with him, nor would I allow him to relocate to Connecticut. Times changed, but I remained very much the same. I also remained hopeful that one day my son would come back to me, and I owed it to him to be ready. I owed it to him to be the man and father he needed.

And then one afternoon in late June I closed the store early. I lit a cigarette and walked towards the colonial on Elm Street. A series of violent protests had been taking place that week in New York City. People were rising up in an unprecedented way. Their courage was inspiring. If they could act in such a big, bold way, then I could, too. For decades, the five steps, paint-chipped, crumbling, had been my albatross. I couldn't climb them no matter how much I longed to.

And now. Now, I was an aging man, myself chipped and crumbling. I had been my own albatross for so many years. Fourteen years since we last spoke. My hair was almost gone now. I smelled strongly of cigarettes and alcohol, not unlike my own father. How many years did I have left? What would I say? What would he say? I had no plan, no words, no expectations. I just knew one thing: my heart would only ever be broken without my son in my life. I wasn't seeking forgiveness —that would be too much to ask for. I'd settle for, "Hello, Dad." My name on his lips would be enough. His acknowledgment would be enough.

I made my way up the steps, walked to the front door, and knocked.

ACKNOWLEDGMENTS

To my family who shared stories and pictures, answered countless questions, and without whom these characters would never have been brought to life. Special thanks to Aunt June, Uncle George, Susan Dimyan, Ferris Nasser, Steven Coury, and the Najam/Jowdy/Hokayem family.

To Christopher Madden, Hayley Battaglia, and Paull Goodchild. Without you, I'd still be rewriting the first scene.

To the teachers, mentors, and friends from my Fairfield University MFA program especially Eugenia Kim, Porochista Khakpour, Nalini Jones, Karen Osborn, Da Chen, Stephanie Harper, Abbey Cleland Lopez, Tommy Hahn and Brooke Adams Law. This book would still only exist in my head without the support, feedback, and encouragement you all gave me.

To the many members of the Danbury community (Lebanese and non-Lebanese alike) especially the "You know you lived/live in Danbury, CT if..." Facebook group. Your memories were invaluable to the research process, and I am eternally grateful for your willingness to share them with me.

To Cody Sisco and Lisa Kastner, thank you for believing in this book as much as I do and for helping me to share it with the world.

To the friends and family who hosted me in Beirut and Aarbaniyee, Lebanon. It truly did feel like I was returning home.

To my parents who taught me to always go after your dreams.

And, finally, to my husband, Greg, for your constant love, support, sense of humor, and mostly, your patience. I promise I won't take eleven years to write the next book!

Running Wild Press publishes stories that cross genres with great stories and writing. RIZE publishes great genre stories written by people of color and by authors who identify with other marginalized groups. Our team consists of:

Lisa Diane Kastner, Founder and Executive Editor
Mona Bethke, Acquisitions Editor, Editor, RIZE
Benjamin White, Acquisitions Editor, Editor, Running Wild Press
Peter A. Wright, Acquisitions Editor, Editor, Running Wild Press
Rebecca Dimyan, Editor
Andrew DiPrinzio, Editor
Cecilia Kennedy, Editor
Barbara Lockwood, Editor
Cody Sisco, Editor
Chih Wang, Editor
Pulp Art Studios, Cover Design
Standout Books, Interior Design
Polgarus Studios, Interior Design

Learn more about us and our stories at www.runningwildpress.com/rize

Loved this story and want more? Follow us at www.runningwildpress.com/rize, www.facebook.com/RW-Prize, on Twitter @rizerwp and Instagram @rizepress